LIKE A RIVER
TO THE SEA

Paul Fisher

For permission, serialization, condensation, adaptions, or for our catalog of other publications, write to Ozark Mountain Publishing, Inc., P.O. Box 754, Huntsville, AR 72740, ATTN: Permissions Department.

Library of Congress Cataloging-in-Publication Data

Like a River to the Sea
by Paul Fisher -1955-

A story of an ordinary man, who, it turns out, has a most extraordinary story to tell.

1. Purpose 2. Spiritual 3. Karma 4. Reincarnation
I. Fisher, Paul-1955- II. Purpose   III. Spiritual   IV. Title

Library of Congress Catalog Card Number: 2022940801
ISBN: 9781950639090

Original artwork "Abyss" 2012 by Kali Emerald Fisher, mixed media on canvas
Cover Art and Layout: Victoria Cooper Art
Book set in: Castellar & Times New Roman
Book Design: Summer Garr
Published by:

PO Box 754, Huntsville, AR 72740
800-935-0045 or 479-738-2348; fax 479-738-2448
WWW.OZARKMT.COM

Printed in the United States of America

CONTENTS

Dedicated to my father, Paul Fisher.

THE VIEW FROM HERE

I recognize that it is a rare opportunity to be able to tell the story of one's life from the perspective I have recently been privy to. I am wise enough to know that this gift, and I believe it to be that, is something not to be squandered.

To be able to describe the events leading up to the end of a life is a substantial enough accomplishment, but then to be given the chance to, as best I can, portray what happens when that earthly threshold has been crossed and one is, well, beyond that lifetime … I'm not sure how you even begin to put a value on that.

My life was not particularly special in any way. By that, I mean that I wasn't famous, I didn't discover a cure for anything. I didn't perform any heroic acts; at least nothing that I felt was heroic at the time. I wasn't a great artist, musician, or inventor. I was just a guy who, for the most part, did what he thought he was supposed to do. I was a husband, a father, a friend to some, and a lover to others.

While I didn't do anything particularly great in my lifetime, I also didn't do anything terribly bad either. As there was nothing extraordinary about it, I would call it an ordinary life, except perhaps for the fact that I am able to tell you my story from both sides of the fence, as it were. That's where the ordinary part is no longer quite so ordinary.

PART ONE

Every story has a happy ending.
It just depends on where you end it.

CHAPTER ONE

I held the picture in my hand and studied it intently. It was a black-and-white photograph, and without the unnecessary intrusion of color, the true essence of the image was enhanced for me that much more. I was immediately and quite magically reconnected to that moment, and the promise it once held of a new day.

I was not sure how long I had been sitting here, comfortably ensconced in my cocoon beneath the leaden sky, as sheets of rain fell beyond the walls.

The photograph—yes, some of us still like to print the occasional photograph rather than keep everything on a memory stick or on a hard drive—was one I had tucked away in a book some years prior. That was back when I still lived with my wife, when I felt confident in the knowledge that she would no more open this book and discover this window to my past than she would have opened her heart to me again. On the cover of the book, against a bright yellow background, is a picture of a rather stout black man wearing a crumpled sports jacket through which his belly protruded; the loud jacket drew your eye away from the look of exhaustion in the man's face. He is cavalierly holding an alto saxophone as if it were an ornament instead of the fountain of music that it became in his hands. The book was called *Bird: The Legend of Charlie Parker.*

The house groaned faintly as it strained against the wind. In my head there were thoughts that danced between the photo I held in my hand, the memories I could not easily let go of, and of the house on the other side of town where I had spent a few thousand nights in what now felt like a different lifetime. My wife and I, I was getting used to the idea of referring to her as The Ex, well, we had not yet severed the legal bonds that tied us together, although we had done a fairly good job of slicing through pretty much every other tie that binds.

As the rainy morning settled in and took hold of the day, I considered the idea that many people confuse bad choices with destiny. It was just too easy to lay the blame elsewhere when something went sideways. Oh, I would have been happy, on occasion, to place some of those bad choices right in the lap of destiny or divine intervention, thereby taking the onus off of me, but that was likely the reason I didn't do too well with religion. As easy as it was to blame something on God's or Allah's will, I just couldn't relinquish the feeling that I—we—were ultimately responsible for our actions.

I gazed longingly at the photograph, this precious moment that had been captured in time for my later pleasure, or was it pain? I recalled with great clarity the way her face rested on the pillow, gently bathed in the chalky half-light thrown by the moon. Like the face of an angel coaxed from a sliver of pale alabaster, she lay there barely breathing. I remembered how, as I took her photograph, I had held my own breath for fear of waking her.

This picture was my connection to a time when I was so terribly happy, and so terribly confused by that happiness. Change, I mused, is always a gift. The challenge is in learning to acquire the appreciation for certain gifts. When it came to change, you had to be careful of what you wished for.

Somewhere off in the distance there was a muffled wup, wup, wup, of a helicopter circling the city. I eased myself away from the warm scent that clung to her like a second skin. The sound of my body sliding over the rough sheets was so loud as if to wake the dead, yet all remained calm within the room. The hotel had taken liberties with the five-star rating they had ascribed to this place. The sheets were cotton, but thick and heavily starched, smelling slightly of bleach; they felt coarse against my skin as I sought to stifle the sound of my movement.

Padding over to the small stone balcony of our hotel room I gently pried the door open. It was made of glass and metal, and generously layered with many coats of paint, that sought to hide the number of years it had sat heavily on its hinges. It complained with a low moan as it gave way beneath my pressure. I stepped through the doorway, the night air carried a slight chill, and I felt a cold finger trail down my back raising goose bumps on my skin.

I was not able to discern the body of the Atlantic Ocean, hidden as it was beneath the shading of the murky sky, but I could taste its essence as it filtered through the other olfactory stimulus of the city. The lights of the Rue de Tunis spread out like a ribbon below and merged with the soft glow that the city cast up to the sky, serving to dampen my view of what lay beyond. To what I determined to be north, a large swath of darkness cut into the city, hemmed in on two sides by a haphazard series of lights that if my memory served me correctly, was the Medina, the old city that was home to the marketplace. The helicopter that I had heard earlier was now just a series of faint thumps reverberating in the night air as it circled somewhere near the Palais Royal where, as the concierge had informed us upon arrival at the hotel here in Rabat, the king of Morocco was hosting some of his neighbors in an Arab Summit meeting.

It had been an exhausting day of travel; the flight up from Nashville to New York, then a seven-and-a-half-hour flight from JFK to Casablanca that turned into nine hours on-board due to the weather delay getting out of New York. By the time we got our rental car and drove from Casablanca to Rabat, then sat down for a hurried dinner in the hotel dining room, we were both ready to collapse. When we got back to the hotel room, we had barely brushed our teeth before sleep took us over. I didn't mean to be keeping score, but I couldn't help making a mental note that this had been the first time we had ever been alone in a room and not made love, since that very first time a year before.

The name of the woman on the bed was Julia. I was still

married at the time, and I will tell you that she was not my wife. That woman was at home with my two children, several thousand miles, and what was truly another world away.

Julia's looks belied her age. At twenty-seven she easily appeared several years younger, as was evidenced by the times she had been carded in a bar back home when we had squeezed in a short visit over a drink when that was all the time we had.

The blonde hair that cascaded about her shoulders was such a beacon in this land of mysterious dark-haired women, many of whom still hid beneath their niqab, that she had attracted the attention of everyone, men and women alike, since our arrival. Children pointed her out at stoplights as we made our way in the rental car all the way here to the Rabat Hilton. I imagined that there had likely been more than a few men who had seen us together today who would readily and gladly defy some vow or another, so that they could be the one with Julia for the novelty of a night or, closer to my desire, to be with her forever.

I turned my attention back to the exotic shaded vista that spread before me, not minding the coolness of the evening air as much now, as I stared blankly into the night. The wind had picked up and moved the clouds around, exposing a cluster of stars that found their way through the canopy of light that emanated upward and outward from the city. In a brush with fantasy, I pictured myself high above in the heavens looking down on the world from a perch hundreds of miles above. I picked out the rounded shape of Northwest Africa where I placed a pinpoint of light here on the city of Rabat. Then looking wistfully across the Atlantic I found North America, noting New York City. From there I drifted downward to zero in on the Mid-South and Nashville, Tennessee, where I placed another light. I connected the points with an umbilical cord and watched to see if any life pulsed between. I stared at the connection for several long breaths. It appeared stillborn.

The old stone floor of the balcony felt gritty against my bare feet and, while I contemplated the life-changing decisions that needed to be made, I rubbed my foot against the coarseness of the stone, worrying away the dead skin that had formed a tiny ridge on the heel of my foot. Here I was, standing in the dim shadings of this fishbowl, sharing a room with a woman I was in love with, while halfway around the world was the woman I was married to, and with her were the two children I loved so fiercely. I wrestled with the question of whether to listen to my head or my heart. There were things you were supposed to know before you hopped on a plane to some foreign shore with the "other" woman.

You might quite rightly consider that a man of forty can be very attracted to a woman of twenty-seven for all the wrong reasons. The term "midlife crisis" comes readily to mind, but then, if you are a fair and reasoned person, you might also consider that he may be attracted to her for a great number of right reasons as well.

I will admit that it was difficult for me initially to decipher the difference between love and lust with Julia, when so much of the relationship was conducted under clandestine rules of engagement. How much did that add to the mystique and heighten the sensuality of every touch, every kiss? Stolen moments are the sweetest. Want and need; love and lust. They are such interesting contrasts to sort through.

As I turned away from my roost on the balcony and looked back into the room at Julia, I could not help but contemplate how innocent, how almost child-like she seemed as she lay naked, wrapped in cotton with the pastel moonlight settling on her like milky morning dew. I moved stealthily across the room and quietly unzipped the suitcase that I suspected held my camera. Sifting through the layers of clothes that we hadn't yet unpacked, my hand found the aging Nikon and I looked around for a suitable spot to shoot from.

I decided against the harsh intrusion of a flash, not wanting to wake her, wanting instead to capture the image before me exactly as she appeared. I wanted to incorporate the sensual shadings afforded by the moon as it poured over my shoulder, flooding the room with its pale ruddiness. I balanced the camera on the back of a chair in lieu of the small tripod that I had brought along. The shutter speed was exceedingly slow as the aperture stretched wide open with the click, gasped through one-one thousand, two-one thousand, three-one thousand, four, before the clack as the shutter finally closed, having swallowed the sight of her perfect sleeping image. The sound of the shutter faded away into the night, the room was quiet once more.

The weariness of the day caught up with me, and after pulling the door to the balcony half closed, I put the camera aside and slipped into bed beside Julia. She did not awaken, but unconsciously twisted and turned like a mechanical doll as she wrapped her arms and legs around me capturing me in her warmth. I felt the soft bristle of the small tuft of pubic hair against my thigh and I reached instinctively across her hip to cup the roundness of her buttock and let my hand nestle into place. Her head was tucked beneath my chin and the smell of her hair was in my face. My other life was a million miles away and at this moment I was at home with Julia. This was Heaven, I felt. I would face my Hell another time.

When I awoke, she was propped up on one arm, the one with the scar from where she had fallen as a child and put her hand through the glass of a storm door. Many times, after we had made love, I would stroke her body, traveling wherever my hand could reach while we remained locked in embrace. Inevitably I would end up running my finger up and down the slightly raised ridge of scar tissue on her arm. The one imperfection I could find, I would often tease.

Her hair was behind one ear, and she had that perpetual anticipatory smile playing at the corners of her mouth.

"I missed you all night," she said and leaned down to brush her mouth against mine. "I love the way you kiss me," she said and her mouth was on mine again and this time she lingered and I knew that this was the invitation to our slow dance of lovemaking, the delicate ballet that drew us deeper and deeper into each other. It had always been this way since the first time. It was always the first time, again.

The room had already been warmed by the balmy Moroccan winds that billowed through the half-open door to the balcony. Later as I welcomed the caress of the breeze on my skin, I rolled to one side with a sated sigh. Her hands ran along my body and traveled down the slickness of my lower back.

"Oh, you're sweaty," she whispered, and brought a finger to her mouth. "And salty."

The trip across the ocean to this other continent also served to allow me to take a journey deep inside myself. I understood later that this had been a watershed moment in my life, one of those intersects where search and discover come together. It is here that you are faced with the realization that all of our important decisions are made on a level of consciousness that is somewhere in the background of our minds. The final answer is not necessarily part of an active debate; we muse upon it and all of a sudden what we are supposed to do becomes clear to us, and we are left with the choice of accepting the gift, or not.

Two nights after our arrival in Morocco we had driven to the city of Fez, and it was here that we found ourselves in a traditional restaurant perched on cushions on the floor, tasting local delicacies, eating with our hands. It was all part of the experience that had been prearranged for the travel story that Julia had been assigned to prepare for the newspaper she worked at, the *Tennessean*.

The evening was not without its surprises; the softened cauliflower that I had enjoyed as one of our starter dishes, turned out to be marinated sheep brain. When I inquired as to what was inside the dessert-like sweet phyllo pastry covered in cinnamon and icing sugar, I was told it was baked pigeon.

Our host for that evening was a pleasant young man in his early twenties, who went by the name of Nabil. He was a guide provided by the tourist board, to show us the city of Fez and to entertain us for the two days we would be here, with the obvious goal of having Julia write about the wonderful times she had on her visit.

"So, tell me, Nabil," Julia had asked. "You've been through university, you speak English, French, Arabic, and a bit of German, what do you want to do with your life, are you going to stay in the tourist industry or do you have other plans?"

He smiled at her; he didn't speak for several seconds, while he afforded himself some time to consider his answer.

"I'm having a great degree of difficulty making a decision about my future." His hand stroked his neatly trimmed beard contemplatively. "My mother wants me to study religion; my father wants me to be an engineer or an architect. I feel like I don't want to do any of those things, but at the same time I keep changing my mind about what it is I truly want to do. Perhaps I haven't heard my calling yet. Indecision is a terrible thing, is it not? Sometimes I think it is better not to have a choice, then there is no question to be answered, you don't have to second-guess anything. There is an African proverb that says, 'Indecision is like a stepchild. If he does not wash his hands, he is dirty; if he does wash his hands, he is wasting water!'" He laughed and rocked backward on his cushion and clapped his hands together. "I do not think I have answered your question!"

We laughed with him, but inside I also agreed with him. There were a number of questions that I had not yet answered for myself; such as, what bridges do we cross, and which ones do we burn?

CHAPTER TWO

So now, dear reader, you are somewhat aware of my involvement with the woman named Julia. This is very important, as my relationship with her is something that carried on until the last day of my life.

For all the days that run seamlessly together, in a careless and sometimes carefree blur of sameness, there are those days, those moments in our lives, when something of true significance occurs. These moments are what shape us, so that who we are when we shuffle off this mortal coil is someone who is different from the person who entered it. I think for the most part that we all hope that the person who leaves is somehow, in some way, a better person because of the experiences of their lifetime, but of course we also all know that it isn't always the case.

In sharing my story with you, it is my desire that it will allow you to have a better understanding of how it is that the seemingly random incidents that occur in our lives are often anything but random. The understanding I'd like to leave you with is that you are the author of your own narrative; you create the characters and situations you interact with, and ultimately, you determine how the story is going to unfold. You are actually much more in control of your life, your destiny if you will, than you have likely ever considered. That truth is a difficult one for many people to accept, because if you accept it, then you have to accept that you are accountable for your own happiness and sadness, your own triumphs and tragedies.

There is no God's Will, there is only your will. You define what it is that creates the happiness and sadness in your life. What a huge responsibility! It's no wonder so many people would rather follow someone else's direction, and attribute what happens to them as someone else's creation or plan, rather than acknowledge that they are following the map that they created. Yes, it is all about the journey, but the truth is that it is your hand that holds the brush that paints the landscape you view along the way. It is you who determines when the journey begins and ends, and you are truly responsible for every element along the way of that journey. So, please allow me to tell you about my journey, during my lifetime, and we'll see how it compares to where you are in yours. With the next chapter I will detail the last day of my life, and how it led to the essence of my story.

Thank you for this opportunity.

CHAPTER THREE

It was at the point where I realized that something was truly amiss that the situation became entirely surreal. I felt as if I had been covered with something heavy, that clung to me like a horse blanket saturated with rain. I could scarcely move beneath the weight of it. It was only with great tenacity that I was able to get any air into my lungs at all due to the pressure that was pushing down on my chest. I felt like I was slowly suffocating, and with that sensation came a rapidly growing anxiousness.

I tried to push myself up so that I could rest on my elbows and shake this covering loose, but my body was not responding to any of my urgings. I formed the command in my mind, but my muscles simply would not respond, like I had been floundering about in freezing water and the icy fingers of hypothermia had wormed their way into those muscles, rendering them useless. At some point, against all odds, I managed to force open my eyelids, but I could not make sense of my surroundings and the whole effort put such a strain on me that I retreated back into the relative safety of my enclosure. Except for the gentle bubbling that I was aware of deep inside my chest, my body was still. My mind was not. In fact, it was exceedingly difficult for me to follow all the thought impulses that were racing around in my head; they appeared to have their own unique energy source as they mingled in a swirling mass of sensations.

"Concentrate on goodness."

I couldn't tell where the voice was coming from. And what the hell did it mean?

"If you are afraid, if you feel confusion, concentrate on the idea of goodness or peacefulness, however you imagine that emotion to be. Surround yourself with good feelings, picture yourself bathed in a beautiful warm white light and it will bring you comfort."

Just hearing those words brought some measure of solace to me. I was aware of a soft droning sound off in the distance that was slowly building in volume. I could sense a vibration in the silky air around me that felt like a large turbine racing up to speed. As it grew, I could feel the pulsing energy spiraling through my mind and body, winding deeper and deeper inside of me. I didn't feel that I could offer any resistance, even if I had wanted to. I couldn't do much more than simply give myself over to the sensation. As I acquiesced, the mist that had been clouding my thoughts began to dissipate like a curtain drawn aside, and I found myself observing an eclectic production unfolding in front of me.

There were a series of dances being performed synchronously on a stage upon which all the movements of the dancers were quite precisely choreographed; it appeared to me to be happening in a state of slow motion. I watched a foot slide languorously across the polished floor; an arm rose to shoulder level before flowing outward in an unhurried extension; the gentle bow of the head followed by a hand gesture that invited me to draw near.

My perspective of the recital began to shift as what appeared to be dry ice began to flow in from the wings of the stage, the haze enveloping the figures as it slurped across the floor, swirling around the feet of the dancers, before it tumbled lazily into the orchestra pit like a listless waterfall.

I had been so caught up in what was playing out before me that I did not immediately notice that the distance between the dancers and I had evaporated. I was now standing on the stage surrounded by the troupe of performers as they continued with their routines. I was no longer simply an observer, I now felt that

I had become the centerpiece of the dance.

The musical score that accompanied the dancers was something that I could not at first ascribe a rhythm or melody to; it was just a jumble of discordant sounds. Gradually, the random notes were not so random, and I began to identify a cadence and a repetition, which led to a melody once the time signature began to fall into place. As the notes connected together, I realized that the song I had been hearing was in fact made up of words.

"He's having trouble breathing, keep that bag going."

"I think we're looking at a haemothorax here."

"There's no air on the left side, I think he's punctured ... yeah, it's a tension pneumothorax, get me a chest tray please and a sixteen-gauge needle, I'll draw it out."

"Let's get some blood, cross and type eight units and get the bank to send down four more units of O right now, he's lost a lot from the leg trauma."

"Ringers lactate going in."

"Let's check CBC and lytes."

"Can I have someone hold his head, I'm going to intubate him."

"Pressure is really low, sixty over ten."

"I don't like the look of that left leg. How's the gunshot next door?"

"I think they're under control there, we're going to be a while here."

"The leg looks like a comminuted fracture. I have a distal pulse."

"Let's leave that for now, just get some pictures of it, is the portable unit here?"

"How's his O2 now?"

"Get ... Thoracic ... Ortho ... Consult ... Chest ... Hand me ... now ..."

A sharp crackle of electricity arced inside and then outside of my body, accompanied by a sound like the tearing of fine silk. I suddenly felt so tired, so utterly drained. My arms would not rise up, my legs felt like they were weighted down with bags of wet cement.

The exhaustion!

I had never felt anything like this before. It swept over me like an advancing tide, and as the waves rose up and crashed against me, I had no choice but to give myself over to them like a hesitant sacrifice whose will had been broken. The waves took me up in their embrace.

Immediately I felt the heaviness lifted away from me. I was on the surface of the water, floating, as the waves and their tender touch washed over me. The water was soft against my skin as it warmed and calmed me. From the vantage point I now occupied, I saw myself floating in the water but I was six years old and was being held in the safety of my father's arms as he bobbed me up and down in the waters of Old Hickory Lake where we used to rent a cabin in the summer all those years ago.

"Kick your legs, Josh, kick your legs, we're going deeper."

I felt my father's hands under my arms as he swirled me through the water.

"Your head will go under if you don't kick your feet, Sport."

Sport was my father's nickname for me as a child, and hearing it now felt reassuring to me. I kicked hard, determined to please my father, and to keep my head above water. My father leaned me into the water and I kicked my legs; I felt total trust as his strong hand slipped under my chest to hold me at the surface. Then the forward motion began to ebb and as my body slowed its advance, I twirled a half turn until I was now floating on my back, supported by the warm water. Rising and falling at the beck and call of the waters touch, I was rocking back and forth in a long slow steady rhythm. I allowed my muscles to go lax and my legs began their predictable drift downward. As my head slipped below the surface of the water and my heels made contact with the sandy floor beneath me, it was like I had brought together the two contact points required to complete an electrical circuit.

CHAPTER FOUR

"Damn he's arrested."

Whatever had happened when my feet touched the ground had created some great spark and then everything went dark for me. It was black, so black that I could not imagine where my body ended and the black around me began.

"Josh, hey, Sport, I'm right here. It's all right, don't be frightened, I'm here to help you. See the light just above you? Look up, just focus on it and you'll be beside me in no time."

The sound of my father's voice brought me immediate relief. Instinctively I kicked my legs and felt myself rise through the warm water, breaking the surface in a matter of seconds as I rose toward the sound of his voice and the comfort of the light. A moment later and I was no longer in the water but sitting by the edge of a pond, the water lapping lazily at my bare feet.

"Josh, don't worry, it's all okay."

Now if there's something a son knows, it is the sound of his father's voice, and yet I noticed a difference in the words I was hearing. I'm not sure how to describe it, except to say that the sound of his words was tinged with a kind of synthesized texture. I looked toward the source of the voice and in the serene light of late day I saw my father standing several feet away from me.

In the years since his death, I had retained an image of him in my mind that captured my memory of him from somewhere in my teen years, I'm not sure how old he would have been then, mid-forties perhaps. The sight of him now was hazy at first but then it sharpened into focus until he was not only clearly visible to me, but he almost appeared as a three-dimensional figure that had been projected in front of me like a hologram. The backdrop of lush vegetation was juxtaposed against his crisp presence and it made his outline shimmer in a way that the light seemed to emanate from within him rather than from around him. He looked positively radiant to me and I stared at him for a long time before I actually found my voice.

"I've missed you so much," was the best I could come up with as my voice finally caught up with the words in my head. I felt a wave of emotion well up in my chest. How do you greet a loved one, my father in this case, all these years after his death?

I was about to walk over to embrace him, but my father was no longer standing those few feet away from me. The pond had elongated into a waterway, a canal or river, that was spanned by a quaint bridge. I remember at the time that the scene immediately made me think of a framed print that had hung in our hallway in the house I grew up in, of the Monet painting of the footbridge and the water lilies at Giverny.

My father stood on the far side of the small arched bridge. I began to walk toward him, but as I did, he held his hand up in a gesture that made me hold my ground.

"It's best that you stay where you are for now." His words were spoken softly but firmly. I recall that it surprised me at the time that he did not want me to approach him.

"I'm not afraid," I told him. "I'll walk across the bridge or wade across the water, it doesn't look deep."

"Josh, there are things that you're not aware of yet. You need to be patient."

"What sort of things do I need to know?" I asked. "What is so important that I can't be there on that side with you and hug you."

"You can, in time," he said to me, and before I could speak, he continued. "Josh, there is so much to our lives, so much meaning

18

that we simply don't acknowledge. We know it deep within, but we often don't allow it to come forth and flourish. We're put on this earth plane to share love and seek the truth and instead we chase a thousand different distractions. Don't cross the bridge yet," he said calmly to me. "It's not time yet."

I didn't mean to disobey him, but I also could not resist the urge to be with him. I took a step toward him and as I did the bridge, the river, and my father retreated an equal measure in order to maintain the distance between us. I remember being put off by this, so I stepped forward again, but as I did a bank of fog rolled briskly in. It was similar to the dry ice that had been a part of the stage production, and the view I had before me was suddenly swallowed up.

"Don't be afraid, Josh."

I think I actually felt my father's words more than heard them. And then there was nothing, absolutely nothing.

Have you ever had that sensation that you were floating? Not in water, but floating in midair. I felt myself floating in a hushed darkness that didn't seem to have a beginning or an end. My hands encountered nothing but empty space as I extended them into the inky blackness. I knew my eyes were open; at least I felt like I was stretching them as wide as I could, but they just stared into abject emptiness. Then, almost imperceptibly at first but growing, I saw a single star far off in the darkness. It was a tiny pinpoint from which my pupils could extract some minuscule amount of light to feed into my retina. It was something, in the middle of nothing.

I stood in place, concerned that I could not see enough around me to venture in any one particular direction without encountering some potential danger. I heard a sound that was like the rustle of the wind in the trees but after a while I recognized it, as I had earlier, as the sound of murmuring voices. My thoughts were muddy, and I had to struggle to piece the sounds together and then, as if I had just unclogged a drain, the voices swirled together and their meaning became clear to me and cut through the darkness like the flash of a hot knife.

"He's breathing again; I've got a sixteen-gauge in under the mid-axial line. He's got a couple of broken ribs here; one punctured the lung, that's why he wasn't getting any air in there."

"Anything back from the lab yet? Let me see how his gases and enzymes are doing."

"Let's get that portable X-ray in here now and get some pictures."

I understood what they were saying, but of course I did not fully understand the meaning of it all from my layman perspective. I managed to piece together that I was in a hospital, but I did not yet understand why or how it was that I had come to be here. I did not feel any pain but truly I really did not feel my body at all. I didn't know if it was intact, or if anything was missing.

"He's having a lot of PVCs."

I had no idea what that comment meant, but at the sound of that voice I opened my eyes and I was staring at a monitor that my body was connected to, and I remember seeing the lines jumping across the screen like jagged cries for attention.

"Hey, excuse me, can you tell me exactly what's going on here?"

No one responded to me. I knew I was speaking aloud because I could hear my voice, but no one in the room paid any mind to me. My heart felt like it was flubbering around in my chest like a jellyfish. Whatever it was doing, it didn't feel right. There was a droning sound that I was aware of that was building in intensity as I felt its approach. I reminded myself to keep track of it, it seemed to be of some significance, when without warning the sound rose dramatically in pitch and spiked. I heard a voice cry out and I think it was mine.

"Oh, oh, he's going again."

The heavy blanket had begun to suffocate me again and I just felt that I had to get it off me now! I grabbed it with my right hand and flung it heartily to one side. Immediately I felt so much better.

I took in my surroundings with a quick glance and recognized that I was in what looked like a small operating room with a group of doctors and nurses, and whoever else, crowded around. There were enough people blocking my sight that I had to stretch up over their heads to get a proper view.

The stress in the room was palpable, to the point where not only could I feel it, but I could actually see it. The best way I can describe it is that I was seeing what looked like undulating waves of energy that expanded out from the center of the group. I watched it spiral around them like a snake. My fascination with the energy in the room had distracted me from the realization that when I had stretched up to see over their heads, I had somehow moved to a new vantage point which involved me hovering over the group from a position near the ceiling.

"Give me 300 milligrams Amiodorone IV push, please."

I felt peculiarly relaxed as I watched the efforts of the medical team. What might be quite obvious to you now, was not so obvious to me then, as I conveniently overlooked the fact that the patient they were working on was me.

"Is that chest guy done in the OR yet? I want him here for a consult; I think we might be looking at a myocardial contusion here."

I scanned the room, taking in the array of medical equipment, tubes and monitors, all of the accessories of this room of life and death. The energy in the room pulled at me like an enormous electromagnet and I could literally see the faint blue fingers coiled around me, tugging like an undertow that held me in place in the heart of the room. A soft vibration came alive in me and began to pulse through my body as if I had taken hold of a low-voltage wire in each hand, providing the electricity with the path it sought. I was floating freely near the ceiling, caught up in the intoxicating sensations coursing through my veins. I was a drop of water in a bucket, a bucket that was poured into a stream that ran to a river, that made its way down to the sea where it emptied out into the greater body of water. I was some microscopic speck of awareness that had tapped into some fantastic source of energy.

"He's started to fibrillate."

"Shit."

"Son of a ..."

"Get the cart, he's crashing."

CHAPTER FIVE

Looking back at it now, I can put all the pieces together quite seamlessly; at the time, however, it was a different story.

I was standing on a small rise overlooking a field interrupted by small scrubby growths. The sky had a mauve tinge to it; the ground, drawing from this light, gave off a dusty rose hue. The fields were quite unremarkable; the landscape quite plain. Imagine if there were some trees, I thought; some kind of greenery. It didn't need to be lush, just something to stimulate the spirit at least.

When I looked up a few moments later I was pleasantly surprised to see that I was no longer surrounded by the desolate setting. In fact, I was quite amazed that the fields and hills had become dotted with trees and a carpet of wildflowers, while grasses now flowed out over the land. Even the sky had changed its appearance; it was brighter now, somehow more alive, more inviting to look at.

My eyes journeyed to the horizon and I saw a winding silver band that sparkled, and I stared at it for some time feeling drawn to the gleaming water that rushed across the terrain. And then, without being aware of any physical movement on my part, the next thing I knew I was standing beside the river.

As I stood looking at the water racing past me, I ran my hands over my body. It felt very solid to me, not dreamlike at all. I was not aware of any pain or injury. I glanced down at my left leg, the one I had heard someone say was injured, and it seemed fine to me. I drew a great breath of air deep into my lungs and let it out slowly and deliberately. There was no resistance, no deflated lung, nothing that would arouse even the slightest suspicion of there being anything wrong with me.

The water shot by at a rugged clip. I could see that by carefully choosing certain rocks to use as stepping-stones, and managing to keep my balance, I could plot out a sort of tic-tac-toe route across the river. It was as I imagined my foot landing on the far shore that I saw her.

Her eyes glowed with an energy that leapt right across the water to me and held me in place. She was clothed in a white dress or gown. I don't know enough about fashion to describe the style, but it clung to her in a very attractive way. She wore several silver bracelets on her left wrist. Her face was warmly familiar to me, but I was not sure from where. It was enough for me that I felt at ease with her right away. I stood there placidly, thinking that I would like to speak with her, to find out about this place, and wondering how I should go about trying to get to the other side of the river in order to engage with her.

"You created the river. You can cross it anytime you wish."

Her voice sounded like it was right inside my head. She was far enough away from me that she would have had to yell or at least speak loudly for me to hear her, and I had been watching her the entire time, she had not moved her mouth and yet I heard her voice as plain as could be.

"What do you mean I created the river?" I said aloud, hoping my voice would carry across the river.

"You have many abilities that you are not using. You can accomplish anything you want," she replied, and again her voice was inside my head. "Thoughts are living things." She said, "If you direct your energy into a thought then it will become a form, a life form of its own. If you speak your words out loud to me of course I will hear them, but if you think clearly of something and direct it at me, I will hear that as well, and with greater clarity."

"Why am I here with you? There was a dream or something, where I thought I was ill or had been injured and was in a hospital, and then I visited with my father, my dead father," I hastened to add. "Now I'm here with you and I'm not sure where one dream ends and where the next one begins."

"If you accept that thoughts are things, then your dream is as much a part of your existence as your existence is a part of your dream."

"I'm not sure I follow ..."

"The knowledge is within you. When you truly want to know it, the truth will be there for you to know. It's like this river of yours. When you really want to cross it, the means will become clear to you. You have the strength and knowledge to accomplish virtually anything, the only requirement is for you to focus on it and desire it."

I hesitated before I spoke while I tried to organize my thoughts, and before I could say anything, she was suddenly face to face with me; she had traversed the river to join me on my side.

I'm sure you know of a particular smell that can effortlessly take you back in time to a situation or a person, and allow you to relive all those memories in a flash. It could be cinnamon buns fresh out of the oven at your grandma's house, the smell of burning leaves from a particular autumn day, the smell of someone's skin. As the woman appeared in front of me, one of the first things I was aware of was the wonderful fragrance that hung in the air around her. I knew the smell immediately, except that I couldn't articulate what it was. Somehow this scent connected her and I, but I could not see the pieces to fit them together.

"You surprise me, Joshua," she said using my name, which further perplexed me. "There was a time, a lifetime, where you were so intoxicated by the scent of Nardos, and the woman who wore it, that you allowed it to change the course of your life."

"Nardos?" I drew deeply on the scent as I said the word aloud. "It's beautiful. Somehow I know it, but I don't know how or why." The perfume excited my senses to the point where I didn't just smell the scent, in my mind's eye I saw it as a color and felt it as a vibration. It was a multidimensional experience.

I was trying to piece together the memory of where this scent originated, but instead the words "Don't forget ..." came to mind.

I said the words aloud. Don't forget what? I wondered.

Miranda. Grayson. Don't forget Miranda and Grayson. Yes, that was it. And Julia, don't forget Julia. Then I understood.

"Clear!"

I heard the word a split second before I felt the jolt. It was like someone had just punched me in the chest and I reeled from the force of it. With that I was once again aware of my surroundings, realizing that I was back in the hospital, I was standing in the doorway that led to the ER. I was being tugged insistently back into that treatment room by a magnetic pull. Now I understood what had distracted me from the memory of the scent. I leaned away from the room, and felt the pull lessen somewhat.

I made my way along a corridor. The edges of my vision were clouded, and it made me feel like I was walking through a tunnel. Julia was nearby, I could sense her presence and at that moment I wanted nothing more than to be with her; she had been the beautiful distraction.

On more than one occasion I needed to pause to steady myself. I did this by stretching my arms from wall to wall for support. At the time I didn't stop to consider the obvious issue of being able to span ten or twelve feet in order to reach out and touch both walls at once. I had other things on my mind. I was advancing at a mockingly slow pace, but I persevered and kept moving forward until there she was, not more than thirty feet in front of me.

I raised my hand so that she would see me and in doing so the gesture had the effect of lifting me up and carrying me forward on a wave, and I was suddenly standing right next to her. I was so relieved to be with her and yet I was aware of the incredible fear and sadness that surrounded her in a smoldering glow. I could see her emotions hanging in the air around her like a smoky haze of shades of gray and brown that pulsed with intensity.

She had just finished speaking and as the last word trailed away from her mouth her bottom lip kept moving in a quiver, like it was reluctant to let go of the word. She stood limply; her head hung heavy; her eyes stared at a point in space somewhere near the floor. Her face was pale, the spark that I knew in her eyes was absent as they filled with tears. A droplet fell from her eye and I watched transfixed as it traveled the interminably long distance to the floor in a state of slow motion, undulating in shape from round to pear-like. The teardrop disintegrated as it burst against the tile and I raised my eyes to her face. I felt like I was looking at her through a magnifying glass; every pore in her skin was visible to me, everything about her was intensified. I was drawn to a line of saliva that clung to her lower lip, swaying in time with the subtle rocking of her body.

"Don't worry, Julia, it will be all right, he's in good hands. Right now, we have to be strong for him and for each other."

His voice startled me. I had been so focused on Julia that I was not aware of anyone else around me, and I had failed to see that she was standing with Dan. His voice lacked any firmness, I did not sense any conviction in his words, and that shocked me as much as anything. Dan and I were friends and business partners since we had graduated from Vanderbilt. I had never known him to be anything but loud, proud, and brash, a pillar of optimism about everything. He was a master of false bravado in the best of ways, and to hear his voice now, so thin and empty, brought a wave of sadness to the scene that was unfolding in front of me.

I was acutely aware of the urgency surrounding this moment. I was torn between wanting, needing, to be here with Julia and Dan, and yet I was feeling this strong pull drawing me back to the emergency room. I became aware of a new sensation. In split-second increments I was standing beside the body being treated in the emergency room, and then in the next moment I would be standing beside Julia and Dan. The air around me in both locations was thick with emotion. I could actually see a molecular storm of charged particles dancing and skipping all around me, colliding in a shower of sparks, the embers floating down to the tile floor where they faded away.

I focused my attention on Julia and reached out my hand to touch her shoulder, but my hand was like a hologram projected into space, and I could not make physical contact with her.

"Hey!" I said loudly, looking for her reaction to the sound of my voice. Julia responded by looking up from her abstract focus and taking a step toward Dan, burying her head against his chest. Her body began to shake with jagged spasms as her anguish seeped out.

"Listen to me," I said in a louder voice. "I'm not sure exactly what is going on here, but I need to speak with you!"

There was no response. It was like talking to someone who didn't understand the language, as if somehow my speaking louder and slower would bridge the communication gap.

"I think there has been some kind of accident; I think I've been involved in something pretty serious. I want to tell you what's going on with me, I'm not quite sure what it is. If you can listen to me just for a minute, please ..." I implored them.

"Look, I'm here with you guys right now, are you aware of that? I don't know what to tell you and I'm not sure how I can be here with you, but I am." I was basically yelling into their faces, but they were only focused on each other. "Julia, where are my kids, do you know? Were they involved in any way with whatever happened to me?"

"Dan, if I didn't have your business card in my bag, I wouldn't have known who to call, you're the only connection I had," she said, her voice a weak trill.

"I'm glad you held on to it, if we hadn't run into each other in the restaurant ... I've tried to call his ex, I left a message saying it was urgent that she call me right away or to just head down here to Baptist emergency. I don't have his kids cell phone numbers."

"This happened because of me," Julia said. "If I hadn't suggested that he meet with me this never would have happened." She sobbed into his chest.

"Look, you can't blame yourself for this. Didn't you say you were in the coffee shop when it happened?"

"Yes, but he was coming to meet with me. I saw it happen; I saw the whole thing. I rode with him in the back of the ambulance, one of the nurses here at the hospital let me into the area where they were working on him. I think she thought I was his wife.

He looked so bad. I thought he was dead when they put him in the ambulance but then I saw that he was breathing. If we hadn't agreed to meet today this wouldn't have happened. Oh God, I wish this was some kind of nightmare I could wake up from, I don't want this to be real." Now she was weeping openly. "They had him filled with tubes; he didn't even look like him anymore."

"No! No! That was before, look at me now!" I shouted at them, leaning forward trying to peer through the shock of hair that was matted against Julia's wet face. I thumped my chest with my clenched fist. "Look at me now, dammit, I'm all right, look at me now!"

"Oh Jesus, what have I done?" Her voice was a pained whisper that carved through the ethereal matter that separated us with the crisp reality of a cold scalpel touching warm flesh. "Oh God, what if he dies? I don't know what I'm supposed to do."

I drew in a deep breath. I was trying to contain my emotions, but in truth I just wanted to yell as loud as I could to feed the scream of frustration that needed to escape from me.

"Clear."

CHAPTER SIX

My eyes opened a fraction, the slits so narrow they scarcely allowed any light to penetrate the cavern that I imagined myself to be in. Somewhere off in the distance I could make out the blurred shapes of figures passing back and forth, floating like specters, in the muted light of the cave.

I felt the urge to swallow and I could not, there was some sort of obstruction in my mouth and throat. I heard a hissing sound that made me wonder if I was in some sort of factory or industrial complex, but then I recalled my earlier memories of the medical staff and what had gone on in the treatment room. I was in a hospital. The hissing sound I heard was a ventilator; that must be why I felt the obstruction in my throat. Okay, I had a certain degree of clarity as to what was going on, although I was still having difficulty arranging the thought sequences that were swimming through my head.

The memory I had of standing by the river with the woman in white was quite dominant in my thoughts. There was something about her that brought a degree of calm to me, though I found that odd considering the fact that she was a complete stranger to me.

"Joshua."

Who was that?

"Mr. Davidson, can you hear me?"

It took a second for me to realize that the voice was coming from outside my head, from somewhere in the cave. The light became brighter as I allowed my eyes to relax and open slowly.

"Mr. Davidson, I'm Doctor Neary. You're at Baptist Hospital in the intensive care ward and you've been in a traffic accident, do you understand me?"

I tried to answer him but all that came out was a gurgle and a muted cough.

"It's okay; I'll take that as a yes. Don't try to fight the tube in your throat, just relax and let it breathe for you. I'm going to take your right hand, if you can give me a small squeeze."

I did as he asked and he seemed pleased by that and asked me to perform a few other minor movements.

"Good, good," he reassured me. "Don't worry about anything right now, we're taking good care of you. We're letting the machine breathe for you just as a precaution, which is why we have you hooked up to the ventilator; you were having a bit of difficulty breathing earlier. I'm going to tell you a bit about what happened to you so that you have an understanding of how we came to this point, would that be all right?"

I nodded yes, I wanted to know.

"So, here's the story so far; the paramedics brought you in, you were in a pedestrian motor vehicle accident. Apparently, according to people who witnessed it, you stepped out into moving traffic and did not see a pickup truck coming up in the curb lane."

I closed my eyes and allowed the information to sink in and register. How could I have done something as stupid as that, just stepping out without thinking?

"You were brought in unconscious with a number of injuries," the doctor continued. "You were in shock and you had a fracture on your left leg, a nasty one where your femur, the big bone in your leg, has been damaged with a number of breaks from the impact. It's pretty serious but at the same time it's something that we're going to worry about fixing up later. Right now, the injury is stable and you shouldn't feel any discomfort from it. More importantly, when you came in you were in respiratory distress, basically your lung deflated when one of your ribs punctured it. You actually went into respiratory arrest and we aspirated your lung to get it back up and it was at that point that we put in the ET tube that you have in your throat right now. We'll remove it soon, but we wanted to have a functioning airway at the time. While we were treating you there was a concern when your heart went into ventricular fibrillation and we had to shock you a couple of times with the paddles and give you some meds to stabilize your heart rhythm. Because of all of that you'll be spending a day or two here in the ICU before we move you to a regular room and then deal with your leg. How's all of this sitting with you?" he asked.

I remember nodding appreciatively. It was okay, it was making sense to me. I wasn't dead, I wasn't a vegetable, this was all good under the circumstances. The only thing that was a bit of a mess in my head were the dreams that I had of my father and of the woman by the river.

"You have a couple of people here who want to see you," Dr. Neary said as he was preparing to leave me. "They've given our social workers the name and contact info for your family; we're trying to reach them. The woman who is waiting rode in with you in the ambulance, I understand she's a close friend and she's been quite insistent on getting in to see you. You can see her if you like, but only for a short time and only one person at a time. Are you okay with that?"

Was I okay with that? I was totally okay with that, but I couldn't say anything to him except to nod affirmatively and point to the tube in my throat.

"I understand that it's a discomfort, let me discuss with the ICU staff and see if everyone is okay with the tube coming out. Give me a minute with them. Stay here," he said and smiled.

I watched as the doctor indulged in a final glance at the monitors and, seeming satisfied with whatever he saw, he left me alone with my thoughts.

Was it reasonable to believe that there was more than one level of consciousness? I had never been a religious person, not terribly spiritual either, but I was leaning toward the idea that something either mystical or spiritual may have occurred. How else was I to explain my feeling of being outside of my body in the emergency room? How else to explain my three dreams; the one with my father, the one with the woman by the river, and the one with Julia and Dan. For now, they would be my dreams, but I suspected there might be more to them.

Even in the forced sterility of the ICU with its underlying antiseptic smell, I could readily recall the fragrance of the woman from the river, wafting about my small room. If she was something from my subconscious, or from a dream, how was it that I could smell her scent as I lay here?

"We've reached an agreement, Mr. Davidson."

The doctor's voice pulled me away from my reverie; he was standing in the doorway with one of the nurses.

"We're going to take out the endotracheal tube; it's actually better to get you weaned off of it sooner than later as long as you're not having any trouble breathing. One thing though, if it needs to go back in, it goes back and stays in, agreed?"

I nodded to him gratefully and closed my eyes as the nurse reached for the adhesive tape on my face and began removing the tube; it came out with a quick but firm yank.

"That should feel better. Breathing's okay?" he asked as he watched me closely for several seconds.

"Okay," I rasped and gave him a thumb's-up sign. "Water ..." I requested. My throat was throbbing and parched. The nurse handed me a small plastic glass with a straw attached.

"Your throat will feel better in a while," the nurse said to me. "In the meantime, let me get you some nice rich air to breathe." She reached behind me and drew out an oxygen tube and slipped it around my neck and under my nose.

"All things considered you look okay, a bit worse for wear, but okay," Dr. Neary said from his place at the foot of the bed. "Are you feeling any discomfort?"

"Not really, not any pain. I don't feel much really, I'm okay." I didn't disclose anything to him about the confusion I was feeling about what may or may not have happened to me. I didn't want to give him any reason to deny me my visit with Julia.

"You can thank Sister Morphine for that," he told me. "You've got enough in you to keep the Titans front four pain free for a week."

I gave him a faint smile.

"Did you say I have a compound fracture in my leg?" I asked. "I don't feel anything there."

"Actually, it's a comminuted fracture. In this case it is where the bone breaks in a number of places but doesn't pierce the skin like in a compound. It's not pretty either way. We've got a good orthopedic team here that will look after you once your overall condition is a bit more stabilized. They'll go in and reset things back in place, probably put a small plate and some screws in. You'll have a scar or two to show off to your friends," he offered with a smile.

My thoughts were still a little scrambled from the morphine and whatever else they had pumped into me. I had to surmise that my kids were not aware of what had happened. The doctor had said that family had not been notified yet. No one in the family, perhaps, except for my deceased father.

I tried again to retrace the progression of events as best I recalled them. The pieces began to flow and fit together in a slow-motion sequence like a 3D graphic model painstakingly assembling itself. I saw myself in the emergency room; then with my father by the bridge at the end of the pond; followed by the woman by the river; back to the emergency room; then standing beside Julia and Dan, trying to connect with them. I had no clear recollection of the accident that had precipitated the entire chain of events.

My attention was suddenly piqued by the fact that not only did the image of the woman exist clearly in my thoughts, she now existed, and very obviously, right before my eyes. To make matters even more interesting, I knew full well that I was laying on my back in the hospital bed with my stare directed to the ceiling. The view I had, allowed me to look directly into the eyes of the woman. She was suspended horizontally above me in midair and I couldn't help but notice as I gazed into her eyes that her hair did not hang down, drawn as it should have been, by gravity. I knew I was not standing erect; I could readily see that I was laying in the bed connected to the various pieces of medical equipment around me. Yet, there she was, hovering directly above me, an inviting smile playing across her mouth while her eyes danced with anticipation.

If anyone were to look into the room, they would have observed me laying on my back staring up at the ceiling, not an unusual sight at all under the circumstances, and yet if they could peer behind my eyes, they would have been aware of this most extraordinary sight.

I was instantly and completely won over by the peacefulness she exuded. It was a feeling of trust, complete trust. I felt myself surrender purely and simply into the moment, with open mind and open arms as I breathed in the intoxicating scent she wore and I felt giddy with the elation.

"Do you remember the scent now?" she inquired gently, tilting her head slightly. "It's a memory, a connection to another time, and it is obviously of significance to you, which is why you are so attracted to it."

I didn't say anything. I really had no idea what to say and instead I simply smiled back at her.

The irony that I was being treated at Baptist Hospital was not lost on me. This was, after all, the same hospital where my father had drawn his last breath and where both of my children had drawn their first. My father had been brought here after collapsing at work with chest pains. His heart had attacked him, and won. Somewhere within these same walls, my father had died without his son at his side. I had arrived just after his departure and had been taken to an operating room where my father's body still lay on a gurney covered by a thin white sheet, neatly tucked under his chin to hide the evidence of the hurried entrance that the medical team had made into his chest cavity, in a frantic attempt to reroute the flow of life force in his body.

One sad good-bye, and later two happy welcomes; how did you balance something like that on your personal score card? And now here I was in an ICU room staring at a bank of monitors, watching the screens as they read off my blood pressure, heart rate, and whatever other notations of my current existence. And then, of course, there was the woman to whom I now turned my attention back to. I was surprised, but not terribly concerned, that she had vanished from my sight. She was nowhere to be seen and yet every corner of the room seemed to radiate her presence. As close as I could describe it, she simply filled the room with a kind of electrical undercurrent.

CHAPTER SEVEN

"Josh."

The word was a whisper, almost a gasp.

My eyes were drawn to the doorway where Julia stood trembling as she swayed delicately on her feet, as if she wasn't sure if she wanted to enter the room or run from it. She looked so fragile that I wondered how her legs were able to support her. I watched her take in a breath and saw it catch in her throat; I could feel it shudder and rattle around inside of her. I followed her with my eyes as she hesitantly approached.

There was a stain of fear splashed across the warmth that I had always known in her eyes; now they had the stare of a caged animal that was searching for a means of escape. She held herself a few feet back from my side as if afraid to enter the zone of medical equipment. I raised my hand languidly in greeting to her, there was none of the rush of feeling myself flying through the air toward her as I had experienced in the hallway when I saw her earlier. She advanced tentatively and reached out to place the back of her hand against my cheek.

Her fingers were cool to the touch, she had not spoken a word since uttering my name. I moved my hand up to meet hers and our fingers intertwined for the ten thousandth time and I could feel her entire body trembling. Her tongue toyed with her lower lip, a trait she employed whenever she was troubled. Her eyes held me tighter than her arms could ever do. She opened her mouth to speak but nothing emerged, not a sound. I did not need to hear her words at that moment; I was acutely aware of everything she was feeling; I could read her emotions as though they were literally being projected onto the pale beige walls of the room. The subtle feel of her hand in mine, the nervous darting of her eyes, spoke volumes.

My throat was dry, and I was concerned about how my voice would sound when I would speak at last. I was afraid that if my voice broke, it would shatter her.

There was so much of what I had just experienced that I wanted to share with her, but I was having trouble determining how and where I should begin. It had not been lost on me, when I first saw her standing in the doorway to the ICU room, that she was wearing the white embroidered blouse, the black pants, and the black leather jacket that I had seen her wearing a short time ago in the hallway of the waiting area.

I felt very conflicted as to how I was going to convey to Julia the significance of what she was wearing and how it legitimized my belief that what I was referring to as "the dreams" were potentially not dreams at all. How should I tell her that I was pulled back here, here to my life, by the thought of her and my children as I stood by the river with the woman.

I kept my eyes locked on Julia's. She had no idea what thoughts I was hurriedly processing. Was it possible, I wondered, that I could have just walked away from this life, my life, by simply walking further into that landscape or by crossing the river? I appeared to have the ability to make the decision between returning to this life or what, of dying? Was that even my decision to make?

I pulled gently at her hand motioning for her to sit on the edge of the bed. She hesitated at first but then, keeping one foot anchored on the floor, whether for support or to facilitate her escape, she sat gingerly beside me. I wasn't sure how I should break the silence; I swallowed, trying to lubricate my throat.

"There is so much more to our lives," I began in a whisper. She looked at me quizzically, I saw the frown form and I tried another approach. "Imagine that there is another place, something on the other side."

"On the other side of what, Josh, what are you saying?"

"On the other side of the river, on the other side of the bridge," I said, quickly realizing that she did not have the slightest clue as to what I was referencing. "Julia, I saw my father, and he was standing on the far side of a bridge. He told me that it wasn't time for me to join him on the other side. And then I was standing by a river and somehow, I knew that if I crossed the river I would be going into somewhere beyond this life, some new and different place. I felt that if I did that, if I made that commitment, that it would mean that I could not get back here and be with you. The moment I decided I wanted to be with you, I was taken away from the river and I was here with you again."

I could tell from the look on her face that my words had fallen well short of their mark. Why should I expect her to understand what I was trying to communicate when even I didn't quite understand it? I chose to hold off on talking about the woman in white or mentioning my fascination with the scent she wore. I could smell it now as clearly as if it were the woman instead of Julia who was beside me. I could feel the presence of the woman, as if she were waiting patiently on the periphery of the room. I gripped Julia's hand tighter, feeling the need to be connected to her. She was like my anchor holding me in place. I was suddenly warm and anxious; I recall that I felt quite hot like I had a fever. My hand was damp in hers.

The scent of Nardos rose around me as the temperature in the room grew and I began to feel nauseous and constrained, to the point where I just wanted to leap right out of my skin. In a brief moment of panic, I found the strength to sit up and lurch forward in bed and I let out a gurgled yelp and a long rope of my spittle fell across Julia's cheek and she jumped back with a shriek as the high-pitched squeal of an alarm sounded.

I remained sitting up in bed, gasping somewhat after the expenditure of energy. Several of the leads from the monitors that had been attached to my chest were now clutched in my hand; I had ripped them from my skin in my attempt to break through the wall of anxiety that had suddenly built up inside of me. I dropped them on the sheet and adjusted the clear oxygen tube back into place beneath my nose and breathed in, letting the cool airflow calm me. As I did so two nurses entered the room, one switched off the alarm while the other came straight to my side and assessed my situation.

"I'm sorry, I'm sorry," I said, my voice hissed and cracked with the dryness in my throat. "I'm all right, really, I just overreacted at being thirsty," I lied. "It was nothing serious, I just felt the sudden need to sit up and the wires got caught up in my movement." I was afraid that they would ask Julia to leave; I could not let her be taken away from me. One of the nurses helped me to lay back down and she began to reconnect the leads that had been stuck to my chest area so they could continue to monitor whatever it was they were doing, blood pressure, heart rate, and whatever else. I felt very weak, but I did not want them to know that. I glanced over at Julia, who was cowering in the doorway.

"Mr. Davidson, an outburst like that is not going to help with your situation. If you're thirsty you can press the call button, we can get you whatever it is you need. Pulling the leads off of your chest sets off the alarm and gets everyone scrambling." She stared intently at me while putting the last monitor pad back in place. "You really shouldn't be having any visitors, particularly if it upsets you."

"No, you don't understand, I wasn't upset about my visitor, it had nothing to do with her. I'd really appreciate it if you'd let her stay just a bit longer. I handled the whole situation wrong. Can I just have some water, please?" I asked in as calm a voice as I could muster.

"Just a few minutes more," the nurse said as she handed me a small plastic cup filled with water and ice chips. "Another five minutes." The nurses left the room and Julia perched on the side of the bed once again.

"Josh, you frightened me when you did that. What was that all about? I thought you were having a seizure or something." She stroked my hand, her touch felt like sunshine on my skin.

"I'm sorry," I said to her. "I just felt, my emotions got the better of me." I paused, I wanted to get it right this time. "I was scared a couple of times; I wasn't sure what I was experiencing with those situations and then somehow I just understood that no matter what happened, that there was nothing for me to be afraid of." I watched for her reaction, she seemed to be accepting what I was saying, so I continued. "When I was afraid or concerned it felt like there was this heavy weight on me, when I finally pushed the weight off of me, the fear was gone and I felt like I stepped right out of my body. I know that sounds kind of crazy, but that's what it felt like." I looked deeply into her eyes, silently pleading with her to understand what I was trying to convey to her. The only reaction I read in her eyes was one of apprehension.

"Josh, honey, you shouldn't be talking too much. Your voice isn't strong, you should just rest, conserve your strength, you've been through a lot. Just rest, baby. I'm so glad that you're alive and okay, right now that's the only important thing."

It was apparent that she didn't share my sense of urgency in trying to understand what I had experienced.

"Julia, you know that my father passed away, but I saw him, I saw him plain as day and he was alive and I just know that it wasn't a dream or a hallucination, it was too real. The doctor told me that I stopped breathing at one point and that there was something else with my heart. I think that is when I saw my father."

She didn't say anything, instead she leaned forward and kissed me on the forehead.

I persevered.

"I think it's possible, I think that I may have been given an opportunity to see that there is something beyond this life, as we know it. I don't understand it exactly, it was like I was totally outside of my body, this body that is injured, and I was in a fresh healthy body. Then there was a river, and as I walked toward it there was a woman on the far side. I wanted to go to her, but there was something that made me feel that if I crossed the river, I wouldn't be able to come back to you and the kids. I think all of those things happened in just a few seconds, but it seemed much longer."

I felt the woman near me, but I did not mention it to Julia. I did not see her, yet I had a picture of her in my mind, like a 3D image of her pirouetting in dance, suspended in a clear blue sky.

"Josh, I'm really concerned," Julia said. "Your words are worrying me and you've got a strange look in your eyes."

I wasn't afraid, but at the same time I cautiously resisted the urge to seek out the woman. Was she meant to be a sense of comfort to me like an angel? I was not religious; I did not believe in angels; at least I never had up to this point.

"Julia, what I'm trying to tell you is that what I experienced felt as real to me as it feels to be with you right now. Maybe some of it was meant to be symbolic, but I honestly believe that if I had not felt so strongly about wanting to be with you, and with the kids again, that the outcome would have been much different. It was like you were my lifeline."

Julia began to weep quietly and I paused, even though I desperately wanted to get all of my words out.

"It was the thought of you that pulled me back, back to here, back to where you and Dan were standing together in the hallway."

"How did you know that Dan was here?" she asked, catching herself in mid-sob. "I haven't told you that Dan was here, did someone else tell you that?"

"I saw you; I saw you and Dan just as clearly as I saw my father, it was all part of the same experience." I recreated the scene I had witnessed; I knew it was important to be as accurate as I could in the information I relayed to her, I needed her to understand, I needed her to believe.

"I remember that you were talking about me and you said to Dan, 'he looked so bad, I thought he was dead when they put him into the ambulance but then I saw that he was breathing.' You also said, 'if we hadn't agreed to meet this afternoon none of this would have happened.' Do you remember saying that? Somehow I was standing beside you and Dan and I could see and hear and feel everything that was going on. I saw you wearing these clothes, I knew you were wearing this before you walked into the room. How do you think that is possible unless something impossible happened?"

"I don't know, Josh, I don't know. I can't even think about that right now."

I could tell she was reeling from the emotional fallout of the day's events, her eyes looked wild. I sensed that it was too much to throw at her right now, but I felt focused on the need to get her to accept what I was telling her.

"I remember you also said, 'Oh God, I wish this was some kind of nightmare that I could wake up from, I don't want this to be real but I saw it, I saw it all. They have him filled with tubes; he doesn't even look like him anymore.' Did you say that?"

She stared back at me, her wild eyes suddenly glazed over with a look of incredulity.

"That's what I said," she sputtered. "You could have guessed how I was feeling, but how do you know my exact words?"

"That's what I'm trying to tell you, baby, I don't understand how it happened, but somehow I was able to go from this body to another body and stand next to you and Dan." I suddenly felt tired and I closed my eyes for a moment to gather my thoughts. As I did this, I became aware of a peculiar sensation. I might have missed it the first few times it happened, but as I caught on to it, I was aware that I was blacking out, but only for a split second at a time. The episodes were like a strobe-light effect; except that the intervals were faster than any strobe I had ever seen. When the light was on, I was here in the room with Julia. When the light was off, I couldn't say where I was, just somewhere else.

I held Julia's hand in mine, the feel of her cool smooth skin became the focus of my attention in the room and I was concerned that if I were to let go of her hand during that split second that the light was off, that I might not be able to navigate my way back to her. She had indeed become my lifeline.

"Can you smell it?" I asked Julia abstractly.

"What do you mean, what is it, Josh?"

Her voice sounded far away. I hadn't meant to say those words out loud, and yet …

"The scent," I told her. I had to try to explain it to her now. "It comes from the spikenard plant. The fact that I can smell it must mean she is nearby."

"Who is nearby, what do you mean?" Julia asked. I regretted taking us down this road but felt I had to continue now.

"The woman I told you about, the one by the river, the woman in white."

My eyes scanned the room for the woman. I knew how ridiculous it sounded for me to be talking to Julia about this woman when I could not offer the slightest bit of evidence to support my claims. Even if I could see her, I was not sure that Julia would be able to.

"Josh, you've passed the point of scaring me. You're not making sense, who is this woman?"

It was happening again; not only could I hear the fear in her voice, I could actually see the physical manifestation of the energy of her fear. Large jagged waves of light quivered in the air around her. I held her hand tighter. I felt that the woman was standing right beside me.

"Josh, honey, you're hurting my hand. What's the matter, should I call a nurse?"

I saw, as much as heard, the rising inflection in her voice. I could feel my own waves of emotion growing in me, like the swells I felt when I was floating in that ocean; it was a force that spread outward in every direction and I was here in the middle of it, rising and falling with the water and it seemed I was unable to control a single aspect of it. I was carried to the crest of a wave and then pulled down into the trough as I fought to keep focused on the light off in the distance.

Was I getting closer to the light, I wondered at one point, or was it getting bigger and brighter? It was growing in intensity and then it crossed a threshold and glowed brighter than anything I had ever seen. I had been concentrating so intently on the light as I rose and fell in the swells that I had not noticed that I was no longer holding Julia's hand. I plunged my own hand into the water and felt about frantically for her. I felt the resistance of the water as I thrashed around in my fruitless search. I had lost her as my focal point. I was now experiencing this event from a perspective that I cannot adequately describe to you.

Flash.

I saw my children, Miranda and Grayson.

Flash.

The woman.

Flash.

Julia.

My attraction to Julia was intense. I felt her pulling at me, trying to draw me near to her, back into the room, back into a body that now seemed so foreign to me. I pictured her wrapped around me like a human vine and I in turn fought to hold on to her just as tenaciously. My hands felt like they were made of clay, they would not function at my command, and they slipped away from her. My movements were sluggish and clumsy.

My prevailing thought was that I was dying. That was the first time I had actually considered it to be a real possibility. I felt that I had to convey to Julia what I was thinking and feeling but I had no idea of how to do this. Where would I begin, what words would I use? All of a sudden time was the most precious commodity in my world.

My body felt numb and rubber-like without true form. I felt that if I were to stretch out my arms, if I could, that they would stretch out to infinity. Words began to tumble out of my mouth even though I wasn't sure of what I meant to say to her.

"Julia, Julia, it's so important that I tell you this." I could feel my breath fighting to form the audible words. "It's so important that you know that there is something else, something spectacular, beyond this life. Do you understand?"

"Josh." She said my name sharply, the wildness had returned to her eyes. "I'm going to get someone in here right now." She started to get up from the bed, but I grabbed her hand. "Something's not right, let me get the nurse."

My hands of clay hardened, and I was able to hold her.

"I'm so glad you were a part of my life," I told her, not sure where these words were going. "I'm sorry for the way things went with us; I wanted us to have so much more. You were the one, the one in a lifetime." I was trying to process the flow of what I felt I needed to say to her, and at the same time I was panicking about my children. "Julia, I don't know where the kids are, I don't know if I will see them. You have to tell them that I said how much I love them. Promise me. And you, I love you so much, I always have."

"Josh, I promise, but please don't talk this way, let go of me and let me get someone in here to help you."

"Julia." My mind was empty, I didn't have words to say to her.

"Josh, let go of my hand, please leave me be. Don't talk, just be all right and let me get someone," she pleaded with me.

I did not want to defy her or frighten her any more than I already had, but there was no way for me to mask the urgency I felt.

"No, please, don't go. Stay. It doesn't matter now." Tears stung my eyes and ran freely down my face burning a path down my cheek; I tasted the saltiness at the corner of my mouth. I recall being struck by my stark acceptance of how this situation was evolving. Without properly understanding it at the time, it felt normal, quite natural; I was surprised, but not shocked, at my acceptance of the organic flow of my thoughts. It was not without sadness, it was not without regret, but I felt no need to struggle at this point.

The woman in white was near me, I felt her presence and with it came a comfort that allowed me, encouraged me, to surrender to the situation without fear. I did not feel that I was giving up or giving in, in fact I felt a sense of empowerment grow in me as I willingly embraced the moment.

"I can't find the words, Julia." My voice caught in my throat. She looked down at me, her mouth was moving but no sound came forth. Instead, there were her tears that fell to my face like a shower of broken dreams.

"I'm here to help you."

I saw the woman clearly now, standing in the corner of the room.

"Julia, just hold me, don't go anywhere," I said to her.

She did not offer any resistance. I could see the dark shadings of her fear and confusion conflicting with the bright yellow glow that projected her feelings for me. It swirled like smoke as it enveloped an intense flame. She leaned toward me and draped her body protectively over mine. The wetness of her cheek felt cool against my skin.

"Julia, I wanted so much for us." My voice sounded distant to me and it caught me off guard. "I wanted to grow old with you." Her hair fell on my face and I hid beneath it. I felt myself tenuously slipping away from her grasp, from this place, from this life. I wanted to burrow deeper into her arms. Her hair still covered my face, and I breathed in the scent of her and it was the scent of springtime, of fresh green buds stretching open with the sweet freshness of new life bursting forth, as my own life trickled away like water through my fingers, spilling away like tiny rivers running to the sea.

My soul ached. Somewhere inside of me I felt the fiber of my being unraveling. A thousand sighs could not have quenched my feelings of sorrow and anguish as I mourned the days I would no longer spend with my children, and their children; and Julia … my life, my love, my breath. I was aware for just a moment that I was no longer breathing as I bridged two solitudes.

I felt my muscles tighten in a gentle convulsion as if I was being squeezed out of my body and then with no further effort on my part I was standing beside Julia, watching as the body in her arms went limp and sprawled clumsily on the bed under its own weight. A high-pitched buzzing erupted from the bank of monitors beside the bed as the alarm sounded. I stood by passively as Julia leapt bolt upright in the sudden realization of what had just occurred.

I stepped aside as a nurse brushed hurriedly past me followed quickly by a second person. The first grabbed Julia by the shoulders and pulled her away from the bedside. She was left directly facing me and then she retreated to a corner of the room, staring right through me, her face stained with terror. I watched intently as the second nurse went to the side of the bed and silenced the alarm as she called my name several times. Then she placed a hand-held ventilator bag over the face of the body and began squeezing air into it.

"Call a code," she said to the other nurse, who activated some switch or button on the wall. She then began to press down on the chest of the body.

"Code Blue, ICU. Code Blue, ICU." I heard the disembodied voice emanate from the speakers in the ceiling as it was simulcast through the various corridors of the hospital. I understood the implication of the announcement, but my focus remained on Julia, who stayed tucked in the corner of the room riveted in place by panic and fear, her arms clutched tightly across her chest. The skin on her knuckles was drawn white as she huddled against the reality unfolding in front of her. I felt powerless to assist her. The body on the bed lay inert; it was a shell that I no longer felt a relationship with.

As I watched the resuscitation attempt being played out before me, I felt like I was observing some far-off movie screen, like an old drive-in movie that you passed on the expressway as you hurtled along on the way to your destination. Beyond the transparent movie screen stood the woman in the white dress. She appeared to be standing in the middle of a field and at the same time she was standing in the middle of my hospital room. I saw the river sparkling as it cut through the field and I realized that I was now viewing the river from the far bank. I had crossed the river. The woman stood silently and welcomed me with a pleasing smile as her clothing and everything about her glowed brighter and brighter with each passing moment until I felt myself swallowed whole by the ball of light. I was overtaken by a passion that enthralled me and begged—demanded—the attention of every cell in my being.

PART TWO

Love and Fear
The choices we make in life are generally based on one or the other.

CHAPTER EIGHT

In this next section of my story, dear reader, I would like to properly introduce you to me, and my life. I'd like to share with you the people and the events that brought us to that ICU room at Baptist Hospital, where my life went through such a transformation. As I said earlier, my life was quite ordinary by most standards. If you knew me, worked with me, or lived in the same neighborhood as me, I don't think you would have thought me out of place at all. In other words, I was just like you, or like someone you knew. Nothing out of the ordinary. Well, let me tell you the rest of my story, and you can decide what is ordinary and what might qualify as extraordinary.

My name is Joshua Davidson and I stand before you guilty of idealism. That said, I would also like to add, that I am guilty with an explanation. Furthermore, I would also like to include that I admit to being a man whose belief in the idea that I could change the world has been severely challenged of late. After going through much in the way of trial and tribulation, I have arrived at the conclusion that it may well be easier for me to get used to the idea of wearing slippers on my bare feet than it would be for me to try to carpet the entire world for my personal comfort.

As strong as my desire was to walk barefoot and carefree, I have given in to this compromise, after having spent an inordinate amount of time and energy trying to lay the carpet and have not enjoyed a lot of success with my efforts. I have finally admitted that either way my feet will be comfortable, and wearing the slippers may indeed allow me a greater degree of flexibility in handling those things that I'm still trying to understand and deal with.

I believe it is true that not a lot of people go about their lives consciously looking to change things about their situation. Many in fact, fight to keep things the same, regardless of whether they are happy with the circumstance or not. It is often their overriding desire to have someone else, some person, deity or organization, government or religion, be responsible for their completeness and happiness. That way, they don't have to contemplate the gift of change. They can go with someone else's flow, float in someone else's river.

Change was that stranger that threatened the safety of their routine. Once you stepped away from the routine of the routine, you had to make your own choices, and the responsibility that came with that could be scary for many.

I was not terribly different from most people in that regard. For me, change was that bogeyman that used to live at the bottom of the stairs in the basement of the house where I grew up. I was the only child of parents who went out of their way to avoid change, even as it occurred all around them. Years later, as a grown man, when confronted with the possibility, or worse the inevitability, of change, I could quite vividly reach back and connect with that feeling. Many times, I had relived those visits down to the damp dusky cavern, feeling the coolness of the cellar swim up to meet me as I descended the stairs. There was a moldy tang in the air and my footing became less sure with each step taken. The light from the landing would never permeate much beyond the bottom of the staircase, and I would rush the distance to the next source of light, where the string was attached with a big knot to the short silver pull chain.

Change was that hand that I was sure was going to reach

out of the darkness and grab me by the wrist, just as my fingers were closing around the lifeline that was connected to the light. I spent so much time trying to avoid that hand that it wasn't until many years later that I ever considered the idea of confronting the hand full on; of actually reaching out and grasping the hand before it could grab me.

Much of what I believed as a child, simplistic as it may have been, actually stood me pretty well over the years. Along the way I learned a lot of boring grown-up things like how to calculate a mortgage, how to plan and pay for a funeral. I learned to play the politics game on many different levels. Very few of the grown-up things I learned brought me much in the way of satisfaction the way my childhood discoveries did. In my smarter moments, I would still rely on the instincts I learned before the age of ten to get me through most things.

The passage of time reveals many things; one in particular is the presence of a weakness. A fissure, no matter how slight in appearance, will suffer through that passage and slowly but surely it will transform into a crack on its way to becoming an expanding separation of the parts of the whole. Sooner or later that seemingly innocuous crack, that troubling mark out of sight but not out of mind, will beg your attention.

I was reminded of that as I reflected on a brief conversation I had one evening with my wife, Amanda, after I may have consumed an extra glass of wine or three.

"I've never understood the term 'irreconcilable differences,'" I blurted out, without really being sure where I was going with my point. We were sitting in the family room, watching one of those reality shows on TV, doing our best to be a family in what was supposed to be a home, but as it would turn out, was really more of a house.

"What is it with these celebrity couples announcing they are splitting up after only a few months due to irreconcilable differences? How the hell do you know after only three or four months that your differences are irreconcilable?"

Perhaps it was the wine, but I did not notice the look in her eye that I would see on later occasions. Later that night when

I did not feel her touch, I did not put the two things together. I didn't see the little fractures that had already developed in our marriage, but there they were, biding their time, waiting, just waiting.

They say that when a relationship has reached the point of indifference that it has lived its lifetime. Later, it would be so obvious to me that Amanda and I had really just been going through the motions of a life together. We lived together, but we lived our lives apart. I think I knew this long before I admitted it to myself. I guess I just didn't want to accept that particular gift at the time. Couldn't you give it to someone else, please? How about another one of those celebrity couples? Instead, we fell into the Pavlovian response to the stimuli in our relationship. We spoke the appropriate words on command, but we didn't really own the words. When one of us would say "I love you" the other would respond in kind, though not necessarily in a kind way. It was an autonomic response, like breathing; something you did without consciously thinking about it, without appreciating it, until it was no longer there.

When the inevitable became, well, inevitable, when the time came that Amanda and I had made our way through a list of counselors that well-meaning friends had suggested to us, when we had finally learned how to break up our marriage, my friend and business partner Dan suggested I talk to this guy named Herschel. The first time I walked into the office of Herschel Allen, I thought I was at the wrong address.

The office was housed in a third-floor loft tucked away in a laneway off West Second. As I stepped off the elevator into what appeared to be a reception area, I think I could have been forgiven for thinking I was walking into an artist's workspace. Hanging from a heavy oak beam was a large wrought-iron birdcage that contained the life-sized huddled wooden sculpture of a man scrunched inside with his knees drawn up under his chin, his face turned downward. A large canvas, it appeared to be about six feet by four feet, leaned against an exposed brick wall that stretched up to the full height of the perhaps twelve-foot ceiling. The painting looked to me more like a Rorschach test than a piece of art, but that may simply have been my lack of appreciation for a lot of modern art. The lighting was provided by what looked like a photographer's lamp that stood on a tripod in the corner with an antique umbrella attached to the front, so that the overall lighting effect was soft and diffused. There was not an actual receptionist, other than the birdman, to welcome visitors. After ringing the bell in the uninhabited reception area, I waited, wondering who, or what, was going to greet me.

An hour later as we neared the end of our first meeting in "the work room," as Hersch called the area where he conducted the sessions, I stared at the sky through the angled bank of north-facing windows and with quiet resignation accepted that it had indeed come to this.

"Communication, Joshua, proper communication between you and me is the key to our successfully resolving the issues you find yourself facing. Once we, and more importantly you, understand the situation, then we can begin to deal with it." And with that he bade me good day.

As I walked back to my car, I chuckled to myself in a dark tone. Communication was supposed to be my strong suit, being part owner of an advertising company and all. Communication was one of the true weak spots in my relationship with Amanda. In the first few months following our breakup, I heard from my ex on the back on my checks, and that was about it. We scarcely talked on the phone; I would pick up the kids and it was rare for her to be home at that time due to her work schedule. It was the day nanny who greeted me.

I would look at those monthly reminders when the bank sent my checks back to me as they were cashed, and I would stare at her signature. The blue ink on the paper was like the blue ink of a tattoo. It was a faded blue, nothing like the brilliant peacock or proud teal it had been at one time. It had become anemic; the color wasted and ill, washed out by too many tears.

I have looked across the way at some guy in a bar who has a tattoo of a woman's name somewhere on display on his person, and wondered how smart that was, how long he had actually stayed with the person he had immortalized on his flesh.

We always think forever means forever.

At our second meeting at the end of the week I had mentioned to Hersch the irreconcilable differences conversation that I had with Amanda.

"Can you imagine? At that point we had been together, wait, let me think." I pulled out my phone and opened the calculator. "We were together one hundred and forty months, give or take. Not three or four like it took those celebrity couples to figure it out, but a hundred and forty! How stupid am I that it took me that long to discover what these movie-star types knew in no time at all?" My thumbs punched away at the keypad. "Averaging it out, let me see, including sleeping, take away work time, that puts us somewhere in the neighborhood of sixty thousand hours of being in each other's space compared to, say, three thousand hours for the movie stars. No wonder they are the millionaires living the high life, and I'm just trying to make a living and sitting here with you discussing my life. Am I right, Hersch?"

"What's wrong with sitting here with me? You're not enjoying it?" he said.

"What's not to enjoy?" I laughed.

"Well, your math is probably accurate based on the number of hours you're tossing about, but I'm not sure your conclusion needs to be quite so drastic."

As it turned out, Hersch was someone I did enjoy talking with. It wasn't that he agreed with me or said things that he knew I would enjoy hearing. In truth, Hersch and I regularly hit some pretty turbulent times with our exchanges of opinion and fact. Hersch was a straight shooter. When he hit me with a revelation, he always showed me where the punch was coming from, and where it was going to land.

"It's the only way you're going to learn to defend yourself out there," he told me. We went through some solid rounds.

Hersch was the voice of reason, the voice that convinced me that I needed to learn to let go of certain things in order to gain control of my life

"You simply cannot control every element of your life, Josh, and in fact why do you want to? Who has the time and energy? You've got to learn to not always try to fight the current, sometimes you need to learn to just go with the flow; you'll get to where you're going that much faster, and in better shape. The more things you try to control, the less control you actually have."

It was Hersch who suggested the idea of me wearing slippers, instead of trying to carpet the entire world.

"Why not aspire to things that you can succeed at, instead of beating yourself up by setting impossible goals that you end up viewing as failures when you don't achieve them? If this marriage of yours is dead, then let's grieve the death and get over it. Life does go on. Josh, my job is not to pull you out of the water every time you fall into something over your head. My job is to teach you how to swim so that you can get out of that mess yourself. I'm not a lifeguard, and you are not helpless."

I had asked him about pills.

"I don't believe in medication except where it is truly warranted. Pills just serve to hide the truth of your situation from you and the fact is, you can only fool yourself for so long. Things are rarely as good or as bad as they seem, it's all a matter of learning how to look at something and then applying yourself to it. I learned something once from a famous comedian who I did a few sessions with. I actually said to him that I thought a lot of what I did was similar to an improv set, because I often didn't know what would end up surfacing from someone and how I would react to it. I asked him what the secret to good improv was and he said it was as simple as this: Accept and Accelerate. Those were his words of wisdom to me, and they are good words.

"In your case, Josh, here's what I think it means, accept that your marriage to Amanda is over and may well have been over for a long time before you realized it, or at least were ready to accept it, but accept it now that it is done; then accelerate. Move beyond it, know that you can't fix it anymore. You don't need to find a new kind of glue; you need to work on building and keeping a good relationship with your kids. You need to move forward, take your life to the next level, your new level."

He was right, of course, that was the thing I had to focus on. Well, two things, actually.

Thing One is Grayson, born May 21, nine years old and a very capable Gemini. Thing Two would be Miranda, Randi almost from day one, born August 30, and at the age of seven was already becoming the kind of caregiver and detail person that would make any Virgo proud. I had acknowledged, in discussions with Hersch, that it was indeed likely that Thing One and Thing Two had kept me and Amanda together for as long as the marriage had lasted. Children, friends, and activities are often the stitching that holds a couple together. How many marriages simply soldier on, as long as they can, because of the routine and distractions that those components bring to the table?

CHAPTER NINE

The very first time I laid eyes on Julia Moore, she was standing there before me all shiny and new, shimmering in the arrogant heat that Nashville summers are known for. I didn't understand it at the time, you rarely do, but later in the cool appraisal that hindsight brings, I would realize that it was one of those moments where my journey had been altered; significantly and forever.

I had just left a meeting with a client who had flown in from New Orleans to meet with me. They were staying at the Vanderbilt Hotel and as I made my way along Broadway, I saw her. She was standing on the sidewalk beside a car, a black SUV as I recall, speaking in an animated manner to someone who was inside the vehicle. In that split second, acting purely on instinct, like a bird turning to follow an invisible line in the sky, I proceeded toward her, armed with the knowledge that I simply had to talk with this woman.

I had never done anything like this in my life. I had absolutely no idea what words were going to come out of my mouth. I thought about it later, the fact that a more rational man might have looked at the situation and decided that approaching this couple in order to speak to the woman was not only possibly rude and inappropriate, but also potentially dangerous. I didn't give it a second thought at the time, going only with my first one, knowing with that quiet confidence that the universe gives you, when you have been offered an insight that only you are privy to. I had to connect with this woman, if only for this one moment, to know what it felt like to catch her gaze in mine just once, and then I would move on with my life.

"Hi, excuse me," I said to her, and realized that I was holding my business card in my outstretched hand, like it was some talisman that would protect me from all things dangerous. "My name is Joshua Davidson. I hope you'll forgive me, but rather than going through the websites of all the talent agencies in Nashville to figure out who you are, I thought I would just approach you. I run an advertising agency, here's my card, and I wonder if you would give me a call to discuss a project I'm working on?" I smiled and kept the card positioned in front of her, daring her to take it.

"Really," she said. It was a statement, not a question, and she regarded me with a glare that froze me in my tracks until a tiny sparkle flashed in her eyes, which released me. "I will think about it." I realized that she was addressing the man in the vehicle and I began to question the boldness of my approach. "What is it that you have in mind?" she asked, turning her attention back to me. "I'm not a model or anything like that."

"What's the product?" her companion inquired from the driver's seat. I didn't like the tone coming from the man that I would learn later was her husband.

"It's a campaign for an office temp company," I answered so effortlessly that it surprised me. I was being somewhat truthful, the client I had just met with ran a temp agency, we hadn't discussed final creative yet. My sudden on-the-spot brainstorm was to include this woman in the ad.

Ten days later, during the photo shoot for one of the South's better regarded temporary office support providers, I was standing once again beside Julia, and I was concerned. Several times I had to consciously pull my gaze away from her. I could not look her in the eye. I was afraid that if I did, I would fall head long into a situation that could very easily become awkward. I was fearful of the consequences of making some kind of advance toward her, and even more fearful of making no advance at all and letting her slip out of my life.

I did my best to rationalize all the reasons why she would not have the least bit of interest in me. I was married, with two kids; I must have been at least a dozen years older than her, I guessed. Everything about the circumstance pointed me toward the obvious conclusion that my desire to have some sort of further interaction with her was a flirtation with fantasy at best, and potentially quite damaging to my personal life at worst. I did the most rational thing I could think of and pressed on regardless.

"I write about pretty much what I want. I suggest pieces and they take them or not, occasionally one of the editors will mention a story idea, but usually it's me pitching them with things that I'm interested in. I have a few friends in the music industry, so I profile them whenever it's a good fit. I do lifestyle pieces often, and once in a while a travel feature," Julia told me after we had wrapped on the set. I managed a few minutes aside with her while we stood at the roadside. As she waited for her husband to arrive, she was telling me about her freelance writing, most of it done for one of our local papers, the *Tennessean*.

"I guess that makes for some pretty nice and probably free vacations," I said, imagining myself running away with her somewhere. "Do you get to take your husband with you?"

"Sometimes," she replied, toying with the thin gold watch strap on her wrist as she glanced at the time. "Actually, we've traveled separately a few times. He likes to go to Vegas and on golfing trips with his buddies. I don't play golf and I've been to Vegas enough times. We do travel, but when I'm working on a travel piece, I'll often go by myself. I like my alone time, and besides, it's still work, after all."

"Well, nice work if you can get it," I said, intuitively sensing that there was an emotional distance between Julia and her husband. I wondered if she was telegraphing this to me, or was it just my overactive imagination?

"And the other thing is, my writing also gives me a certain amount of free time to explore other things; I'm trying to get to the point where I can be more involved in the music business."

"What do you play?" I asked.

"I'm more of a songwriter than performer," she said, and again I had to consciously avert my eyes. I was sure I was staring at her way too intensely for this casual conversation. "I play guitar and write lyrics; I'm trying to learn a bit of piano."

"Country?" I inquired.

She nodded.

"Figures." I laughed. "It's one type of music I have a bit of trouble with. Seems like every second person you meet in Nashville is a songwriter or performer."

"Does your work in advertising ever bring you into the music business?" Julia asked, tilting her head to glance up the road at an approaching vehicle. She turned at an angle that exposed the silkiness of her neck, and it was everything I could do to look away. I had already started rocking on my heels looking for the momentum to lean forward and kiss her neck.

"Not so much," I blurted the words out awkwardly as I caught myself in mid-motion, while pushing away the thought of the feel of my mouth on her skin. "My business partner Dan is sure he's going to write something big one day, so he gets close to the music business every chance he gets. He's written a few songs but hasn't really been able to do much with them so far. I'm not really much of a country fan," I conceded, as the SUV pulled up to the curb.

"Well, between me, you, and your partner Dan, I guess your assessment of every second person being in the music industry would be fairly accurate." She flipped her hair with her hand and let it settle into its natural fall line. "Too bad you don't like country music; it's kind of my favorite. I'm going to have to see about converting you; maybe I'll just write a song for you one day."

That day would indeed come, and with it would be the lesson that is one of the basic tenets of a country song; they do a very good job of telling the stories of the hurtin' side of life. It is true that the people you love the most are also the same ones that can hurt you the most. I didn't realize it at the time, but I had already fallen in love with Julia. I was not yet aware of how painful things were about to become. I did have a brief insight into it when, a few seconds later, I watched her walk toward the car where her husband waited. I felt a fanatical urge to run after her, grab her by the arm, and spin her around so I could spirit her away with me. As she got in the car and drove off without a backward glance, I realized how terrible you could feel over losing something that you never actually had.

Over the course of the next few weeks there would be the occasional note from Julia in my work email. Sometimes it was just a simple greeting, "hope you're keeping out of the heat today," once it was a copy of one of those brilliant European TV commercials that somehow managed to sell you on the attributes of their latest car design while making light of someone's flatulence. Perhaps you've seen it.

At the time I did not read too much into her communication with me. Perhaps she thought I would be a good contact for her down the road. I did, however, scan the *Tennessean* daily, looking to see if one of her articles happened to grace that particular edition. It was a secret indulgence of mine to sit in the big armchair in the living room, which at one time Amanda and I used to fit in together, before the distance between us grew too great. While the kids wandered in and out of the room on their various missions, I would read Julia's column when it was there and humor myself with my wishful thinking.

It was on one of those quiet, rather nondescript afternoons at the office, as the day quietly ran down to quitting time, that I was reminded that when one door is closing, another door is often being kicked in on your behalf. I had stepped away from my desk for a moment to refill my water bottle and when I returned, I was greeted with a red light on the phone signaling a voice message.

"I'm going to the dentist today at 4:30 and I realized that he is very close by your office; maybe I could buy you a glass of wine after work as a thank-you for putting me in the magazine ad. My gram loved it by the way; I had to buy several copies for my relatives."

I replayed the message a second time, taking great delight in the fact that Julia had taken our communication to a new, albeit still quite innocent level. We had moved from the relative safety of an email message, to the slightly more personable voice mail. I marveled at how the sound of her voice had created such a warm and sensual reaction in me.

We met for that glass of wine, which became three. The feeling that had come over me at the photo shoot returned with a vengeance, and as we sat on the small couch in the lounge of the bar, I had to continually remind myself to maintain a suitable sense of decorum.

We left the lounge just after six, I was heading home and Julia was on her way to pick up her husband from wherever he was having after-work drinks with friends. As we entered the parking lot, a car backed up suddenly from its space and in a reflex action, based on many years of dad training, I instinctively grabbed her hand and pulled her back. At that moment I was introduced to a sensation I had never experienced before.

The feeling was this: In that split second as I slipped my hand around Julia's, I felt my feet leave the ground. Not figuratively, not metaphorically. I actually believed that my feet physically left the ground. I had never before known this incredible feeling of lightness, except perhaps in a dream. I had certainly never felt it with Amanda.

It was like I was being levitated, and when we arrived at her car I stood there, a few inches off the ground I'm sure, not sure what to do and concerned that anything I might say would dispel the magic of the moment.

"I'm going to need my hand back so that I can get in the car," Julia said playfully to me, with a smile that made me feel like I was bathed in warm sunlight.

"I'm sorry," I stammered. "That guy came out of that parking space pretty fast."

"You mean that car that backed up a few minutes ago?" The smile remained. "I have to go now to meet up with my husband, and you have a wife and kids to go home to."

I did not speak. My response was to lean forward to kiss her, unable or unwilling to fight the feeling any longer. At the last

moment she turned her face away and my lips brushed her cheek.
"You can't do that, I'm married, remember?" She adjusted
her hair but I saw that the smile remained.

"I know, I'm married too," I said. "I think one cancels out the
other like a double negative becomes a positive, or something like
that." I doubled down and leaned in again, only to be presented
with her cheek once more. I compensated by angling my head
and I kissed her neck instead. I knew I was crossing a line, but
I didn't care to stop myself as my mouth touched her warm and
fragrant skin. I took half a step back from her. I would have fully
accepted a slap in the face from her, but instead she regarded me
for a few seconds; her head was tilted slightly and I wondered if
she was waiting for me to try a third time.

"Sorry," she said, pushing her hair behind her right ear,
something that I would watch her do a thousand times in the
future. She observed me with interest across the short distance
that separated us. "I'm usually a more enthusiastic kisser."

CHAPTER TEN

There was a time when I loved Sunday afternoons more than any other day. This was especially true in the fall, when I had the luxury of crashing out on the weathered brown leather couch in the TV room for a couple of hours to watch football, while I watched my family go about their day all around me. At some point Grayson would find his way over to the couch to watch part of a game with me, usually falling asleep within minutes, tucked into the curl of my arm like a gangly football. His hair, slightly damp with sweat, nudged into my face and I was surrounded by that little boy smell that I knew would soon fade.

I realized later, that as much as the games brought me pleasure, in truth they were simply the soundtrack and backdrop to those times when Gray and I would share our warmth, all the while drifting in and out of that narcotic haze that came over you as you flirted with sleep, and then teased yourself awake again. They were perfect days.

Of course, I did enjoy the games too. There was something akin to artistry and pageantry about football that appealed to me. While you might never go so far as to compare the NFL to, say, the Dance Theater of Harlem, if you carefully observed those muscular-yet-lithe wide receivers as they leapt into the air, performing a three-quarter pirouette as they snagged the ball into those hands so artfully extended, and then landed miraculously with both feet inbounds, it could easily be considered an artistic form, or so I thought. To close the routine the player then tucks his head down while executing a graceful tumble to the hard ground, scattering the phalanx of photographers and cheerleaders on the sidelines in his wake. Then, to the cheers of the assembled multitude, especially those in the balcony seats, he would leap back to his feet in grand exclamation, followed by a bow to the appreciative audience while other members of the team fondled the player's buttocks and slapped him on the side of the head. Come to think of it, football shares a lot more with ballet than you might think at first glance.

I enjoyed football as much for the show within the show as I did for the actual game itself. The play by play, when done right, was such an integral part of the afternoon, that I often wished I could get hold of a set of those magic pencils that drew white scribbles all over the screen. I would have liked to be able to draw a bunch of lines in midair to show my wife how all the little things in life are connected to the big play happening on the screen in front of us.

"See how this line connects my mood at the end of the day with your reaction? See how us not talking about things at the right time opens up this hole in the offensive line? Look at the play clock running down, spoiling our chances for an on-side kick, which is our only hope of pulling a win out of this marriage. And … look at these two kids standing forlornly on the sidelines while we argue over the placement of the ball when there is no time left on the clock anyway."

There was a time when I would have paid a small fortune for a set of those magic pencils. I wanted a re-do on the play-by-play portion of my life. Of course, in my postgame analysis I would have had to acknowledge the fact that you can't expect to score on every single play, that we couldn't win every game, every time. Somebody always had to lose; in fact, no one really won, it's just that one person lost slower than the other.

I had made it a point to not discuss my personal life with clients, and so I could not readily explain why it was that over a business lunch, I spilled my guts about my situation at home to a client. Later, when I learned that there are no coincidences, it all fit into place like those notorious jigsaw puzzle pieces of our life. At the time I simply chalked it up to some very good luck, as a phone call was made and arrangements quickly fell into place. It was one of those situations where you just sat back and kept out of the way as the pieces moved about the chess board, seemingly of their own accord.

Who would sublet a furnished condo to a complete stranger just like that? The person who would, it turned out, was a friend of my client who had also recently become single again. For him, this was the third time, and he had decided to explore a different passion in life and to relocate to Florence, Italy, in order to study painting in a nine-month program.

The apartment, an eight-hundred-square-foot place of solace, was my saving grace. After all the conversations with Amanda that had led us to this moment, for all the anticipation I felt as Julia and I discussed this major change in my life, the bottom line was that I was afraid; afraid of what I had left behind and equally afraid of what may lay ahead. A few days into the move, as I stood in the late-day sun that streamed into the southwest bank of windows ten floors above ground, I finally began to feel some small comfort in the sanctity of my new surroundings.

The man who owned the apartment had retired early, at age fifty, after selling off the small chain of auto body shops that he had started up in his early twenties. After exiting marriage number three, he had bought this place and spent the last year or so deciding on what to do with the back half of his life. Somewhere in his ruminations he had discovered a love for painting that had never presented itself to him before. I only met him a few days before I moved in, and he moved on, to his next adventure.

He took great pride in the fact that he had furnished the apartment himself, and when I first saw the place, it was obvious, even to someone like me who knew next to nothing about decorating, that a guy had made the choices. The pieces were large and deliberate and sat proudly in their places. There was nothing subtle about it, no nuances or artfully placed arrangements. It was all upfront and open, kind of how he wanted his life to be, he had said to me while showing me around. If this apartment were a dinner plate, it would be a honking big steak with a massive baked potato beside it.

"I used to believe that you could not make love with someone without kissing them during it," I said to Julia during one of our brief encounters at the apartment, just prior to an event she would be attending with her husband later that evening. Almost from the day I moved into this place, we had made it a point to rendezvous here where we, often hurriedly, made love before she had to get home or to meet up with her husband somewhere. "I guess I proved myself wrong on that count with Amanda."

"I've been doing it that way for the past year at least, with Mike; that is, when we even bother to have sex," she responded, as though we were discussing a mutual hobby, like photography. "It's at the point now where I don't even think about it or miss it. I hadn't thought about it until you just mentioned it."

"Why would you stay in a situation like that?" I asked.

"Why did you?"

"Well, I've got kids, responsibilities. I wasn't prepared at the time to break up my family just because the kids' mother didn't kiss me when we made love."

"First of all, if we're going to have this silly conversation, if you're not kissing during the act, we shouldn't call it making love, we'll just call it having sex, and probably not very good sex. Secondly, refer to part one; if you're not kissing your spouse, especially when you're having sex, you likely don't have much of a marriage left at that point. You're done, you just haven't worked out the details yet."

"You're quite the pragmatist, aren't you?" I said. "If it's as cut and dried as that why don't you leave your marriage?"

"I feel like I already have," she said wistfully. "I wouldn't be here with you otherwise. I'm certainly not there in spirit, I'm just there because I took a vow and I haven't decided to undo it totally yet."

"Define totally."

"Sometimes I think that if I tried a little harder, if I took my happiness out of the equation then it would be different, though not necessarily better. I just need to sort through a few more things before I do something about it. I'm not very good with failure."

"Tell me again why we're still debating our situation? You're twenty-seven, with the world at your fingertips, and you still can't decide if or when you're going to leave Mike," I said to her. "I'm forty with two kids, wonderful as they are, and a soon-to-be ex-wife who is going to be who knows what to deal with. Are you sure you want this?"

"You don't get it, do you, Josh? I want to be with you. I want—watch my lips—to be with you. I could not be with you, while I'm still married, if I did not want to be with you more than anyone else in the world. The fact that I am not moving at your speed is immaterial. If being with you means having your kids with us every second weekend, or whatever you work out, and having to deal with your ex is the way it's going to be, then so be it. What price do you want to put on happiness? Being happy doesn't mean that everything is perfect. Personally, I think perfection is overrated; I'm a big fan of excellence, I'm a big fan of happiness.

"I know I'm happy when I'm with you, happier than I've ever been with anyone else, and I believe I will continue to be happy with you no matter the circumstances. One of these nights when you're not lying awake half the night trying to solve every problem at once, trying to make everything in your world perfect at the same time, perhaps you will learn what it is like to be happy too. I believe in you. When I am ready, and when I think you are ready to move forward, I will leave my marriage to be with you. What is so difficult to understand about that?"

Somewhere over the mid-Atlantic as we flew toward New York City aboard the Royal Air Maroc 787, with our time away together in Morocco fading into the jetstream, I had awoken from my half sleep and caught Julia quietly sobbing. She was staring out into the blackness where ocean and sky merged, and as I watched her shoulders gently tremble, I looked into the blackness that merged my head and heart and shuddered.

It seemed that the fantasy we had enjoyed overseas had run its course as the plane slipped out the air and took hold of firm ground once again. She held my hand as the plane eased its way into the final approach; she was not a good flyer, but she quickly released my hand as the roar of the reverse thrusters began to fade and the plane slowed and coasted the final part of our journey along the runway.

She had that uncanny knack of being able to glance at me and know intuitively where my thoughts were. As we waited in line at customs, we did not exchange a word. We were both exhausted, and not simply from the busy itinerary of the trip.

We had determined, before we left for Morocco, that when we arrived back at Kennedy airport that I would continue on home to Nashville, while Julia would remain in New York to meet up with her husband, who would be there for meetings at his company's head office. There would be a two-hour wait between flights for me and after checking my luggage through for the final leg home I walked Julia outside to the cabstand. I remember how appropriate it felt that it was one of those dreary and damp late fall days in New York, and how it matched the emotions living inside of me at that moment.

As I prepared to release Julia back to her husband after spending these past nine days with her, I stumbled to the conclusion that it appeared that I was about to release her fully and completely. I didn't see any other way that I could offer my children the stable family environment that I wished for them. I had not yet shared this conclusion with Julia, but I knew that she had simply known, as she always seemed to know, that this outcome was all but established.

"I thought that this trip would be the make or break for us." She sighed, cracking the skin of the awkward silence, as we stood just outside the terminal building amid the hustle as the world came and went all around us. I felt her thin fingers stroking my wrist as she spoke. She was always touching me; her hand resting on my arm as we watched television in the apartment; her foot against mine in a restaurant; her breath falling on me as we slept entwined.

"Tell me the story of how going back to a loveless marriage scares you less than being happy with me," she said.

"I'm not scared of being happy with you," I said, watching as the tears began to well up in her eyes. "The idea of me putting my happiness above that of my kids is what scares me."

"I understand that, Josh, it's one of the reasons why I love you. I don't mind coming in second behind your kids, as long as that is the only reason."

"What do you mean, what other reason could there be?"

"If you are still in love with your wife, then tell me and we can be done with this once and for all. If that's not the case then I'm prepared to wait for you, to see if you change your mind about being with me." She looked deeply into me and I felt uncomfortably exposed. "I don't know if I will wait forever, but I will wait, for now."

It was during the drive through the Atlas Mountains as we wound our way through Morocco, that I had resolved to try one last time to convince Amanda that we should attempt to put our lives, our kids' lives at least, back together. For the sake of the children, and well, for the sake of trying. It just felt too easy to split up this way, and I was afraid that we had moved too far, too fast.

Without speaking another word, she stepped forward as the taxi eased to a halt in front of us. I placed her luggage in the trunk and held the rear door open for her. She did not look at me as she got into the car, and for that I was strangely thankful. I watched, despairingly, as she was whisked away from me and swallowed up by the city. Why, I wondered, were we always leaving each other?

CHAPTER ELEVEN

There is something I have always found quite enchanting about the sound of wind-driven rain; I have been drawn to it for as long as I can remember, perhaps similarly to the way a baby will listen to its mother's heartbeat.

To me the sound of rain drumming in rhythm against the roof of a car, or the thoroughly drenched material of your raincoat, was like the sound of nature's heartbeat. It was amplified for all to hear, like the microphone they put on a pregnant woman's belly when they do an ultrasound, and you hear the galloping heartbeat of the baby tucked away inside of that little body, tucked away inside the body of the mom.

The sound of the rain was my unspoken mantra that soothed and cleared my head. There was no need for me to assume the lotus position (as if I could) or chant away; I only needed to sit near a window or better yet beneath a covered porch, the mist of the rain delicate upon my skin, while I listened to, smelled, and tasted the downpour. The scent of the rain was almost a sexual thing for me. When I took in that first rich earthy smell, I would feel a stirring inside, like the reaction you get when you pick out the scent of a woman.

If nothing else, it knows how to rain in Atlanta. The thunderstorms that I reveled in during my time there were etched in my mind. It was not unlike the way the image of a bolt of forked lightning was burned into the storm-soaked murky backdrop of the sky, hanging there like a ghostly blue-white specter until it was washed away by the cleansing rain.

The first time I physically laid eyes on Amanda was at a photo shoot there in Atlanta. I had moved to that city two years earlier to work at the Anderson-Baker advertising agency as their creative director. I had been riding the crest of a pretty good wave, with several successful campaigns under my belt. I had chosen Mandy, which was her name on her modeling head sheet, when I was looking for someone to be plastered on billboards all over the northeast as the face of Georgia tourism. The moment I saw her picture amid the two dozen other women on the head sheet I was drawn to her. There was something tantalizingly familiar about her, but it would take another twelve years for me to realize that sometimes you had to really get to know someone in order to understand that they were, in fact, a stranger, after all.

I have always retained in my memory a picture of the front porch of the house where we did the photo shoot. It was one of those splendid homes from a bygone era that ring the city of Atlanta. These homes, mansions really, were a testament to the history of the South that existed before that little North South misunderstanding that I think still lingers somewhat today. I had chosen this house because it said "American South" in an understated, yet loud and proud way. If I had shown a picture of this house to someone of a certain age in Mumbai or Moscow, or most anywhere in the world, they would have said "America" or at least "Clark Gable" without the slightest bit of prompting.

I had checked the weather for the day of the shoot, and it was supposed to be on our side. However, in one of those moves that is not supposed to surprise you in that part of the country in summer, a weather system snuck in from somewhere in the Gulf. It gathered up an armload of the humidity that hung about us all day like damp cotton, and then presented us with a spectacular late-day thunderstorm that delighted me as I watched the crew drag lights and tripods and cameras into the garage of the house, while I sat on the majestic front porch, taking it all in.

I have always cherished that tranquil feeling when you were

enveloped in the sanctuary of that false sense of peace before the sky tore open and all hell broke loose; caught in the quiet trough as the air pressure went through its spastic gyrations and seemed to push away all sound in that tiny vacuum of space and time. Just prior to the onset of the storm I would feel its seductive touch on my skin, it was not all that different from the anticipation I felt as a lover moved toward me. It was something to be savored, which is what I did as I sat rocking gently on the swing chair on the porch. As the hurried activity of the crew fell away from me, I was busy falling into the eye of the storm.

To me the distant rumble of thunder was like the spark that was ignited when your eyes connected with a woman across a room; a signal that an engagement was about to commence. I let the storm come to me across the two-hundred-foot spread of lawn that lay between the house and the roadway. I watched it approach the way a woman would advance on you in her strong, confident way; knowing full well what was about to unfurl around you, wondering only at the nuances that would be incorporated along the way.

The first splatters of rain on the hot dusty ground were like those initial flirting touches of her fingers on your arm. As the intensity of the rain grew, so did my level of intimacy with the storm. Later, when the thunder had detached itself from the affair and rattled off into the distance, the slow silky hiss of the rain, its steady pulsating rhythm, would become the catalyst for my brief meditation.

And so it was, on that oppressively hot day with the relief of the cooling touch of the rain on my skin and the soft whispers of its voice in my head, that I underwent a profound experience. I was taken back to a time when I was introduced to the vision of a woman, one that I believed I was meant to be with later in my days; a woman who would have a dramatic impact on my life. That day I heard the voices of children who had not yet been born, but who would come through me and be mine to love and care for. I felt the touch of a woman's hand on my face, a touch that was accompanied by a familiar sadness that I would later know all too well.

Looking back, as I sat in the midst of the storm on that grand porch in Atlanta, I thought that I recognized Mandy, Amanda later, and I embraced the sadness I saw in her eyes. I saw things that were broken and set about fixing them because, after all, that's what I did. I took damaged things and put them back together and gave them new life. I was the magician; I was the alchemist.

I find it curious how we look for ways to justify the things we do. Like a religion, we interpret events to assuage our fears, to meet our desires, and then we pronounce it to be a truth and prepare to defend it to the death.

When I returned from the Morocco trip I lobbied enthusiastically and as it turned out, successfully, and managed to convince Amanda that one last effort to breathe life into the dead body of our relationship was not a lost cause. I thought that if I could only bring a sense of routine back to our world that it would be enough of an accomplishment. Sometimes best intentions just aren't enough.

Routine, after all, was the glue that held many a relationship together. In time I realized that routine alone was a fragile bonding agent. It was the soccer tournaments, the dance recitals, the birthdays and holidays that kept us on track, kept us distracted from the obvious.

The days rolled into weeks and we lurched from one event to the next, stumbling forward through the calendar with no clear goal in sight, as we reeled backward in almost every other way. It was draining.

On the days when there were no activities planned, Amanda and I would stare across the room at each other like strangers on a train who felt too awkward, or disinterested, to begin a conversation. I was reminded that expectation will breed resentment, and it was clear to me that our relationship, what remained of it, had begun to atrophy.

In one last attempt to see if anything could be salvaged from the wreckage of our marriage, I let Dan talk me into bringing Amanda on an upcoming client trip to Jamaica. This was nothing new; we had organized one pretty much every year since we had formed the company. Don't tell the IRS, but we selected the clients (and their partner or spouse) who would join us based on how well we liked them, rather than how much they spent with us. Our company paid all expenses for everyone; usually we went down to the Caribbean, sometimes Mexico.

It was a chance to get away and enjoy some sun and sand. What else could one want for? Well, I knew the answer to that; regardless, I worked at convincing myself, and then Amanda, that this year's trip would be worthwhile.

To be quite honest with you, it didn't seem to matter whether we were home in Nashville or away in the Caribbean, things did not particularly change for Amanda and me regardless of the surroundings. Lying in bed at the resort on the Saturday morning of our trip, in a moment inspired by the warm salty breeze slipping through the open sliding doors, my thoughts turned down an amorous path and Amanda, somewhat reluctantly, accepted my advance.

There was no passion in our lovemaking, there had not been for so long that I had basically become used to the idea that we would go through the motions, literally, without spending too much time on the preliminaries or post party. Frankly it was quite efficient in a cold, clinical, sort of way.

In another relationship, that I knew so well, this setting with the sunshine pouring into the room, the sweet ocean wind, that all-too-overlooked gift of knowing that the phone was not going to ring, that no one was going to be crying out for immediate attention outside of this room, well … this would have been a moment to savor. Instead, I found myself resting on my hands in a kind of push-up position so that our bodies were only barely (but specifically) engaged, and as I thrust inside of Amanda's body, I wondered what the point of all of this was.

"Are you even present in this room?" I blurted out, without applying any filter to my thought. I stared down at her face, bereft of any emotional display that I could read, and in that moment, I confirmed all that I knew and feared. In that brief flash of unmistakable clarity, I was left with the realization that we could no longer fool ourselves about the state of our marriage. I extricated myself from Amanda, in every sense.

There was no response from her. Not a word, not a muscle in her moved; she stared back at me with the lifeless eyes of a statue. There had been little in the way of a response from her in years, why should today be any different? I was guilty of the same sense of indifference, I knew. As I looked at the seemingly lifeless form on the bed, that so obviously represented our lifeless marriage, I realized that we had reached bottom. We had reached the point where, fixer that I professed to be, there was nothing left to fix, nothing left to do but to pay respects to what had been.

Amanda remained in her pose, naked, looking drugged, her legs slightly parted like a mannequin waiting to be posed for the next position. I turned away and went into the bathroom where I showered away any evidence of the abandoned lovemaking and then went to find a breakfast table for one.

A short time later, looking out at the cool serenity of the hotel swimming pool from the sanctity of my breakfast perch, the one emotion I did not feel was guilt. The air was soft, the water in the pool, unencumbered by bathers for now, was still and aquamarine. As I gazed up into the sapphire sky, I allowed myself the one indulgence I had done my best to avoid during this soul-searching trip.

The truth was that Julia had been in my head the entire time; in the days leading up to this trip, the flight down, my every waking and sleeping moment. Up to this point I did make every reasonable effort to banish her from my thoughts—I had to in order to have as clear a picture as I could of the finality of my relationship with Amanda—but now I stopped the fight. I had lost the battle, there was nothing left to do but surrender.

CHAPTER TWELVE

Around four that afternoon, as I sat on the beach beneath a thatched shelter looking out across the sea, I began to picture how my life would begin to look when I returned to Nashville.

I felt comfortable in my skin for the first time in forever, and I felt okay with the idea that I might be able to embrace my own happiness without cashing in at the expense of my children and theirs. They knew, the kids always knew, try as we might to hide the extent of the distance between their mother and me. It would be a relief not to have to pretend any more, I reminded myself.

In time the warm breeze, no doubt assisted by the large scotch I had procured from a passing waiter, a blended scotch with a bit of ice since there were no single malts to be had, these all-inclusive resorts did their best to make up for quality with quantity, and I was brought to the edge of sleep. As I sank into the welcome siesta, I felt myself slowly drifting in and out of awareness until at last I was carried off on the gentle wave of my dream.

In the dream I was snorkeling with a group of people I did not recognize. I could make out their shapes as they moved through the water, but their faces remained obscured by their masks and breathing tubes. In my peripheral vision I was attracted to a glint of sunlight that rippled along the length of a woman's body, the light reflecting streamers of copper, yellow, and gold. The other swimmers moved ahead of me, their flippers leaving a trail of tiny bubbles like phosphorescence in their wake.

I looked down at the ocean floor, taking in the flowing shapes of coral that covered the bottom. Ocean plants undulated in time with the rhythms of the water, it was as if the ocean was breathing and the plants were her lungs. Breathe in and pull at the plants, breathe out and push them away. I felt myself floating peacefully above it all, watching the bottom recede as the ocean floor gradually fell away. It was difficult for me to judge the depth of the water; it was so clear and the sunshine from above so intense that the depth could just as easily have been ten feet or a hundred.

I lifted my face from the water and surveyed the surface area for the protruding snorkels of the other swimmers, but I saw none. I had somehow drifted out into open water.

I felt my heart move up into my throat and I was afraid that I would choke on it. My pulse was thumping near the top of my breastbone, and I felt that I needed to concentrate on my breathing. What had been a slow controlled rhythm was now a shallow gasping, and I had to exert effort to keep from panicking. I tried to focus on the slow rolling motion of the ocean, trying to find the tempo of it, so I could time my movements in order to go with it and avoid fighting it. Conserving my energy quickly became of paramount importance to me. I was having difficulty taking air into my snorkel; the sound of my breathing was amplified in my head. Every time a bit of spittle entered the breathing tube, it sounded like a handful of marbles rattling around in a tin can. I tried to swallow down the spit, which only upset my breathing pattern that much more.

I began to tread water; I forced my body vertical and raised my head fully out of the water. The view that greeted me filled me with dread. The rolling of the ocean had morphed into seven-foot swells that began to toss me about like some insignificant bit of detritus.

When I had been stretched out horizontally, my face just below the surface, I had felt the moderate flow of the energy of the waves. Now, in this upright position, I cut across the grain of the swells, and I was being tossed about by the roller-coaster effect of the waves. As I rose above the crest, I could see the great expanse of sky above me. Sliding back into the trough I saw nothing but the dark blue-green mass of water, oxygen boiling white across the tip of a wave as it pulled me into its bosom. I had no real point of reference on which to base my movements as I was pitched about. The shoreline had disappeared from my view and the sky offered no comfort. The once warm water began to chill me, and I could feel myself shivering—as much from the fear of drowning as from the cold.

I put my face back into the water and stretched my body across the surface. I had no strength left to fight the waves, I knew I had to conserve energy and I tried to remain floating with as little effort as possible. I had no idea which direction to swim in, even if I could find the strength to do so. All I could think of was that sooner or later, when I totally ran out of strength, the cold water would begin to paralyze my muscles and I would simply sink beneath the surface as the water filled my lungs and took me to the bottom.

An image of Miranda and Grayson formed in my mind and I raced to find a way out of this situation. I was suddenly startled by the realization that this was a dream. Just a dream. Why was I letting it take control of me? I tried to calm myself, all the while trying to wake myself up. I began to hum, I needed to distract my thought process and as I did, the vibrations that I heard in my head were amplified along my jawbone to my inner ear and it countered the chattering of my teeth.

What was the song I was humming? Oh yes, "Blue Monk," Thelonious Monk's tune. Do do, do do do do do do, da dah. I kept repeating the opening theme of the song. I needed to wake up from this dream.

Peering through the water, my mask allowed me a clear view, I saw a figure gliding toward me. It was Julia, smiling and waving as she passed below me. I did a kind of breaststroke, propelling myself along with newfound energy, moving toward the welcome sight of her. I followed her long graceful movements, not sure where she was leading me, and then I saw the seabed begin to rise up to meet me, and before too long my feet touched the sandy bottom and I was finally able to awaken myself.

The only sound I heard was the soft lapping of the water at the edge of the beach. The sun hung heavy in the sky and my head was cloudy with scotch and sleep.

The following evening Amanda and I, and the rest of the crew, arrived back in Nashville. At the baggage carousel Amanda and I stood beside each other in our separate worlds. Later, as I finished loading the bags into the trunk of the car in the parking garage, I went over to the passenger door and held it open for her. The gesture, one that had been performed uncounted times before, somehow struck us both as a bit odd and we attempted to smile at each other. I closed the door and went around to my side and slid behind the wheel. The car felt damp and chilled. I started the engine and stared ahead as Amanda flicked on the seat warmer and kept poking at the temperature control for the heater. I didn't bother to remind her, as I used to, that the engine had to warm up first before the heat would flow out. The drive from the airport to the house was one I would always remember for the sheer emptiness of it.

We pulled up in front of our house and I waited while the garage door lumbered open. The silence hung over us like a sodden rain cloud. Have fewer words been spoken at the end of a marriage? I wondered.

"So that's it?" I asked.

There was a long pause.

"I guess so," was her reply.

"I have waited forever to talk to you." Those were the first words I spoke to Julia when I heard her voice at the other end of the phone connection.

I had called her mobile several times and left messages with no response. I had finally called her office number and was met with an "out of office on vacation greeting."

"Where were you? I left messages."

There was a hesitation that I marked.

"I was away last week," she said.

"I know. I finally called your work number and figured that out from your message. Where did you go?"

"I hadn't heard from you since you told me you were going away with your wife, and kind of last minute I ended up going with Mike down to Turks and Caicos, he was looking on-line and found a last-minute deal. We just got back yesterday."

"You go on vacation now with your husband?" I asked, somewhat incredulous.

"Josh, yes, he is still my husband. Did I mention I hadn't heard from you for several days, knowing that you were going away with your wife? What was I supposed to do, call you for permission or to see if you had a better offer for me?"

"No, no, of course not. I just, it's just that well, and first of all I'm sorry that I didn't call you before I went away, I just didn't have anything new to tell you, but I do now."

It's funny how you know something instinctively and intentionally choose to ignore it. I chose not to press her, but the spark, the playfulness in her voice, was missing. Something was not right. I didn't question it when Julia presented me with a series of scheduling conflicts that would keep us from seeing each other this entire week. I thought, naively, that she was punishing me for going away on the trip with Amanda, even though I had assured her it was a business trip, and necessary.

When we were finally in agreement about when to get together, I suggested we meet at the lounge where we had that first glass of wine together. It felt appropriate to me that our relationship should come full circle. We had essentially launched our relationship in there, and I thought we should finally take it to the next level in that same location as well. Knowing Julia, I was sure the gesture wouldn't be lost on her.

I arrived a bit ahead of our meeting time and I ordered a bottle of St. Francis Cabernet Sauvignon from Sonoma County, one that had always been a favorite of ours. Perhaps I could suggest we find a few days to fly away to San Francisco and drive up the highway to Napa and Sonoma to celebrate the new road ahead of us. We had not traveled together since the trip to Morocco; this time I would not compromise the experience with my guilt.

I had asked for the wine to be decanted and as I sat looking anxiously at the two empty glasses I wondered how I should present my news to her. Should I blurt it out? Get down on one knee? I wasn't asking her to marry me, yet, but I was asking her to finally leave her husband so that we could get married one day. I wanted this moment to have a unique twist to it; I wanted it to be one of our stories when people asked, "So how did you two get together?"

As Julia entered the lounge, I was once again reminded of how much I loved watching her walk toward me, the idea that this woman was intentionally making her way to me was such a turn on.

"Well, I see that we've returned to the scene of the crime," she said, beaming and presenting me with that magnificent smile. I stood to greet her, took her hand in mine, and leaned in to kiss her. "No kissing in public, remember?" she chided me and sat down on the couch beside me. "You look good, looks like you got some sun."

There was that strange tone in her voice again. I poured two glasses of wine and noticed that she averted her eyes when mine sought hers out. She could look at me from across a crowded room and lock me in place with her eyes, just like that. Now, the fact that her gaze flitted to everything in the room except for me, made me shiver.

I slid Julia's glass in front of her in preparation for the small toast we did each time we opened a bottle of wine. Perhaps I would present my news to her in the form of a toast to our future.

"You're going to need that glass of wine in your hand if we're going to do our toast," I said, not at all comfortable with the fact that she had not reached for her wine until I suggested it to her. She picked it up by the stem but seemed indifferent to the glass in her hand. Before I could begin my toast, she put the glass back down on the table and began to speak, directing her look, and her words, to the glass of wine.

"The last time I spoke with you, the last time you called me, a couple of weeks ago, I asked you how things were going at home and you said fine."

The word "fine" hung out there like something unsavory. I did not like the feel of where this seemed to be going and I wanted to quickly defuse any landmines that I may have inadvertently placed around us.

"Julia, fine means nothing, it's an empty word. It's a word you say when you want to be polite or noncommittal about something." I shrugged my shoulders for emphasis. "In this case it meant things are bearable, they're day to day, routine, basic, nothing special. Great, fabulous, those are words that mean something definitive."

"Let me finish, please," she said. "You left me with the understanding that you were going to continue in your marriage, that nothing of significance had changed between us. When Mike and I went away on this trip, I thought I would make an effort to see if I could make things better between us because it looked to me like you were never going to be available to me properly, completely."

"What are you saying?" A wave of nausea came over me as I realized the words she was about to say. I didn't know how that burst of insight had come to me, but when it did the whole room felt upside down. I felt small and everything loomed large and magnified like I was in an Alice in Wonderland set.

"I didn't see you last week because I was concerned about something and I wanted to look into it before we got together."

"You're pregnant," I whispered. I didn't mean it as a stage whisper or to be dramatic, I said it that way because it was the only sound I could generate.

Her stare had not wavered from the wine glass that sat in front of her on the table. She nodded yes and then hung her head.

"Did this happen a week ago, on Saturday afternoon?" I asked, when at last I found my voice.

"What does it matter when it was?"

"It matters because I was sitting alone, on a beach, looking out across the water and thinking of you, of us, and some of the bad mistakes I've made. I had this really weird dream that afternoon, that I was in trouble in the ocean and thought I was going to drown, but then you swam by and led me back to the beach. As I sat there on the beach, half awake, I decided it was time to finally make things right between us, but then I had such a sinking feeling about it, about us. I felt like someone had died and I was somehow aware of it and it left such a hole in my life."

"No one died. Someone was being conceived," was the hushed response as she finally looked up at me. "As soon as it happened, I knew, or at least I thought I knew. I waited till I got home and did a home pregnancy test, then I went to my doctor for a blood test to be sure. It's so ironic, the entire time I was away with Mike I was wishing it was with you; the entire time."

"We have to do something about this," I said, assuming that I was still part of the plan here.

A stormy look crossed her face. "What do you mean?"

"There are things you can do about this," I began, and then realized that I was, in fact, not part of any plan. When that sperm and egg had fused it had created a force field that kept me on the outside.

"Josh, I would not have an abortion. I can't, I couldn't, and you should know that about me."

"Then what should we do?" I held my glass out at an angle toward Julia. "Shall I just toast the end of our relationship, is this our good-bye toast?"

"No," she said quietly. "I am supposed to be with you, there is no such thing as a good-bye toast between us. You don't choose who you are going to fall in love with, but I can't help that you gave me every indication that you were going to stay with Amanda, and I also can't help that the one time in God knows how long, that I have relations with, and I might remind you, he is still my husband, and this pregnancy occurs. You seemed to be getting on with your life; I was attempting to get on with mine."

"You know," my breath did not come easily, "you know that I am the eternal optimist, the 'anything is possible if you want it' guy, but what do we do about this situation if you and I are meant to be together?"

"I don't know the answer to that right now. I know that I will have this baby. This baby is coming for a reason."

"This baby is coming because you had gratuitous sex with a man you don't love anymore and probably never did," I said, through clenched teeth.

"I know that. I'm not a fool. But you did not let me into your life, and I just wanted to get on with mine. I wasn't planning on getting pregnant at that time, I wasn't even planning on having sex on that trip, and that time, for your information, was literally the only time in I don't know how long that I had been intimate with Mike."

"I don't think frequency is the issue here," I responded.

"No, I don't suppose it is. Look, you went back to your wife, I waited for you for a long, long time. Now this has happened, and it might take a bit more time until we can be together now. I was patient, now it's your turn. If we are meant to be together it will happen. That is what I believe."

CHAPTER THIRTEEN

That night, when my perfect dream had been shattered into a thousand perfect shards, it had not seemed out of place at all to me that following the dinner, Julia and I would end up back at my workplace. It was long after the cleaning staff had left, and we made love on the couch in my office.

I did not rationalize it as "one last time for old times' sake" nor did I feel that with this act I would erase or "best" another man's seed with my own. The fact was that the father of her child simply did not exist in my mind at that moment. Nothing existed except for Julia, and me, and the sanctity of the bond between us. The pregnancy was just another disturbance along what, from day one, had been a challenging road.

I have since learned that the majority of the decisions we make in our life are based on either love or fear. At the time, I knew that I loved Julia enough that I was willing to do anything to overcome the fear of losing her.

The time that had passed from when I arrived back home in Nashville from the Jamaica trip to when I had located and moved into a new place was pretty much a month to the day. I saw Hersch several times during that month and it was during one of those sessions where I joked with him that I had felt so despondent lately that I thought manic-depressive people were hanging around me just so they could feel better about themselves. It received a small laugh from him.

"It was the worst of times and the worst of times." I was finally able to laugh with him. "Once again, I get to watch my family fragment apart, this time for good, I think; and now, to have Julia choose to stay in her marriage for the time being ... for the first time I fear that my idealism might just be running out of steam. I feel like I'm spinning my wheels, Hersch, spinning on sand and just digging a deeper trough by the second. The more aggressive I've been with the situation, the deeper a rut I end up in. When am I going to learn to stop digging holes only to fall into them?"

It had not all been doom and gloom during that time—it only felt like it. Amanda and I had managed to pretty much keep out of each other's way during what would be the transition period. I had slipped back into the happy yet bittersweet custom of seeing Julia almost daily for lunch. There had been a few evenings when Mike had been out of town, as he was suddenly spending a lot of time at the company head office in New York. For those few hours in the evening as Julia and I lay together in the bed in the guest room at her house—the bedroom she shared with her husband being off limits—I could pretend that we had crossed that bridge and were now together. How ideal it all felt, as long as I was willing to engage in this willing suspension of disbelief.

The realtor I dealt with had called it a distress sale. It was priced to move, and I jumped on it. A lot of comparable homes in the neighborhood had sold for a lot more as the sellers waited for the right price to come in, but these people wanted out as fast as I wanted in. I will admit to feeling a twinge of guilt as I willingly took advantage of their tough situation; there is some small degree of honor among the walking wounded, after all.

The house had been built around 1928, a two-story Cape Cod style with the distinctive roof and dormers. It was a house where

I immediately felt at home as I stepped through the front door for the first time. These are the feelings we are supposed to take note of as we go through life, and thankfully I had the presence of mind, or just the plain good luck, to do so.

The house had a mostly stone exterior; the density of the stone certainly made the house feel solid, and that in turn helped me to feel more rooted. It was a three bedroom, four when you factored in the small room that had served as an office on the second floor. It had a good-sized principal bedroom with an updated ensuite bathroom. Much of the house had been redone on the inside sometime over the last few years, with updates to the kitchen and the bathrooms. The addition of a small sunroom off the back, which overlooked a nicely landscaped yard, added further to the allure of the house.

The couple that sold the house were splitting up. There seemed something poetically apropos about that to me, although their circumstances were not due to the apathy that Amanda and I had been afflicted with; these two really were breaking up over irreconcilable differences. This was one of those situations where all the counseling in the world wouldn't change a thing.

It seems the husband had decided to go and play for the other team. Personally, I didn't have any problem at all with his lifestyle choice, but I thought you were supposed to have those preferences sorted out before you got married and had a kid. Still, I was no one to judge any one about anything.

I did wonder how long he had wrestled with his decision. A lot of people, Amanda and me included, just lived our lives in a type of quiet desperation, hanging on to the marriage by your fingertips, just trying to get to the next holiday, the next family event, the next anniversary, and sometimes, the next day. You try to put on the happy front but you wonder exactly who it is that you're fooling.

About a week after I moved in, in order to make the house a bit more mine than theirs, I performed a simple ceremony that an acquaintance had advised me on.

When Grayson was about three years old, we had taken him

to his first dentist visit. The dentist was a woman named Shalene and she specialized in treating kids. We have taken them to her ever since. It was just after the Jamaica trip and I had taken the kids in to see Shalene for a checkup and before I knew it, I was telling her about Amanda and me, and the new house I would be moving into and how it was that I came to own it so quickly.

Shalene was a full-blooded Cherokee, and she shook her head and appeared to frown as she listened to my story.

"I feel badly for you and your family, and for all the sadness that was in that family that you bought the house from. I hope everyone will be happier in the future. You know, Josh, there is probably a lot of energy in that house that you don't need in your life right now. There's a Native tradition that removes old and negative energy from a place and allows new and healing energy to flow in. You should really clear out that house, get rid of the old energy patterns that still live there."

"You believe that?" I asked. "What am I supposed to do, hire an exorcist?" I joked.

She laughed. "No, nothing quite that dramatic, you can do it yourself. It's called smudging and my people have been doing it forever. You take a mixture of dried sage, a bit of cedar, and some sweet grass; you can buy a premade bundle at any new age store. You light it up, blow out the flame, and keep the embers going while you fan the smoke through the house while you send out positive thoughts. You have to be serious when you do it; these thoughts are living things so you have to be consistent with the message you are sending out."

Was this really going to accomplish anything? I wondered. I had looked up a few sites on the internet to get a better idea of how I was supposed to conduct this little ceremony, and on a Thursday evening, the day before the kids came to the house for the first sleepover, I became a temporary medicine man. I hoped I wouldn't set off the smoke alarm as I lit my smudge stick.

Shalene had told me that when a memory is strong enough or lingered long enough, it almost seemed to acquire a personality of its own. The whole idea creeped me out.

I started by going to the entranceway of the house and, sitting quietly on the floor by the front door, I tried to let my thoughts run clear, as she had suggested. The hot coal at the end of the smudge stick glowed brightly in the semi-dark entranceway. The smoke had a pleasant smell as it curled upward in its lazy spiral; not quite like incense, not quite like weed. Following the directions, I began offering the smoke to the four compass points, then I stood and began to walk through the house. I went from room to room, fanning the smoke with my free hand while I sent out thoughts asking for a blessing and a cleansing for the house and all who would live in it going forward.

If you were to ask me then, point blank, I would have told you that I was not a man generally concerned with religious or spiritual matters. I had grown up with a mother who followed a stern approach to life based on her Southern Baptist roots, and though she had exerted as much influence as she could over the religious teachings of my youth, I can tell you it was to little avail. I had chosen, at my first opportunity when I was old enough, to forego the church visits that had been instilled in me as part of the routine.

I smiled as the thought of my mother found its way into my head. She would have had a fit if she had walked through the door and witnessed me engaging in this "hocus pocus" stuff, as she would refer to anything that was not in line with her good upbringing. I knew it broke her heart that I did not follow her religious dictates. I did not attend her church, or any other, except for weddings and funerals.

The smoke flowed out around the house, taking with it, I hoped, the negative feelings that had settled into the floorboards and seams of the house. As the aromatic smoke cleansed the house, I glided in and out of the rooms on the second floor. I paid particular attention to the couple's bedroom, where I imagined so many of those painful discussions must have begun. I pictured the two of them walking though the darkened house in the middle of the night, when their bed had become too uncomfortable for them to remain in it together. I saw them closing the door to their child's room as they tried to keep their voices away from her, while they attempted to sort through the sudden storm that they had found themselves in.

I followed the purging smoke as it danced through the rooms going about its purpose of casting out any demons that might still dwell in the fabric of the house. When I was finished, I felt comfortably at ease, and the house seemed as if an unpleasant odor had been carried away on the cross breeze. Perhaps I was fooling myself, but I believed I could feel a shift in the energy of the house, and in me.

I had brought Julia to the house the day I had taken legal possession of it. I needed her to see the house, to be inside of it, to make her a part of it.

We stood in the bedroom, the liquid late-day light trickling into the room, covering us in its soft diffused glow. I felt Julia shift slightly on her feet, her stomach brushed against me, and I felt the slight prominence. The only thing wrong with this picture was the fact that this woman was carrying the wrong man's child in her womb. I did not, however, let that small point move me from my moment.

I drew her closer to me, and we let ourselves down to the carpeted floor in the otherwise empty room. I gently undressed her, caressing the soft swell of her belly. She was like a being of light in my arms and I was careful not to crush her gossamer wings. We began making love, for the very first time, again.

CHAPTER FOURTEEN

"There's been a change, a change in plan that I did not have any control over. I did not have any say in the matter."

Julia was four months pregnant at this point. We were together at my house, in which I now felt quite comfortable. We were sprawled out on my bed, cuddled against one another, my arm protectively cradling her slightly swollen tummy.

"What are you talking about?" I sat up, disengaging from our tangle of arms and legs. "What are these plans that you have no say in?"

"You know Mike has been traveling to New York a lot over the last few months, it's why you and I have been able to spend so much time together. Apparently, he was there to help restructure parts of the company and it turns out they've decided to just close down the Nashville office and transfer him to New York. This has been in the planning stages for some time, but he only let me know about this a couple of days ago. The house will be listed within the week and we'll move there right away. They'll put us up until our house sells and we can buy up there."

I was silent at first, struck dumb more precisely, and then I slapped my hands together in one loud clap.

"This is perfect! Let him move to New York, you can stay here in Nashville. Live in your house until it sells, then move in here with me, or just move in right now and let the other house sit until it sells. You don't have to keep beating yourself up over the guilt thing about leaving him, he is going to be leaving you! We couldn't have planned this any better if we'd tried!" I remember feeling elated, and I remember it lasting barely a second or two.

"Josh, I need you to think about this. I'm about to give birth in a few months to my first child, his first child. What would you have done if Amanda did that to you with Grayson? I can leave the marriage later, but I have to let him be there for the birth of his first child. You're a father; one of the things I love about you is the type of father you are to your children. You've got to know that this is one of the things I couldn't and shouldn't do to him."

I admit, I didn't really care too much about how Mike might feel right then.

"So then what are we supposed to do? I bought this house with the idea that you would move into it with me one day."

"You bought it for you and your kids," Julia said. "If I get to live in it one day with you then that will be perfect. I believe you and I will be together, but for now I have to move to New York. It's not going to be forever, that's for sure. I'm thinking six months, a year tops. I feel like I owe it to Mike to help him get set up and settled into a new house. That way I won't feel guilty when it is time to leave. For all the things I do not like about him, for now he is still my husband, and he will always be the father of this child."

"What are you talking about?" I challenged her, and I was quite abrupt about it. "What do you feel for him, do you love him?"

"Of course not. I wouldn't be here with you, especially now, if I did. I would never have been with you if I did love him. I didn't sit down and plan it out this way, this is just how the situation fell together. I didn't plan on getting pregnant with Mike, I was on the pill, it shouldn't have happened. It could just as easily have been you a few weeks before, it was one of those one in a million chances, what can I say?

"You need to understand that I am going to move to New York, I am going to have this baby, and then I'm going to plan what to do with the next stage of my life. I expect that next stage will be with you, but if you are not available at the same time then I will have to live with that decision."

It was a few months after Julia had moved to New York when my phone rang one morning just before 7 o'clock. I was sitting in my kitchen, having a coffee, getting ready to head out to the office. The sound startled me, but even before I had a chance to glance at the screen, I knew what the call would be about. Baby John had been born two hours earlier, she would tell me. Her husband had just gone down to the cafeteria at the hospital to get them something, it was the first chance she had since the birth to pick up her phone and call me.

She was so exhausted, we only spoke for a few precious minutes, just long enough to let me know that she was all right, the baby was all right, and that we were all right. I was the first person to receive a call, she told me, even precluding the news to her mother. It reestablished my belief in what existed between us. Even in the face of my abject despondency I had never truly doubted it, but like many potential disbelievers, I needed the occasional miracle to restore my faith.

Two hours later I placed an order for a dozen roses to be sent to her room at the hospital. I asked for the card to read, "Life's a mountain, not a beach. I'm enjoying the view." I knew she would recall the quotation from a card she had sent to me early on in our relationship, and I knew that there was no need for my name to appear on the card with the flowers.

I spent many hours over the next few days pouring over every aspect of the bond that joined Julia and me. I wondered openly if I could have been with Julia had Amanda not presented me with the coldness that had become such a mainstay in our marriage. Had she not done so, would I have been able to suppress that urge to be with Julia? Could unfaithfulness live within a happy marriage? If you were truly in love with your partner, would there be any oxygen available to feed another lustful flame?

My mind wandered to a story a neighbor had shared with me

about an affair that happened early on in her marriage. We had all had a lot of wine that night at the dinner party. To be honest, she had occasionally indulged in friendly flirtation with me in the past. I wasn't particularly surprised when she told me the story; however, I didn't think at the time that it would lead to anything beyond her narration.

She had been away on a business trip, the way she told it. She was walking through the lobby of her hotel when she inadvertently made eye contact with a man. She claimed she had never seen him before or since. In that split second she decided that she absolutely had to be with that man. She said it felt like an alien being had fired a laser beam into her head and scrambled her thought process. She was acting purely on animal instinct. She walked over to him, boldly introduced herself, and made it very clear that she was both interested and available.

She claimed to not know a thing about him beyond his name, the smell of his cologne, and that after their lovemaking session they had watched part of a Cincinnati Reds game in bed in his hotel room before parting company, with him leaving town the next day and her returning to what was left of the commitment of her marriage.

It occurred to me, as I recalled her story, that an incident like the one she described would likely not be easily forgotten. It would always be present, perhaps often in the background, but there like a tiny grain of sand forever caught somewhere under your eyelid, floating on a wave of saline. It might escape your notice for a time, but every now and then it would slip and slide around and hit a tender spot, reminding you of its existence. I suspected that most people would rather just get used to the feeling, and the temporary inconvenience, rather than confront it. No point in going out of your way to embrace change, unless you really had to.

I did wonder, when her grain of sand invariably worked its way to the forefront, as it would from time to time, whether she replayed that little indulgence and considered what it would have been like if she had up and run off with Mr. Cincinnati Reds. Did she ever watch a Reds game on TV and scan the crowd when the opportunity allowed, when the cameras followed those looping foul balls hit down the first and third base lines, looking for one particular Reds fan? What would she do if her phone rang and the voice on the other end said, "We should take in another Reds game sometime." How would she handle that separation between want and need, that thing we call desire?

I rubbed at my own little grain of sand and speculated on what might have been had I decided to remain with Julia after the trip to Morocco, instead of attempting one last reconciliation with Amanda. I could not deny that I did what I thought was the right thing at the time, yet I could not escape the realization that for all that I had hoped to gain that day, I had sure lost a lot.

Let me tell you the rest of the Cincinnati Reds story, not that it has anything to do with a baseball game at this point.

A funny thing happened one evening when I dropped the kids off at their mother's house. A neighbor, Laura, the one who had told me the Reds story, surprised me by walking over as I was getting back into my car.

She wanted to talk to me about a fund-raising function that was being planned at our kid's school. The company she worked for had offered, through her, to print up a bunch of flyers for the kids to take home. She wanted to know if I, with my art director background, would be willing to use the agency to take care of the layout and design, gratis of course. I was fine with that, I told her, and probably would not have thought twice about it, had she not then suggested that we get together the next day after work for a glass of wine to discuss the project. Was I being a little too brazen in thinking that Laura had something in mind above and beyond the school fundraiser? I wondered. Was I being called out of the bullpen to pitch for the Reds?

When I was at home later that evening, I realized that I was humming the signature song from the movie that bears her name. It was an old movie, I couldn't think of the year, but the mid-'40s came to mind. I knew the song a long time before I had ever heard of the movie, and quite a few years before I met my alluring neighbor, my introduction being courtesy of Coleman Hawkins. When I started listening to jazz in my late teens, "Bean," as

Hawkins was nicknamed, was one of my early favorites and his version, recorded back in 1957, was one of the songs that had stuck with me ever since my first listen.

I chuckled at how the brief run in with Laura had brought that song to the forefront of my evening as I went into the kitchen to pour a small glass of Lag to unwind. The "Lag" was Lagavulin, a wonderfully mature sixteen-year-old single malt scotch that was my preferred drink. My father was a bourbon drinker, like many good southern men before him, but I had strayed off that well-traveled path and ended up all the way over in the damp fields of the Scottish West Isles.

Lag was such a deep drink, that when you released the cork the smoky iodine bouquet wafted up to greet you with its brash personality and just grabbed your attention like a firm slap on the back. I once managed to get Julia to sample a little sip, but she screwed her face up in disgust at the taste.

"I can't drink this," she sputtered. "It tastes like a campfire. I prefer it second hand, when it's on your breath and you kiss me." I assured her I could handle that request.

Hearing her voice in my head made me want to speak to her, and just for a moment I considered phoning her but since it was evening, and her husband was possibly home, I shelved the idea. She had made it clear that I should not call outside of "office hours" just in case. I poured a good two ounces of Lag; no ice, no little drop of water, just nice and neat the way I'm sure the Scotch gods had intended.

I had a large rack of CDs in the family room, I had joined the download-your-music-to-your-phone club, but I generally just used that to listen to music in the car. The MP3 files were convenient, but the truth is, you missed a lot of the sound with all the compression they used. CDs were a bit better, but for my money nothing truly replaced playing from vinyl, on a good sound system. I bypassed the CDs this time and went over to the slightly larger rack of albums that also occupied that same corner of the room. I knew exactly what album I was looking for to accompany my mood. I looked through the H section; I had about a dozen albums by Coleman Hawkins as a leader, and a bunch more where he played as a sideman. When you listened to Bean, you were listening to music history. If it hadn't been for Coleman Hawkins, what path would John Coltrane, Sonny Rollins, Charlie Parker, Zoot Sims, and all the others have had to follow? Bean introduced the tenor sax to jazz the way Sidney Bechet had introduced the soprano sax and Django Reinhart and later Charlie Christian had brought the guitar to the jazz scene. Angels sent from on high, all of them, bringing forth that beautiful music that was made to appeal to the spirit within. They were angels with dark sides to be sure, but angels nonetheless.

I located the "Hawk Flies High" album, ignored the double entendre, and placed the disc on the platter, watching the damper on the tone arm delicately lower the stylus on the aging Thornes turntable, where it would embrace the grooves and release the music locked away in the ridges and crevices of the vinyl. The first song on the side was "Laura," a not-so-subliminal inspiration to be sure, and it began with Hank Jones caressing the piano which led to Oscar Pettiford on bass, and then Jo Jones, very restrained on drums, as he brushed away on two and four. And then Bean came in, cementing the sound, and everything felt right in my world for that moment.

CHAPTER FIFTEEN

I sat in my office at the agency, staring at the phone, turning over thoughts of Laura while I toyed with the business card she had slipped to me yesterday, during our very brief but very interesting encounter. I leaned forward and keyed in the digits of her phone number. She picked up on the fourth ring, and I heard the fading words of the conversation she was in the process of ending before her greeting.

"Laura DaSilva."

"Joshua Davidson," I said in response.

"Josh." The tone in her voice softened perceptively. "Hey," she said, like an old friend.

"Hey," I parroted back. "It was nice to run into you yesterday," I said, and I meant it. She had been in my thoughts half the night as I had sipped an extra glass or two of Lag, and listened to music late into the evening.

"Thanks, yeah me too. I hope you don't mind me asking you to help with this project for the school. I thought afterward that I may have been a little too direct with my request."

"Happy to," I said. "And when have you ever been anything other than direct?" I said, and thought of the secret she had shared with me about Mr. Cincinnati Reds. "What can you tell me about this project?"

"Well, basically it's a sales flyer for the school. I don't have a lot of time to offer to the parents committee, so I told one of the fundraising moms that if I could ever help with something through work to give me a call, and she followed up. Instead of selling those chocolate-covered almonds, they want to sell some school wear, hats, fleeces, hoodies, that sort of thing. They thought they'd like to send home a flyer that might sit around on a counter or on the fridge to generate some orders. I suggested an email blast to all the parents, but they wanted something on paper for this. I thought if you could help with the design and layout, then I could arrange to cover the printing costs of it here."

"Sure, that sounds good, what sort of timeline are we on?" Hmm, maybe this was just a neighborly request, after all. My bad, for having all those naughty thoughts last night.

"Soon, week to ten days and ready to be printed, if that's okay."

"Shouldn't be a problem," I told Laura. "Do you want to email me specs and I'll start to work on some ideas?"

"I can do that, but I was also hoping that your schedule would allow us to grab a quick drink after work, maybe tonight, and I can share some of the comments from the fundraising committee in terms of what they had in mind, might be more helpful than just some bullet points in an email."

"Of course, tonight would work for me." Bingo, maybe I wasn't so far off after all. We agreed on a place near Broadway and 30th. I placed the phone back in the cradle and smiled. Batter up?

At four that afternoon, just before leaving the office a bit early for my, ahem, appointment, I called the kids' house and the part-time nanny answered. When Amanda went back to work, we had arranged for this woman to be at the house from 3 till 8 until Amanda made it home from the TV station where she did the weather, live for the dinner news show, and then taped the late-night forecast.

The woman was a widow, who was happy for the income and the fact that it gave her something to do to take her mind off her late husband, who had forgotten a few of his wedding vows and instead entered into a pact with Jack Daniels, which as it turned out, was the vow that led to "till death do us part." They found him one December day, curled up on the cold ground off to the side of the James Robertson Parkway, near the state capitol building.

Grayson took the phone from the nanny; I could hear Randi in the background trying to wrestle the phone away from him.

"Hey, Dad," then off to one side, "Randi, wait your turn, I'm older and I'm first."

A little too old for his own good in some ways, I thought.

"What's happening, Gray?"

"Not much. Stuff. Are you still coming to the school tomorrow night?"

"Sure am, wouldn't miss that show for the world."

"Good. I told Mom she could bring the A-hole guy but that I would be sitting with you."

"I'm glad you'll be with me, Gray, but you shouldn't really be calling him that name." I'll call him that name, I thought.

"When she asked me if she could bring him, I told her he was an A-hole but I said it like that, I didn't use the real word."

"Well, it's still close enough, it might be better to avoid that sort of word with your mom, I'm sure she didn't appreciate it."

"Can I come to your place after the show and sleep over, just you and me? You can drive me to school in the morning."

"We'll see, I'll have to talk to your mom, but I think it will be okay. What about Randi?"

"Just a boy's night, Dad, just you and me, okay? You work it out with Mom," Grayson said, tossing the ball to me. "I'll have my bag ready when you pick me up for Randi's concert."

I was quiet for a moment, we both let the silence sit there like a great big lump and then I heard Gray's breathing change and I felt like he was trying to suppress an urge to cry. He was trying to hold it in, but it was determined to squirrel its way out. The big lump that was the silence moved into my throat and my eyes started to burn as they moistened.

"Gray, it's all right, honey," I whispered into the phone. "I'll make sure we have the sleepover tomorrow. I'll talk to your mom and work things out."

I arrived at the lounge for my meeting with Laura and took a corner seat in a booth and ordered a beer. I waited, lost in contemplation, sifting through the ashes of my conversation with Grayson. Our words hung in the air like the acrid reek of smoke that remains after the building has burned to the ground. I was reminded once again that my role as "the fixer" was under fire from all sides. I could not fix my marriage with Amanda; I had certainly done a piss-poor job of fixing my relationship with Julia; and I could not fix my children's fears and concerns. I felt the sting of failure. I was like one of those new age occultists who believed that they could use the power of their concentration to move the clouds around in the sky. Sounded great on paper, and I had certainly spent enough time blindly staring into the heavens trying to work my magic, all the while forgetting the other side of the equation. As much as I wanted those clouds to move, what if someone else was quite happy with them exactly where they were?

"You look deep in thought."

Her voice startled me, and I almost knocked over my beer glass.

"Laura." I stood up to shake her hand.

"A handshake?" she said, and leaned forward to kiss me on the cheek. I leaned in to embrace her. "I'm so glad we have this chance to sit down and talk today." The fragrance that hovered about her was quite enchanting.

"Good to see you too." I was momentarily caught off guard by the intensity of her presence and I leaned back a half step to admire her, and to gather my thoughts. I was used to seeing her dressed in a much more casual style; track pants and a sweatshirt were not out of the ordinary, or jeans and a t-shirt or light sweater. I found the look of her in a business suit quite arresting.

Our server came over and Laura ordered a glass of wine then turned her attention back to me and I was locked in. I could not get over how she could be the cute mom across the street one day, definitely worthy of a fantasy or two, and today be this very sexual woman, dressed for business, perhaps even some monkey business, and here she was, sitting across from me. To me a man was pretty much who he was, what you saw was what you got; I had briefly forgotten that a woman could be many people, depending on her mood and intention.

"Let's get this business out of the way first," she said, opening her leather briefcase and extracting some rough artwork and copy points. "Then I want to know all about how you've been and what you've been up to. We didn't get much of a chance to talk yesterday."

"Fair enough," I answered, taking the papers from her and realizing very quickly that this bit of layout work would be a no-brainer. I wasn't sure she really even needed my help with it, it seemed pretty much put to bed already. Still, I told Laura how we might put the piece together, and did a quick sketch on the back of one of the pages showing her a layout and suggesting some color and font ideas.

"You see?" She reached across the table and patted my hand, then allowed her hand to remain for just a moment longer than necessary. "I knew you were the person to go to on this. This will look great and I'll make sure that you and your company are properly thanked in the next school letter."

"Well, that will make it all worthwhile." I laughed. "Now I guess I'm going to have to buy a whack of this stuff for my kids."

"No doubt," she smiled. "How are the kids doing with the split, and how are you doing? You two aren't divorced yet, are you?"

I was mildly surprised that she did not ask, as many did, if Amanda and I were going to try to work things out.

"Not divorced, not officially, but I guess in every important way we are. It's really just a matter of process and paperwork at this point."

"Well, at least Amanda has her job at the TV station, always better when the ex-wife is working, I suppose."

"I guess her landing that job was a blessing in disguise," I said. "It was a bit of an adjustment at the time, since she had taken a few years off before that to be with the kids, but it was all for the best in the end, I guess." I smiled as I recalled how Randi had recently managed to mangle that phrase and add a whole new twist to the saying. "Daddy, when I missed the tryouts for the play, when I was sick that day, I thought I wouldn't end up being in it at all, but later when one of the other girls had to miss the performance, I ended up with the best part in the play. When I was sick it was really a blessing in the sky!"

"The kids are doing okay for the most part, I think." I didn't bother to tell her about the conversation I had earlier in the day with Grayson. "I think they kind of get it that we split up, tried to work things out, and then split up again. No third time lucky for us, I guess."

"Well, I'm sorry then," she said, and patted my hand again. This time her hand stayed. I looked down at her hand on top of mine and for a moment was torn. My gaze lingered and I noticed her nails, not long but nicely manicured and polished; not bad considering all that yard work I had watched her do over the years. I did not spend much time looking at her wedding ring, instead I traveled up her arm, hung a left at her shoulder, pausing at her breasts and enjoyed the way they shaped the front of her crisp white blouse and then, because I am a polite man, for the most part, I looked into her warm eyes.

Women's eyes have always fascinated me. They were, for me at least, easily one of the most sensual elements of a woman's physical being. I had, on many occasions, been both beckoned and dismissed by nothing more than a glance, or an eyebrow that simply leaned one way or the other. I respected the power that resided there in a woman's eyes. As I looked into Laura's eyes, I was satisfied with how at ease I felt with her, and how I believed those eyes would forgive me any transgression. Now I just needed to forgive myself for what I was about to do.

"I spent some time thinking about you last night after our brief run in yesterday," I said, testing the waters but knowing that her hand, still on mine, was giving me all the encouragement I should need.

"I'm happy about that. Tell me everything."

"I was having a scotch when I got home and I was listening to some music, thinking about that time you told me that story about your trip to Cincinnati."

She smiled and I watched as a flicker of amusement flashed across those eyes.

"Imagine, a man who listens and remembers! I must remember not to drink too much wine the next time I'm in a storytelling mood, especially around someone I'm attracted to."

Well, there it was, out in the open, just like that. I would not deny that the attraction was there for me as well, and I took a moment to consider that this would not be a faceless crime. I knew her husband, her kids played with my kids. Did I want to be responsible for some man wondering if his wife had taken a lover? Well, we were down to the wire on that one, I reminded myself. Did I want to be the guy that her husband might one day want to kill? Maybe Doug would just walk into his den one fine day, a den I was familiar with, having watched the occasional football game in there, and take out one of his hunting rifles from the locked cabinet and pop a couple of rounds into my back as I picked up my kids for the weekend.

Who would blame Doug? Oh sure, a court would still likely convict him; this wasn't Italy, after all, where crimes of passion apparently had their place within the judicial system. Doug would probably think it was worth it; a couple of years in jail after time off for good behavior, because, after all, he was a very decent guy, for exacting his revenge.

Did I think it was worth it? I considered the many angles to it as I felt the softness of Laura's hand on mine. Yeah, yeah, probably worth it, I told myself. Not the getting shot in the back part, but likely worth the guilt part. Really, it was not like I had pursued her, convinced her to do something she didn't want to do or anything like that. I felt badly for her husband, Doug, but obviously not badly enough to not sleep with his wife. Her hand on mine warmed me from the inside out, and all I could think of was that a bit of risk really does sweeten the treat.

I moved my hand slightly so that hers slipped into mine and I held her lightly, but with enough conviction, to let her know that I was a willing partner in this soon-to-be liaison. She did not say anything to me right away, but when she did speak to me it was a quieter, more sensual voice, that I had not heard from her before. The tone of her voice was confirmation enough of the arrangement we had just entered into, even though we did not speak of it directly. The signing of the deal was consummated by the gesture of a raised eyebrow, a tilting of the head, and the casual touch of skin on skin.

"So, tell me," her words were caressing me. "I hear that you've bought a house, where are you living?"

"Not far, Green Hills."

She glanced at the silver watch draped around her thin wrist. "I've got to pick up Alicia from dance class at seven."

Not tonight, I reasoned, though I noticed that my heart was thumping in my ears like a big bass drum.

"Randi's been asking about dance classes," I said, feeling a bit odd that in the middle of planning the start of our affair, we were discussing my daughter's interest in dance classes.

"She'd enjoy the classes, Alicia sure does," Laura said, gently tossing the comment aside. "Tell me, are you seeing anyone in particular?"

The question caught me off guard, and rather than answer immediately my response was more of a chuckle than a comment.

"You don't have to answer." She smiled. "I don't have to know."

"That's okay, I think we'd should both be okay with a question like that, all things considered. Yes, and, well, no. Along the lines of your Cincinnati story, I had one of those relationships except it was more than just one meeting. I met her just before Amanda and I split up the first time, well, actually nothing happened until after we did split up, like with me moving out. The first split lasted about six months and I saw this woman a lot during that time. Then, I went back to Amanda, trying to work things out, until we split up again. When she and I split the second time I reconnected with the woman."

"And?"

"And, yes, and … you know how they say the secret to life and comedy is timing?"

"Are you going to tell me a joke?"

"No." I laughed, although my relationship with Julia was

truly a dark comedy. "By the time this woman and I got together again so that I could tell her that Amanda and I were done, her life had changed dramatically. Turned out she was a couple of months pregnant."

"Was she married?"

"Yes. Not happily, I suppose."

"Not your child?"

"No."

"Hmmm. Are you in love with her?"

"Yes, I mean, I guess I thought I was. It's complicated."

I gave her the background story on how it was that Julia had moved to New York.

"Really?" was her response.

"She doesn't deal with guilt very well," I offered, and realized how feeble my answer sounded. "She felt that if she refused to go then he would not go, and he would miss out on a career opportunity. I don't think it was about her loving him, I think it was more about obligation."

"It doesn't have to be about love, Josh, I think you've already learned that from your own experience. A lot of people stay in relationships for reasons other than love. Sometimes it's guilt, I'll give you that. Sometimes it's fear of the unknown or of what other people might think of them. Sometimes there is this strange bond, and not necessarily a healthy one, that keeps people in relationships that you'd think they would be better off out of."

I recall wondering how much of what she was telling me was germane to her relationship with Doug.

"It's difficult for me to explain it, so it must be equally difficult to understand it from the outside," I said, and quietly acknowledged to myself that if Julia truly didn't want to follow Mike to New York, that there were at least a half-dozen ways she could have handled it. "I guess my final answer to your question is that I'm not seeing any one person on a regular basis."

Laura smiled. "Well, then, I'm glad that we got that question settled."

"I would like to get together with you," I finally said. "This past while, I've probably seen Amanda more than I have any other woman, on a regular basis."

"Well, I don't think I would call that dating, so I'm going to assume we're okay there," Laura deadpanned.

I laughed. "No, I don't think I'd call that dating either. What about Doug?"

"Well, if you want to get together with him, you're going to have to work that out yourself."

CHAPTER SIXTEEN

The school was in relatively easy walking distance of the kids'
house, but I decided that I'd drive over with Grayson so that
we could make a quick getaway after. As we walked from our
parking space, I lamented the fact that my little man had already
grown self-conscious of any public displays of affection with
his old man. No more holding hands when we walked down the
street; kisses, even on the top of his head, were strictly forbidden.
Randi was still as affectionate as ever, bless those little girls, but
Gray was on his way to becoming a man. I think it's too bad
for everyone that somehow the lesson gets out that hugging or
kissing Mom or Dad in public is something to be embarrassed
about, well, at that age anyway. We all miss out on a lot because
of that.

Grayson led me through the maze of hallways to the gym that
also served as an auditorium for events like tonight. It seemed
we were a little late and it took a few moments to spot two seats
together as we squeezed our way to the middle of a row. It was a
crowded room and we smiled and apologized our way past people
who had to stand to let us by. It was warm already and from past
experience I knew it was only going to get worse. Did no one in
the design phase stop to think that on occasion there would be a
few hundred adults jammed into this not-so-big room and that a
slightly more efficient air-conditioning system might have been

a consideration? And the sound system! Designed in such a way that it was usually more effective to yell from the stage rather than try to get the tinny microphone to work properly. Ah, the joys of the school talent night, these nights were the true test of a parent and their patience.

Of course, I knew that my perspective on the evening would alter dramatically as soon as my beautiful Miranda would magically appear on stage, with twenty-two of her fellow classmates, so that they could warble their way through the two songs they had been painfully rehearsing. Randi had given me a sneak preview of the songs on the weekend; belting them out every chance she got because she was so concerned about forgetting the lyrics. That was her crisis for the weekend, and no weekend was complete without one. When she wasn't singing them out loud, she was mouthing the words, silently committing them to memory.

We settled into our crowded seats and I helped Gray take off his hoodie and I slid awkwardly out of my sports jacket. It had been raining a good part of the day and even though the temperature outside hadn't gotten much above 60 I knew that it would soon feel like the tropics in here. As I wiggled out of my coat, I felt a tap on my shoulder and I turned around to look directly into Laura's eyes. My excitement quickly dissipated as I heard Doug's voice over my shoulder.

"Hey, Josh, good to see ya, buddy." He offered a meaty hand. It was a firm grip, a guy-to-guy handshake. "I was wondering how you were doing; you haven't been around to borrow anything lately."

I laughed, recalling the many times I would wander across the road to borrow some tool to facilitate my attempts at being a handyman around the house. "Well, not a lot of stuff to fix at the new place, the kids haven't had a chance to break much yet." Apparently, I'll be borrowing your wife from time to time, I heard my inside voice say.

"Did you get to talk to Josh about the flyer, babe?"

"I did," Laura answered her husband and smiled at me. "We talked on the phone yesterday morning and got everything worked out," she said, as relaxed as could be.

Take note, I told myself, that we did not have a drink yesterday; it was just a phone call. I noticed a bead of warm sweat sliding down the groove of my back and I squirmed at the sensation it caused. I felt like I should say something about the flyer, but I couldn't drag a word out of my mouth to save my life, so I just smiled dumbly and nodded my head in agreement. A moment later and I was saved as the school band struck the opening notes to the "Star Bangled Banner" and everyone rose on cue; we sang while the band cranked out the music and the sixth-grade choir erupted into song about bombs bursting in air.

Until Randi's class finally trouped out to the front of the stage, I had not paid too much attention to what was going on up there. I had two other major distractions going on.

Behind me sat my former neighbor and his wife and one of their two kids (the other being with Randi for the performance about to begin). There I was, exchanging pleasantries with Doug and joking with him about neighborly things and meanwhile I knew that I was two days away from a clandestine rendezvous with his wife, having set up the details as we parted company at the end of our "flyer" meeting. Every time Doug poked me in the shoulder and I turned around to speak with him, I tried desperately to look him in the eye and to keep the blood from draining from my face. As the evening went on it began to bother me a bit that I seemed so well versed in this duplicity.

The other distraction began when I stared across the crowded room and my eyes locked in on my ex sitting there with Carl, her new beau, with them looking every bit the happy couple. The events of the evening felt totally out of sync, like watching a movie where the sound doesn't match up with the movements of the actor's mouth, leaving me feeling disoriented and off balance.

During Randi's two songs I focused my attention solely on her, and I kept my eyes riveted on my little girl as I strained to sort out her voice from the twenty or so others up there filling the room with their beautifully discordant serenade. As I found her voice, and then separated it from the rest, I laughed quietly while remembering a documentary we watched together from National Geographic or somewhere, showing ten thousand penguins on an ice flow and the mother bird who was wandering around, carefully listening to all that squawking, and finally identifying her baby through its voice in the middle of all of those tuxedos.

For those five or six minutes of song, I was comfortably lost in my own little world, where none of the anger or sad reverie could intrude. It was just Daddy and Randi as we enjoyed our own private concert, totally oblivious to the couple of hundred other people who just happened to be sharing the room with us.

Just me and she, curled up in the big green armchair in the living room with the late afternoon sun pouring in on us like sweet nectar, her eyelids drooping like petite leaves heavy with the dew of sleep. They fluttered like little butterflies in defiance of the drowsiness that was coming over her, and because she was a child, she saw sleep as the enemy. She was still years away from the idea of welcoming a pleasant nap in the quiet hollow of a lazy afternoon.

It was just the two of us, with her head tucked into the pocket of my shoulder; her face snuggled into my shirt, her hair matted with the dampness of her sweat that brought forth the warm scent that a small child radiated. In the dark of the auditorium, I felt the warmth of her little body curled against me and heard the rhythm of her breathing as she took me with her to that peaceful place of dreams where we were shielded from the harsh light of our realities.

CHAPTER SEVENTEEN

I sat in the calm embrace of my Thursday evening waiting for Laura to arrive at the house, and I found myself contemplating the various relationships that I had been a part of over the years. I had never truly considered how interwoven two people could become until Amanda and I began to extricate ourselves from each other's lives. I hadn't really noticed it in my parents' situation, although they stayed married while ostensibly living separate lives.

I was nursing a small glass of Lag and nurturing my newly formed theory of Amanda and me, that we were like a cluster of plants, root bound in a pot that had proven to be far too small for what it was attempting to hold. For all that we might have looked like individual plants above the soil line, we were a terribly tangled mass beneath. Taking this root ball apart required that we tear apart the fabric of our lives. What had been a garment that protected us from any storm was now a tattered rag flapping in the whirlwind that was upon us. The more you clutched at the cloth, the more it fell apart in your hands.

To be fair, I had also witnessed couples who separated their lives from each other with the cold precision of a medical procedure. They appeared as emotionally removed from the process as a surgeon was from the blood and guts of the patient hidden beneath the green surgical wraps of the operating curtain. Just the affected area was exposed, and then it was cut away.

There was nothing personal about it.

Some couples seemed like they had never put down roots with each other, like tumbleweeds that had collided and become entangled until their brittleness snapped and cracked and finally broke apart the attachment to each other. They went wherever the wind carried them, and then when they broke apart all evidence of them would be carried away, not unlike an encroaching surf would wipe away the footprints on a beach.

Laura arrived at the house around seven, which had allowed her time to head home after work to get her family settled for dinner before she went out for her "girls night."

"You found it okay?" I asked as I welcomed her inside and returned her kiss, our first actual kiss.

"Not a problem. You have a great place here, Josh." She handed me a small bouquet of cut flowers. "Men never buy themselves flowers, I hope you have a vase here for them."

I watched as she did that quick, but oh so thorough assessment that women do when they meet a man, or move a fold or two deeper into his world. They seem to do this intrinsically, bringing into play thousands of years of instinct and insight, to assess whether the man in question was a worthy sire to keep the family line strong, and to see if he had the ability to protect and provide for. Hey, hold your politically correct thoughts on this, it's just an evolutionary thing.

"Well, it's coming together slowly," I offered. "I've got to get some decorating magazines or something to help me get the place together a bit better. I look at those magazines and I think, man my house doesn't even come close to that!"

"Don't get too caught up in the deco-porn." She laughed.

"And what is deco-porn?"

"All women know the truth about those home decorating magazines; they're like the women in men's magazines. The rooms and homes they feature, do you really think people live that way day to day? It's like the hot girls in the other magazines, do you really think those pictures are real and untouched? Sure, they look good in the shot, but take away the lighting and makeup and photoshop, add in a couple of kids, a job, and a cranky husband.

By the time they're done with a room in those magazines it's about as fake as the boobs you see on most of the women in porn."

"I'll never be able to say Brazilian flooring again with a straight face," I joked, leading her to the kitchen where two glasses of a Cab Shiraz blend awaited us.

Laura's phone made a sound from inside her purse.

"A text," she said. "I'd better at least look at it. I'll just be a moment." She disappeared into the other room.

How odd is this? I thought. What happened to the flirting and small talk that led up to the conquest? Instead, it was, "let me check this text and I'll be right back to hop in to this affair with you." While I was not a complete stranger to affairs with married women, okay I only had the one so far, I suppose I still retained a preference for a bit of seduction. That feeling of slight apprehension when you played your card and wondered if you'd get an invitation to proceed or receive a slap in the face. Ah, well, I reminded myself, one shouldn't complain too much about the methodology when one was about to get laid.

CHAPTER EIGHTEEN

I have fallen in love many times in my life. What might make my situation somewhat more unique than others is that I always fell in love with the same woman. I don't mean the same type of woman; I mean, the same woman.

The first time it happened I was about thirteen years old. I had felt restless all day, I had no idea what to attribute that anticipatory feeling to. All afternoon I had that buzz you got when you drank two or three Cokes one after the other, which was not unheard of at that age. I couldn't keep still. Finally, after dinner, I decided to go for a walk to clear my head and to burn off whatever it was that was fueling me in this way.

All day the humidity had hung heavy in the air, and the sky threatened rain at a moment's notice. Sure enough, several blocks from the house, when it really didn't matter if I turned back or not, the sky opened up like a canvas bag filled with water that suddenly split its seams. I didn't care that I hadn't brought an umbrella with me. The point was reached very quickly where I went from wet to wetter to wettest. In a matter of seconds, I was completely saturated by the warm deluge, soaked to the bone, and I could not have been more content or at ease. It was a wonderful feeling.

At that tender age I'm sure I did not have the slightest idea of what a serious relationship entailed. There may have been a few frustrating attempts to get to first base, so to speak, but I really did not know much about involvement with the opposite sex. It's funny, to be honest, that all those years later some things just didn't change all that much.

All of which is to say that I found it terribly intriguing, as I made my way through the rain back to my house, as I began to paint a water-color picture in my head of the woman I somehow knew would be the perfect mate for me one day. Perhaps it was the insistent drumming of the rain on my soaked head and clothes; perhaps it was the scent in the air as the rain brought out the smells that had been hiding away from the heat of the day; it might have been the ozone scent in the air created by the lightning charges flashing across the sky. The entirety of this stimulus conspired to create a meditative state for me from where I saw myself much older, standing beside this woman, and I knew, simply knew, that she was the one I someday would be with. Even at that young age something inside of me allowed me to know that when you know, you know.

I remember telling this story to Julia one evening when were at the apartment back in those early days, curled up in each other's arms. I told her that day, at thirteen, was the first time I fell in love with her, well at least I fell in love with the idea of her, and that now I recognized her as the woman from that magnificent rainstorm. I had started to tell her of other times that I had fallen in love with her; like that first time I actually saw her standing there talking with her husband on Broadway. Then there was the time when I had felt myself floating across the parking lot, after we had that first drink together. She put her finger to my lips to shush me.

"Tell me more about that first time. Are you sure you were thirteen, and are you sure it was August?"

I told her everything I could recall about that day. I told her I was sure it was August and as I continued my explanation I paused for a moment and began to smile.

"Yes, I know it was August, and I think, I really do think, that it was August 17."

My fanciful walk in the rain that night had aligned with

Julia's arrival into the world. Twenty-seven years later I would meet that woman face to face on Broadway Avenue in Nashville, Tennessee.

With the absence of Julia in my life, I found myself looking forward to my next rendezvous with Laura, however brief and clandestine it might be. I was quite sure that Laura had no desire to leave her husband or to disrupt her family. With Laura, there was no expectation that might lead to resentment; there was no pressure to "move things to the next level." We did not have to offer each other those perilous promises of "someday" or "if only things were different."

I told Hersch about Laura one afternoon while we were in session.

"Are you in love with her?" he asked.

"Oh God, no," I blurted out. Love was the last complication I wanted from that. "I feel very close to her, but no, not in love. I have no intention of creating any long-term plans with her, and I think she feels the same way. I think that's part of the allure of being with her, she's like one of those serendipitous treasures you find when you're not really looking for anything in particular." I paused and considered. "Hersch, she's a wonderful refuge from my back-to-back disasters."

"Shelter from the storm."

"I think so."

"Nothing wrong with that, I suppose," Hersch said, touching his fingertips together in that slow rhythm that I had watched him do on occasion. It was a sign that we would be coming back to this topic at some point, either later in the session, or not too far down the road in another meeting. "You're both grownups, you've both chosen to enter into this freely, it's entirely consensual, from what you've told me."

"Consensual and sensual." I chuckled.

"And sensual I'm sure." Hersch smiled. "If her husband were to find out it might end up being more consequential."

I laughed uneasily at the thought of that. "I know, I haven't totally forgotten about that, and it does bother me sometimes."

"Sometimes, but not enough to stop?"

"No," I said, pausing to consider. "No, not enough apparently."

"Are you having this affair to get back at Julia for leaving you and staying with her husband?"

"No, of course not." I honestly hadn't contemplated that angle. "She doesn't even know about it; how do you figure that it's me getting back at her? Maybe Laura is just someone that I need to be with right now. This way I'm not out there playing the field and possibly getting caught up in a relationship that might one day get in the way of me and Julia, when she's ready. Maybe it's the right thing for Laura, to allow her to keep the rest of her life on track in the meantime. I don't expect it to last forever."

"Well, Josh, they say that people come into your life for a season, a reason, or a lifetime. Guess we'll see which category this one ends up in," Hersch said, closing off the topic for the time being.

The trouble with making promises to someone, is that the other person actually believes that you are going to keep them. Despite what Julia had told me about returning to Nashville after she had helped her husband establish a home for himself in New York, the window of time that she had promised for her stay there had long since closed. As I had feared all along, the theme of our phone calls and emails began to follow the all-too-familiar pattern of the reasons, or more realistically the excuses, that I had all but perfected at the beginning of our relationship.

How could I fault her feeling the way she now did, since I had offered her the same reasoning following our trip to Morocco? How do you suddenly flip sides and dispute your own argument? I would have made a lousy politician; I just didn't seem to have the necessary double-jointed integrity bone.

For all that I am a man tied to my past, I readily embraced the novelty of the relationship with Laura; in part because it did not demand that the past or present be part of the future. Laura allowed me to move forward, to give myself permission to move forward, which for some reason I seemed to require. Without Laura coming into my life, I wonder if I would have welcomed the idea of dating Missy?

Her name was Melissa, Melissa Margaret Hamilton, and I have many memories of her mother modulating those three words across many a warm evening to gain her daughter's attention from across the way. She never yelled of course; southern women don't yell; instead, they have that way of transforming their words and voice so that the end result is so much more effective than a crude bellow. Except for the times when her mother was calling her and apart from her driver's license and other legal documents, to all the world, her name was Missy.

I first met her in ninth grade and without much fanfare we fell into that terrible purgatory of becoming "best friends." When Missy was swept off her feet at twenty and married a year or two later, I pretty much lost track of her. I lost faith in a lot of things that day when I just couldn't bring myself to attend the wedding. I just couldn't stand the idea of seeing her up there on that day that she was dressed to kill. I ended up sitting at home in my suit, and a part of me just up and died.

Cut to several years later and as fate would have it, well, we'll talk more about fate later. As it turned out, Missy decided that Mr. Right was anything but, and she ended up leaving the marriage and taking her five-year-old daughter with her. Of course, by the time I heard of her leaving her marriage I was happily married, or so I thought. I remember that there had been that phone call out of the blue from Missy the day her daughter was born, and then five years later there was another call, the day after her divorce became final. Each time we had promised to get together "real soon" but of course promises like that are often just words written in the air, and they fade as quickly as they are spoken. Life, and just things in general, had gotten in the way, and we did not speak for many years.

Now, cut to just a few days ago, and picture me sitting in traffic, checking my voice mail out of boredom as I crawled along Briley Parkway, when that voice emerged. In that split second, I was drenched in a cascade of thoughts about everything Missy. In that half a breath of time I was bombarded with such a profusion of memories that I thought my brain was just going to up and crash. You would think that it would take forever to wander through all those pictures and accompanying emotions, but somehow your mind just shoots them all into your head at once, like a confetti cannon going off, and you can see all those years in the second or two that it takes for her to say, "Hey, Josh, it's me."

That's all it took, just, "It's me." In that moment I became sixteen again and I could feel the bite of rejection, the anguish of every failure, and the surging ecstasy of every faint-hearted hope. In the time it took her to say four words I relived a life that I thought I had buried long ago.

I had not laid eyes on Missy for the better part of twenty years. The last time I actually stood face to face with her was about a year after her marriage, when she had asked me to lunch. I recalled sitting across the table from her, untouched food occupying the empty space between us, thinking to myself that I could not believe that we were here at this juncture again. Here, where she needed my shoulder once again to ease her pain, and me just needing to be needed by her.

I did not return her call from the car, I waited until I got home and busied myself turning on some music and getting myself ready. I decided that it wouldn't hurt to have a bit more courage before I listened to Missy's entire message one more time. I poured a healthy shot of Lag, I sipped the smoky scotch and went over to the shelving unit and searched until my eyes settled on the "Miles Davis in Europe" album and I placed it on the turntable and let the sounds of the 1961 Antibes Jazz Festival fill the room with its captured history. After a brief introduction, by the heavily accented French master of ceremonies, the band launched into "Autumn Leaves" and I tapped into the mystical energy source that I drew from as I listened to jazz.

As best I could recall, the first time I actually sat down and listened to jazz, I was seventeen. It was a recording by Charlie Parker, playing a piece that I would later learn was called, "The Song Is You." It just spoke to me; it made me feel instantly good, a little high even, and I fell in love with the music.

The person playing the music was a mechanic named Otis who worked for the Davidson County School Board, where my father was an electrician under contract to the board. From time to time my dad would drop off the old family Oldsmobile to Otis, to have one thing or another looked after. Otis was happy for the extra cash and my dad was happy because he had found a great deal, and more importantly a mechanic he could trust!

One day, my father had asked me to go and pick up the car before five pm, since Otis had to close up; that was the day I was exposed to the magic. Otis kept a record player in the shop, an old Seabreeze with a detachable speaker and along with that, a couple of plastic milk crates filled with jazz albums.

Otis was probably close to sixty by the time I met him, a light-chocolate-skinned man originally from Oklahoma. As I waited for Otis to finish up with the Olds, I sat transfixed, listening to the music, reading the back of the LP cover and seeing that the song was recorded in 1952. I was hoping that it might take Otis a bit longer so that I could hear the entire album side, and when he saw my interest in the music, he obliged me. He actually lent me the album that day to take home and listen to, which I later learned was a pretty big thing for Otis to do. While we listened to the last two songs on the side, Otis talked to me about "Bird," which was Charlie Parker's nickname.

"See here," he said to me in his Oklahoma drawl. "Listen to how he sets up the phrase; listen to how he glides from one note to the next. How you get from one note to the next is as important as what the note is, if you want it to sound right. It's what he plays, but it's also how he plays it that is so important."

And in this way Otis became my guide into the jazz world, and I made a point of visiting him on a regular basis. He would play me different albums each time, and in this way, I discovered the contents of the milk crates. Thelonious Monk, Dizzy, Bird of course, Miles, and more.

"Now you take Zoot Sims," Otis would say. "There's a white boy who plays like he was raised on pigs' feet and corn bread. You go buy some of his albums, but first you have to buy something by Prez, anything you can find will do. See Prez, his real name was Lester Young, but Billie Holiday called him the President of Jazz and ever since then he became Prez. Now Prez influenced Charlie Parker, Charlie Parker and Dizzy were the ambassadors of Bebop, but Prez, he also influenced Zoot Sims but his sound is much more mainstream than Bebop, but Zoot still swings the way that Prez intended the music to swing. Now if you're going to listen to Zoot, I think you've also got to listen to Bean, that would be Coleman Hawkins, because Bean and Prez, man, that's where so much of the magic flows from."

So, instead of my parents complaining about me playing southern rock too loud in my bedroom, I began hearing about the volume of Sonny Rollins, Bird, Monk, Trane, and so on. My father never seemed to mind too much, in fact I think he had an ear for jazz, but my mother despised the music.

"What are doing up there listening to that colored music?" She would shout up to me so that half the neighborhood could hear her. She lacked much of the class of Missy's mother in that regard.

Few people would accuse my mother of being subtle, fewer still would let it be said that she was tolerant of other people's views or skin color, if it differed from hers. I had always meant to ask my father, if the right time had ever presented itself, what he saw in my mother as a chosen companion, but he died before that and all the other conversations that we should have had, could be had. My mother was the grandmother of my children, and for that reason I continued to suffer her commentaries on everything from race relations to Yankee ways undermining the sanctity of southern life. I often thought that my mother was born about two hundred and fifty years too late. She would have been quite at home living in the South before the Civil War came along and disturbed a perfectly good way of life—for some anyway.

Whenever I indulged myself in memories of growing up in the family home it always sent me in a hundred different directions at once, like a skyrocket bursting out of its skin on the Fourth of July. Oh, we did our best every now and then to put the fun back into dysfunctional, but it had always been quite the challenge with the three of us under the same roof. While water flowed downstream, blood, it seemed, had to be pushed and dragged, kicking and screaming. That was how we lived, in a constant state of conflict.

For the first few years after I was married, and after Thing One and Thing Two had come along, I fooled myself into thinking that my own family would survive the car wreck that in my parents' house had masqueraded as a happy marriage. Ultimately, I found myself trapped in the twisted metal of our own car wreck, smelling the gas fumes, and knowing that someone was about to strike that match.

I pulled myself away from that rather unpleasant thought just as the song "Milestones" ended in an embrace of passionate applause and the group started into a song written by Victor Feldman called "Joshua" that I would admit a faint bias toward. Sitting back, feeling mellow, with a second splash of Lag in my glass, I felt comfortably numbed to the outside world. I liked it much better, here on the inside, with some good scotch and some good jazz. Listening to jazz music was akin to meditation to me, good jazz that is, and that is arguably a subjective term.

This was some of the good jazz, to my mind. This was a good band, one of the last good Miles Davis bands at least as far as I was concerned. His first recordings were laid down in 1945 and up until he released "Bitches Brew" in 1969 Miles did no wrong in my book. It was at that point, I decided, that he took a weird turn on that music highway and he lost me. Whether Miles went the wrong way or I just didn't want to follow him was something, I'm sure, that Miles never lost one bit of sleep over. If you were to check the record and CD collection in my living room you would note that it did not contain any of Miles's recordings after "In a Silent Way."

I think now that it was unfair of me to automatically assume that a person, notably a performer or artist, had to continually climb that curve for the audience, but at the same time, never go beyond the top of the arch and into the great decline. I now believe that when someone achieves that position of greatness, that supreme accomplishment, we should not insist that they out-do themselves again and again for our enjoyment or amusement.

Some running back rushes for a thousand yards in a season and we want them to do twelve hundred next year; Paul Gonsalves plays twenty-seven choruses of "Diminuendo and Crescendo in

Blue" in one of the most outrageous solos ever recorded, and someone will want twenty-eight next time. And, hey, painters are not exempt from it either. Hey, Van Gogh, paint us another "Starry Night" and this time put some sunflowers in the painting.

Too often we don't allow those we admire to evolve gracefully through their life. We don't allow them the downside of the curve, well not very often anyway. The sad thing is, we don't even allow ourselves that courtesy. We're always trying to push higher, to be bigger and better, and then we teach it to those closest to us. We forget to appreciate what has been accomplished, and sometimes, to just leave it at that.

CHAPTER NINETEEN

The day I helped bring forward a life into the world I learned a dark secret about myself. In that delightful, and somewhat intimidating moment of beauty, I realized that if I had to I would, and likely could, kill to protect that life.

I had never known that about myself. I had never known where those boundaries lay within me. Touched by the love I felt for the little soul I cradled in my arms I knew, simply knew, that I would put my life in front of theirs if need be. I would take the life of another if they threatened this new life. I made that promise to Grayson, and later to Miranda, as they each took their first tentative breaths, only seconds into their life, their new life.

That was the flip side of loving your kids so much, or anyone else for that matter. The inverse of the depth of your love for them would be mirrored in the depth of the sadness you could expect to feel if they were harmed or taken from you. It took me a long time to understand that when you took love and turned it upside down, the balance on the other side of that was anguish.

I had learned two other things, more recently. One was that you really cannot count on anyone else to create your happiness for you; the other was that you can't just sit back and wait for things to change for you. Hersch had been very good at presenting that truth to me.

"There is no such thing as spontaneous combustion," he had

told me. "You actually have to set yourself on fire if you want something to happen. Those who want to accomplish something will make it happen, those who don't will make an excuse."

He continually reminded me that his role as a therapist was not to be the person continually putting me back together, I was the only one who could do that. He saw his role as the observer, the cheerleader, the crowd waiting at the finish line at the end of the marathon. He used the day-to-day things in my life to put things into perspective. When I told him about the house purchase, he used it as another building block.

"Think of yourself as being in the same rebuilding process as you are in terms of upgrading the house and garden. Rip out all that dead stuff that lived its entire life last summer and died over the winter. Clear out the old and make room for this year's coming growth. If you don't make room for it, how is it supposed to develop and grow?

"The constants in your life, your kids, your friends, your work, these are the perennials that will come back year after year and make the garden a place where you are happy and want to be. The annuals were just meant to be there to add a bit of color, to live for their season, and that's that. When you plant your garden outside your home, think of how you can now begin to plant a new garden within yourself, and think of how you'll feel as you begin to see it flourish. Let go of the past, let go of the annuals that have had their time. I know you're having a hard time letting go of Julia, but let her, let it, go. Make room for someone else to one day set their roots in your world.

"Remember too that you are going to plant this garden, no one is going to do it for you. You are going to take great pride in it and receive great pleasure from it. Accept your defeats when they happen, because you and your garden are not invincible, but remember to celebrate every success that you create as well. Understand that some things you plant will be around next year and some won't, and that's okay because that is part of their plan."

The Lagavulin, miracle potion that it could be, had allowed me to cultivate a bit of much-needed courage, and I listened once again as my voice mail replayed Missy's voice.

We keep a time capsule inside of us that is filled with all the sights and sounds and smells and emotions of our life, and all it takes is that right combination of events to tumble the lock and whisk us back to those magical, sometimes painful, memories that make up our life story. Missy's voice was one of those triggers.

I wrote down the number that she left at the end of the recording and I recognized it as her home number. Every year, back when we used to get a new phone book delivered to the front door, I would go through and look up her name and think of a dozen reasons why I should call her, but never did. I was afraid to. Afraid that I would be left feeling just as empty after the call was done and I had been left so many times in the past. When it came to Missy, I had finally learned not to put my hand on the open flame. But now, being the foolish man that I knew myself capable of being, I was going to leap barefoot back onto that bed of hot coals, and dance for her once again.

I entered the number on the phone and I heard the ring begin at the other end. I felt my stomach tighten like it used to when I was back in the basement of my parents' house, reaching for the string connected to the light.

"Missy," I said casually, well, as casually as I could muster when I heard her voice. "It's Josh."

"Oh," a pause. "I think you want my mom, just a moment, please."

I listened through the open connection into Missy's world and I heard my past walking toward me, heels clicking, across a hardwood floor.

"Hello?" Her voice washed over me, and I could not help but to enjoy the sensation.

"Missy, it's Josh," I managed to repeat.

"Josh, hon, it is so good to hear your voice in person. Thank you for calling me back."

"Don't I always?"

"Yes, but I remember a time when you used to call me all the time." She purred into the phone, and in that second, she had me right back in her hip pocket again.

"Well, we used to have a lot more to talk about then, I suppose."

"Then it's time we did some catching up then, don't you think? I've lost track of how long it's been, sounds like a couple of marriages ago for both of us now."

"So, you've heard about my recent adventures?" I asked.

"I sure have, and I'll tell you what, I'm sorry about what I've heard," she said, in that totally disarming way of hers. "That woman was a complete fool for letting you get away."

"Thank you. It's been an interesting year."

"How are you doing, hon, are you out of the woods yet?"

"Hon" was her term of affection for just about any man. I could imagine her batting her eyelashes to the empty room as she spoke them to me. "Would you hand me that box from the top shelf, hon? Could you get someone to carry these bags out for me, hon?" Never honey, just hon. She'd drop that word the way a petal would casually fall from a rose, and before it hit the ground some poor fellow would be falling all over himself trying to help Missy with whatever it was that she wanted. It had always been that way.

A couple of days later, with a slight quiver in my knees, I walked the path to her front door. I don't think there was any dramatic music playing in the background, but it wouldn't have been out of place if there were. Every step carried me back, over bridges that I thought we had turned into ashes long ago. It had been about fifteen or so years, and so it was not without a fair degree of trepidation that my hand, heavy with the weight of time, tentatively reached out toward the doorbell. In that moment I was seventeen again, calling on Missy Hamilton, most popular girl in the world.

The front door opened and the woman who stood there was Missy, minus the passage of about a quarter century.

"Hi, I'm Shannon," she said, extending her hand into my stunned silence. "You must be Mr. Davidson, it's very nice to meet you. My mom is almost ready, please come in."

I shook her hand, resisting the urge to blurt out that I remembered the day she was born, and allowed myself to be welcomed into the foyer. A spitting image of her mother, I thought, and I wondered if she had yet to command a room the way her mother always had. There was no doubt she had the looks for it, but looks were only part of the equation. A woman commanded a room because she wanted to, because she believed that she did, in fact, command it. Shannon led me into the living room where I waited for Missy to make an entrance. Missy always made an entrance.

The house was a comfortable two-story with a Georgian feel to it. It was furnished in a very traditional style, which is to say that it was quite similar to the house she had grown up in, that I had visited many times. For all her outgoing personality traits, Missy was just a good southern girl molded very much in the image of her own mother. To the right of the living room the hallway split to accommodate the stairs leading to the second floor. It wasn't quite a Scarlett O'Hara staircase, but with Missy gliding down the steps you could very well believe that it had been carefully removed from Tara and placed here for Missy's convenience.

My gaze was drawn to the top of the stairs and the sight of Missy transfixed me as she began her descent. I felt my mouth go a little dry as she presented herself as royalty to an adoring subject. Shannon stood by, smiling, obviously taking pleasure from her mother's premeditated behavior. I chuckled aloud as I sought to calm my nerves. I was sure Shannon had observed this entrance any number of times.

"Hi, hon, it's been way too long."

She breathed the words into the air around me as she stepped toward me, kissing me on the cheek as she held both my hands in hers. In spite of all the feelings of failure that had dogged me through those high school encounters, I could not help but smile and revel in the grand feeling of being in her presence once again. There was just something that happened to me when I was around her; there was something about her being Missy, the way her eyes flashed like lightning jumping across a humid summer sky that let you, made you, forgive her any trespasses she may have made.

Later that evening, as I sat across from Missy in the restaurant,

I delved into the well of retrospection. Many times after a few drinks in the company of a good friend, when the talk ran to past loves, I would wax on about Missy and wonder aloud how it was that I had let her out of my life, and here's the kicker: how many times I had let her back in.

"You realize that we're forty years old and this is our first real date," Missy said, delicately coaxing a sliver of baked salmon onto her fork. "Whatever took you so long to ask me out?"

"Before or after you were married?" I asked. "And, for the record, if we're going to be accurate here, you called me."

"Both," she responded. "And, for the record, I did call you, but you were the one who finally asked me out on a proper date."

"Fair enough," I conceded playfully. "I asked you. I don't know." I glanced back at our past as it flowed out behind us. "Maybe I was afraid of the failure. We seemed to get too close, too fast, as friends. I remember you saying that you didn't want to complicate our friendship; lovers come and go, you said, but a friend always remains with you. You said that to me more than once and I guess it stuck with me."

"If you had tried, you might have convinced me I was wrong," she said, slipping the piece of salmon between her lips. She had done that several times over dinner, I noted, saying something to grab my attention and then taking a bite of food or a drink of wine, leaving the onus on me to continue with the conversation. This time I waited her out, not speaking while she took her time, continuing to regard me from across the table.

"You really should have tried to convince me; you just might have," she finally said.

"Just like that?"

"Pretty much." She shrugged. "I wanted you to, I tried to give you all the hints I could, but when you didn't pursue, I didn't push the issue."

"What was the issue?" I wondered.

"Having sex with you," she said nonchalantly. She began to fidget with her meal but then placed her fork down on the plate.

"And you would have?"

"I might have. Probably. There was that one night in particular that I recall."

"You remember that night?" I did not want to tell her how many times I had revisited that night when we had come so close to leaping into that chasm.

"I have thought about it on occasion. I believe I may have thought about it on my wedding night."

"At what point in the night was that?" I asked boldly.

She laughed and the tension that had been building in me was immediately disarmed.

"Later. Ha, later while I was listening to the snoring, when I was thinking that I may have just made a big mistake. You were, I think, the only one who told me that I was making a mistake. I was thinking about how you avoided the wedding and for a moment I wondered what it might have meant to us if we had gone a bit further that night. A lifetime can be created in an instant, so can a lifetime of regret. I suppose I was entertaining a few regrets at that point on my wedding night."

I was taken aback by her candor. This was not a side of Missy I had been introduced to before.

"I thought you were the one who told me that you did not have regrets for anything that you had done, only for things that you had not done. And there you were on your wedding night, thinking about me."

"Yeah, how about that. I was also pretty angry with you that night when you didn't show up at the wedding. I kept looking around the room most of the night, fully expecting to see you at some point walking across the floor toward me." She smiled a sad smile. "It would have meant a lot to me. You were right. I suppose I knew it that day, that night, that I had made a mistake in my choice of a husband. I realized that I was marrying him for all the wrong reasons. When I cried at the altar, and could hardly say my vows out loud, everyone said they were so touched by it, but I was crying for me, crying for the love I had not yet found. I knew he was marrying me for all the wrong reasons too, I knew I was the trophy wife, and he was handsome and represented security to me. It seemed like what I was supposed to do, I just assumed that we would get used to each other and that I'd feel more secure about the choice I'd made."

"Since when did you ever feel insecure?" I asked, having difficulty with the idea of Missy being anything but feeling secure in her way.

"Always," she answered, directly and then quieter. "I was always insecure. I needed all those boys to ask me out to reassure me that I was pretty enough, popular enough, desirable enough, to matter to them."

"You were always the center of attention," I said, feeling empathy for her, marveling at how well she had masked her fears.

"And always desperately needing to be. I thought marrying him would take care of my insecurity, but I stayed empty, I fooled everyone but me. Every night when I went to bed, I was wishing I was there with someone else, someone who would take the time to know and understand me. Maybe someone like you."

I can't recall now, at what point in the evening it occurred to me that we would be sleeping together that night. I had spent a good portion of the last two and a half decades fantasizing about what it would be like to make love with Missy. I would admit, under duress, to picturing Missy beneath me on occasion when Amanda and I had made love, particularly in the last couple of years of our union, when there wasn't a lot of love in our lovemaking.

I was also willing to admit to myself that for the first time in the past year that I had not been with Julia, that I did not find myself sitting across from a woman, wishing for all the world that it was Julia sitting there with me. What was it Hersch had said to me? Ah, yes, that people come into our lives for a season, a reason, or a lifetime.

"Some people are just meant to flow through our lives, Josh," Hersch had said. "Perhaps they have other purposes with other people, perhaps they are teachers who bring us a lesson, perhaps they just need us for a short time to facilitate a plan of their own that we may know nothing about. Not everyone who touches your life is meant to be with you forever. You can't collect and keep all the pretty shells on the beach, or you destroy the beauty that is the beach."

I will tell you that the events that followed later that evening took a rather familiar, if not well-worn path, that has been followed by lovers forever. We made our way back to Missy's house, entering noisily and carelessly since Shannon had already told her mother that she would be staying at a friend's house that night.

We stumbled our way upstairs and sprawled out on the bed and I began to undress her, finding my way clumsily across that exotic terrain for the first time. Years of emotion flowed like a rising tide. I felt like I was on an intense high, like some drug had been injected directly into my bloodstream and was blasting like napalm through my veins, racing to the roof of my brain, straining against the ectoplasm that lay just beneath the smooth ivory of my skull.

We devoured each other's mouths as clothes were tugged at and discarded, and when we were laying naked beside each other, as we continued our explorations, she suddenly shifted her leg and, without any discernable effort on my part, I was leveraged on top of her. I could not resist the impulse to enter her. This act had been programmed into my DNA every day since the ninth grade. It was not going to be denied.

I felt myself enter her soft warmth and I sank in to the hilt. Once in, I did not move. I held my breath and remained absolutely still for a few seconds more until I felt my hardness swell and I spilled my essence into her. It was as if half of my being had rushed out of my body and into hers, and I felt drained physically, emotionally, and perhaps even spiritually. My entire body, not just my erection, went limp and I lay almost lifeless on top of Missy. The French were right about the orgasm; they called it "le petite mort," the little death. With that one action I felt years and years of tension dissipate in an instant. The weight that was lifted from me was such a welcome relief that I began to smile and despite my weakness, and growing self-consciousness, the smile broadened into a throaty chuckle.

"I think I just added a whole new definition to the term premature," I said, breathing deeply, feeling quite empty and yet fulfilled at the same time.

"It was quick," Missy offered gently. "But really I'm quite flattered."

"I think that was twenty-five years of foreplay rolled into five seconds," I mumbled into the back of her neck where I had buried my face, half by way of explanation, half in apology.

"Was it really that long?"

"Twenty-five years, give or take," I said.

"No, hon, I meant the five seconds."

I recall how I had lain there on top of her, feeling utterly used up. I began to tell her how she had been ever-present in my thoughts for so long, but she hushed me and started to stroke the back of my neck with her fingers. She did not say a word, but continued her feather-like massage while I lay there breathing in the warm scent of her neck. It had taken me two and a half decades to reach this point in the journey, and then just a few seconds to reach the finish. I decided that there was much truth in the adage about enjoying the journey and not so much the destination.

I was embarrassed by my performance, or lack of it, but Missy did nothing to draw attention to it, continuing her administrations in silence, and within a few minutes I could feel something begin to stir inside of me. A little bit of electrical current was being generated. I was still inside of her, soft and warm, and then I began to feel that familiar quickness developing, and I began to feel more like a man, and not some teenage boy experiencing his first awkward sexual encounter with Missy Hamilton.

When I told Hersch of my evening with Missy, the first question he put to me was whether my recollection of the past had held up over the years.

"Being the nostalgic creatures that we are, we tend to swathe the past in this glorious wrapping paper that makes us think we have some wonderful gift bundled away in there. Then when we finally open the package and expose it to the harsh light of today, we sometimes find that it isn't quite the way we remembered it."

I told him about my not-so-stellar performance.

"Happens to the best of us," he said.

"Really?"

"No, not really." He chuckled. "Sometimes. Well, the good news is that you got back up on that horse and rode again! No disrespect intended." We both laughed. "What do you make of this relationship with Missy, if it is at the relationship stage at this point? What do you want from this, or is it just something to cross off your bucket list?"

I had to think about my answer. When you've wanted something so much, for so long, you sometimes forget why you wanted it in the first place. And, as often as not, when you finally do get what you always wanted, you don't always know what to do with it. Kind of like the dog who chases cars and finally catches one!

I was quiet for a while and Hersch let me have my silence. This was often our way; Hersch would stir me up with the right question, and then wait while the contents of my thoughts swirled around inside me until the heavier particles began to drift toward the bottom.

"I think part of me has always wanted to be the guy who can magically go back in time and be the one who finally gets the girl of his dreams."

"Well, you got her! You caught the big one. Now what? Are you going to keep her, or throw her back in?"

"I don't know," I told him. "I don't know if I want her." My candor surprised me; I wasn't expecting to hear myself utter those words. "I might want her; all I know is that for half of my life I've carried around the idea of wanting this woman, not just sexually, but wanting to be her partner in everything, and as long as I couldn't have her, I've wanted her more."

"Maybe it was the same with Julia." Hersch left the sentence hanging there in midair while he put his fingers together and let the tips bounce lightly off the other hand. "Maybe the reason you're still carrying such a torch for her is that you can't have her. What if Julia suddenly showed up tomorrow, child in tow, would you still want her?"

CHAPTER TWENTY

I think it can be safely said that just about every waiter or waitress in Nashville is also an aspiring singer, songwriter, or musician. It is also likely true that just about everyone else in this city is not more than one or two steps removed from someone who is either in the music industry, or wants to be. It's like six degrees of Country Music separation.

A couple who Missy was close to had invited her and a guest to a Saturday Night session where their friend was being featured. Lee Ann Harris, a performer with a big enough status that even a country music nonbeliever like me had heard of her, would be trying out some new songs in front of a small and friendly audience. Missy had invited me along, setting the stage for our second official date.

"The Dove? Oh boy, country music, my favorite." I groaned good-heartedly when she told me about it. I did not mean for it to sound quite as sarcastic as I'm sure it did, I did my best to affect a recovery. "Hey, a night out with you is a treat; I don't care what we do or where we go, and I can certainly enjoy a night of country music if it's with you."

"Josh, you hated country music back in high school, I know that. I just thought that it might make for a nice evening. I'm not a huge country music fan either, but I do like some of Lee Ann's songs. Would you do it for me? One day you might even get me to listen to some jazz. Okay, not really." She laughed, and I was in.

The Dove was a small club where big names who were already "up there" as well as those who were still "up and coming" liked to play for the crowd, which for most of them was a relatively small, but comfortably intimate one. The big names were often anonymous, listed under a pseudonym, at least until they walked out to the stage. When an act wasn't advertised, or when it sounded like a made-up performer's name, it was usually a good night to be there, that is, if you liked country music. In all my years of living in Nashville I had never been to The Dove.

We arrived at the club around eight thirty and left the car with the valet, who promptly jammed it into the parking lot of the now-closed furniture store next door, along with a bevy of BMWs and Lexus SUVs; there was not a pickup truck in sight, dispelling another myth. Whether you had been to this place before or not, you could not live in Nashville and not know that this place existed. It was legendary in its subtleness. As we approached the front door, I realized just how small the place was as we brushed by the people in the lineup and headed over to the VIP line. I smiled at the thought of how excited Dan would be if it were him spending the evening here, glad-handing all around, making connections in the hope of getting one of his songs in front of some of the right people. The doorman checked our names off the list and unhooked the heavy red rope from the stanchion, and we made our way into the main room where there were about twenty tables for four. Missy scanned the room quickly and waved to the couple who were hosting us for the evening.

Susan and Robert were their names, Missy reminded me, as we navigated our way through the small maze of tables. She had mentioned that Robert did Lee Ann's taxes, and they had become friends along the way. The club began to fill in quickly behind us as we sat down and formal introductions were made. The noise level of conversation grew around us and Susan commented on how everyone was getting the small talk out of the way before the music started.

"You can hear a pin drop during the performances here," she said, nodding her head for emphasis. As I listened to the conversation going on between Missy and her friends, I scanned the room, taking in the sights, and my thoughts, without any prodding, wandered toward Julia. She had spoken fondly of The Dove several times. She had apologized, unnecessarily, for not taking me to the club.

"I know a few people there. One day when we're both out of our marriages I would love to go there with you, but not until then."

Well, I was definitely out of my marriage, and here I was, live and in person at The Dove. I remembered joking with Julia, "So this is a good news, bad news story, right? The good news is you want to take me out, the bad news is you want to take me out to a country bar."

"Ah, you silly handsome man." I could see her face; I could hear her voice as she had gently chastised me. "It's not just a country music bar, it's a place where special things happen. It would mean so much to me, to be sitting in that place with you. The Dove inspires dreams in me about my song writing, and I want you to be proud of me when one of those songs gets performed, or better yet, recorded by someone."

"Then we'll do it," I declared. "And I will love every second of it."

"It's a real treat to be included tonight, isn't it, hon?" Missy was patting my hand as she pulled me back into the conversation. I smiled and thanked Susan and Robert again for the invitation.

"You know I've heard that the staff have actually asked people to leave for talking during a performance when they were warned once to keep it down," Missy said, matter of factly. I nodded my head in earnest and put on my best concerned face in what I hoped was a measured show of empathy for the artist and their craft. Somehow, I could not bring myself to equate a set in a country music bar, venerated as it may be, with the reverence that was due, say, a Bill Evans performance, had he still been alive. Hell, I thought you were supposed to make noise when a country band was playing, wasn't that an integral part of the ambience?

We filled the next half hour with polite but idle chat, while we enjoyed some finger food from the menu and went through a couple of rounds of Coronas as we waited for the set to begin. I was asked to tell the story of how Missy and I had met back in the day, and with some additional input from Missy we took Robert and Susan through that great gulf of years that we spent apart. Missy made a big point of telling the table, and everyone within earshot, that my ex was the weather girl on Channel Two. I did get to use my favorite line when asked how long Amanda and I had been together. "Twelve years," I said, "but with the wind chill, it felt like fifteen!" I always laughed at that line, but I really didn't need to be reminded of my ex tonight, any of my ex's.

I had been proud of myself of late; I had finally reached the point where thoughts of Julia did not occupy my every waking, and many sleeping moments. There were actually days when I only thought of her half a dozen times. I could not recall the last time that Julia and I had spoken.

After what seemed like an eternity the crowd suddenly detected a bustle in the back of the club and a wave of energy rolled through the room. The level of conversation rose and then fell precipitously as the lights faded the room to black and a woman, who appeared to be the MC, made her way to the stage in the center of the room where she was held in the glare of a solitary spotlight. We listened as she welcomed us to The Dove and reminded everyone to respect the performers by not talking during the set, and that picture taking, videos, and sound recording were prohibited. No danger of that from me, I assured myself.

It turned out that there would be an opening act before Lee Ann Harris's set, and we sat through about thirty minutes of some good old hurtin' songs, by a guy whose name I cannot recall. I will, however, give him credit where it is due, and concede that by about the third song I had decided that he was actually pretty good. Either that or the Coronas had kicked in.

The Dove was essentially an acoustic club, and that by itself made the music a bit more palatable to me. I resisted my urge to whisper my country music joke to Missy at the end of the set. "What happens when you play a country song backward? The truck starts, the dog doesn't die, and the wife comes back home." Kills me every time.

142

I tried not to be too obvious about glancing at my watch as the proposed fifteen-minute break between sets ran to half an hour and then some. The talk at the table remained animated during the break, carried mostly by Missy and Susan. Robert wasn't overly talkative, even by accountant standards, though I did pull him into a loose thread of conversation as we discussed the relative merits of the Titans season. Finally, the house lights dimmed and a trio of spotlights that hung from the ceiling above the stage came to life.

There was not an MC for this section of the show; everyone in the room knew who Lee Ann Harris was. A burst of applause and whistles erupted from the hundred or so souls in the room. I had done a head count of those seated, including those at the bar, during one of Susan's stories.

A follow spotlight sprang into business from the front part of the room and caught a thousand particles hanging in the air with its beam and traced a path through the club to the dressing room area to pick up the shock of hair, streaked with white blonde and gray, which adorned Lee Ann's head.

She was dressed in a one-piece black suit and it made her appear like a cat, slinking through the gaggle of tables and chairs as she made her way to the stage in the center. She was quite a stunning woman; one who did command your attention even more than her CD covers and that big billboard I had driven by on a regular basis about a year or so ago near 8th and Demonbreun, supporting her last release. The spotlight that followed her to the stage caught the bright strands that were woven into her hair and made them glitter almost electrically. I decided that if I didn't enjoy listening to her that I would at the very least enjoy watching her.

She carried a big Gibson acoustic guitar in front of her, parting the sea, as she walked through the growing applause that became a standing ovation. Perching herself atop the bar stool center stage, she adjusted the microphone and plugged the guitar pick-up into the house system and offered only the briefest of greetings before she began to strum the guitar. Another guitar player quietly slipped into place beside her, and he would accompany her through the set.

As she began to sing, I surprised myself by not only listening, but I may have actually been enjoying what I was hearing. Perhaps it was the idea of an acoustic set that appealed to me; the absence of twangy steel guitars was certainly a plus. Whatever it was, as I listened to this woman sing, her voice tinged with the plaintive shades of emotions that I had known all too well lately, I offered up an acceptance and let myself surrender to the moment.

She knew how to manage and please a crowd. She opened with a couple of songs that seemed to be well known by all in the room, save for me, and as the set grew to several songs, she introduced some newer material.

"This is a song that we're thinking about for the new release and I'm going to debut it for y'all here tonight. It's kind of a trial by fire, and y'all are the judge and fire department," she said to fresh applause.

The lyrics resonated with me, and I was caught up in that magical wave when a piece of music spoke to you personally in such a way that you wondered how this person, this stranger, was able to capture your feelings so intimately, and put them so succinctly into words and music. It stirred up a goodly amount of sentiment in me; the fragile river bottom that had not been disturbed in some time was suddenly churning and shifting with a new current flowing through. The thought of Julia sat like a metallic taste at the back of my throat.

We generally don't like to acknowledge the truth, that many of us, essentially, live in a house of cards. It often came down to the realization that the right card, removed at the right time, could bring the whole house down around you. When that happened, you were just a trailer-park off to the side of the highway, waiting for the tornado to wind its way along the road, settle upon you, and scatter you across the fields.

I never saw the funnel cloud coming, but I could sense it. A change in the air pressure in the room, that "all too quiet" feeling. I waited in anticipation for I knew not what, when everything went eerily quiet and the dark cloud appeared and poked its skinny finger down out of the sky and stung me, uprooting me and flinging me into oblivion like a spindly stand of poplar trees.

"I'm really glad you liked that song," Lee Ann said and was beaming, the applause slowly drained away as she spoke. "The first time that song was played for me by the writer I thought that it was one that really deserved to see the light of day. I'm happy to see that y'all seem to agree with me. I think it's found a home on the next release. The writer is actually a friend of mine from way back, and I know it's been a dream of hers to have her songs recorded by someone and I guess I'm going to be that first someone, and that's quite an honor for me. I'd like to introduce her to you, she's originally from Nashville but moved away recently and she flew in tonight for this show. Please give a warm welcome home to my friend and songwriter, Julia Moore."

The applause rose up and my heart sank as the spotlight left Lee Ann and poked into the crowd, highlighting a table near the dressing room. I wondered at first if I had misheard the name, but it was my Julia who rose to her feet, smiling that smile, basking in the glow of approval. I stood up as well but was rooted in place as I saw the face of her husband in the peripheral glow of the spotlight.

I suffered the instantaneous sensations of euphoria and acute shock. My head swam with confusion as I tried to process too many discordant thoughts at once. I felt the last year of emotions suddenly weigh heavily on my shoulders and I sank back into my chair. I could not make sense of this evening; I could not bring myself to accept that the relationship with Julia may have reached its destination some time ago, and that the two weary travelers had wandered from their shared path and each begun a new journey. I had envisioned us as two exotic birds, each with one wing, and that by embracing we could fly as one. At this moment, I felt nothing short of crippled.

"Earth to Josh, come in, please."

I turned toward the sound of the voice and realized that it was Missy sitting there beside me, tapping on my arm.

"It's not polite to stare, hon, especially when you're staring at another woman while you're out of a date with me."

"What?" I looked away from Missy back to where the

spotlight had captured Julia, the table now empty.

I felt totally disoriented and had to stop and think about what had just occurred. For a moment I wondered if I had imagined that entire situation with Lee Ann introducing Julia. It couldn't have been that, I told myself.

"Oh, don't look like such a lost puppy dog," Missy's voice chided me. "C'mon, hon." She shifted gears and presented me with a warm smile followed by a firm grip on my arm. "Show's over, Lee Ann is just doing the one set, there's no encore. Let's go home, you look like you need to get a real drink into you."

She must not have ever considered that I would be in a country music bar when she planned this visit; this is how my line of reasoning was shaping up as we made our way toward the door. I scanned the valet area to see if I could catch a glimpse of Julia, but she was nowhere to be seen.

Twenty minutes later, I was standing in Missy's living room, still shell shocked, as she emerged from the kitchen balancing two martini glasses that were dangerously full.

"You can only have one of these, any more than that and you'll be useless to me after," she purred. "I'm sorry I don't have any scotch for you, I'll remember that for next time."

Somewhere between the second large sip of gin, and the last moment before our bodies touched the sheets, I wrestled myself into the headspace whereby I did my best to forget the earlier events of the night. Julia had told me to go on with my life, until she was ready to join me. It was now apparent to me that she was following her own advice. I felt like a fool for chasing after the ghost of her for so long.

Missy, of course, knew nothing of the emotional turmoil that was racing through the sinew of every muscle in my body. I was relieved when her efforts began to have the desired effect on me. What I truly needed was an outlet for the immense frustration I had been harboring inside of me for the past several months. That outlet was writhing beneath me in the form of my very enthusiastic partner who, if nothing else, was deriving a considerable amount of pleasure as a direct result of the anguish and pain I was desperately trying to expunge.

Afterward, on the leeward side of my emotional storm front, I lay on my back with Missy curled around me, soft and pliable like a ribbon threaded through my arms and legs. I thought about what Hersch had said to me about not hurting anyone else with my own hurt. As she lay beside me, limp as a rag doll, deep in her sleep, I surprised myself with the admission that I wanted to get up and go to my home. For half of my life I had fantasized about a night like this, laying here with Missy, and now all I wanted was to be alone. God damn you, Julia.

CHAPTER TWENTY-ONE

The next day gave way to a warm evening as I sat in the sunroom at the back of the house, where the sun had only just vacated the space, leaving behind a mothering warmth. The room was perhaps twelve by twelve feet, not extravagant by any measure, and yet it had quickly become my favorite room in the house; a space where I was happy to do everything, and nothing. When Grayson was here last, curled up with me in the large green armchair that occupied an entire corner, he had snuggled up against me and declared that "this was his best room" because it was so cozy. I knew exactly what he meant; it was my "best room" as well.

The walls were covered with a coarsely applied coat of raw plaster in a type of Santa Fe style. The floor was a rough slate, not manufactured tiles, but cut from a slab of stone in rough rectangles with layers of deep green and gray that ran through it. It still felt warm beneath my bare feet as it released the heat it had been storing all day. The window beside me was cracked open, allowing the perfume of the garden to filter in through the screen. The backyard lights were on and from my corner view I could see the mass of white petals from the Chinese fringe tree that anchored the far corner of the garden.

This was the setting I was enjoying in the relative serenity of my sanctuary, as I contemplated my life in exile from Julia. That's how I felt, exiled, like Napoleon stranded on the little island of

Helena, with all the basic creature comforts, yet craving all that he could not have. He couldn't have his beloved France; I could not have my beloved Julia.

I sometimes felt weak when I considered how I could not resist the thought of her, how I longed for her as if we had spent a lifetime together, instead of the relatively short time we had actually shared. An autopsy had never brought anyone back to life, yet I continued to sift through the layers of our dead relationship, somehow believing that if I could understand where things went awry, that I could somehow fix it, somehow breathe life back into the dream.

By my definition, a relationship was over the moment you no longer cared what the other person was thinking or saying. It had always been my belief that from that point forward you were basically living with the corpse of a relationship. It was still there, the same way a dead body was still there. You could dress it up, prop it in a chair, but the simple fact was that it was no longer a living, breathing entity. You could take that dead relationship to Christmas dinners, weekends at a friend's country place, even family vacations with the kids; but when you held a mirror under the nose there was no evidence of condensation, no breath marks. There was just the shadow of a smile that used to be there.

I had observed these relationships many times over the years; at dinner parties, kids' soccer games, and all kinds of other social and family gatherings. I had watched these couples go at each other like snipers in an abandoned building, trying to find the perfect angle to squeeze off a kill shot at the other person. It had been a low point for me when I had finally admitted to myself that I was one of those people in the abandoned building.

Two nights later, it was another warm evening as I waited in my car, to meet up with Missy. I kept the engine running in order to keep the air conditioning on. Several minutes later I saw Missy pull into the parking lot and ease her car into the vacant spot a few cars down. I turned off the engine, got out, and walked over to her car.

We were meeting up with my business partner Dan and his wife, Amy.

"It's been a while since the company bought us a nice dinner," he suggested, out of the blue, earlier in the day. "Think you can scare up a date?"

It had been one of those oppressively humid days that Nashville was famous for and now, in an encore performance, the warm clamminess of the day lingered into the evening. The air was heavy, signaling the thunderstorm that would almost surely come upon us before the night was done.

Missy stood by the side of her car and smoothed her hair back in place with her hand, using the tinted car windows that captured her darkened reflection in the glass.

"What a glorious day!" she exclaimed as I approached. "I couldn't resist driving with the windows down so I could feel the air on my face, even in this heat."

"Glorious?" I whined. "I feel like I've been fully dressed and in a Russian steam bath all day." My shirt was already beginning to stick between my shoulder blades as my dark jacket soaked up the day's heat. The humidity pushed its way beneath the fabric and the rapidly fading cooling that the AC in my car had worked so hard to create.

The evening was pleasant enough, and I relaxed into a comfortable frame of mind as we made our way through the appetizers, and the first of what would end up being a couple of very nice offerings from a vineyard somewhere in Sonoma County.

The talk was light, and I was enjoying the veal chop that had just arrived with fingerling potatoes, creamed spinach, and okra on the side. I was a lucky man to have teamed up with Dan all those years back, that decision had afforded me a good lifestyle and a job that I liked getting up for in the morning.

Dan, for his part tonight, was regaling the table with his story about how close he was to getting someone or other, I had never heard of this person, to record one of his songs.

"I'm more of a lyricist," Dan was explaining to Missy. "I think I'm better focusing on my strength, which is telling the story of the song. Sometimes I'll write basic chord changes under the lyrics but really I prefer to let someone else interpret the music side of it."

"Do you sing as well?" Missy asked.

Perhaps I could see myself with Missy, after all, I had thought at that point in the evening. The only thing she really had going against her was that she was not Julia. Since that acknowledgment included every other woman in the world, well, maybe that was something I should finally come to terms with. I smiled at my dark predicament.

"He sings, but not so well," Amy interjected, amid Dan's protest.

I noticed Missy's gaze shift suddenly away and flash at someone or something across the room and my eyes followed hers like a laser. I felt a shiver run down my spine and the hair on the back of my neck sprang up.

She was still all the way across the room, but her energy hit me like some kind of metaphysical force field. There was the shock, and the feeling of being stunned, as if I had walked into a thick glass door, totally unprepared for the intersect with my path. I did my best not to telegraph my surprise outwardly, while inside I was reeling from the blow. I had scarcely had any contact with her in the last few months, and now to be in the same room with her, unannounced, twice in the last few days, was too much and my surprise and sadness was quickly turning into something that resembled anger.

"Hey, Josh, isn't that the woman we used in that photo shoot for that office temp company way back?" Dan had been aware of my involvement with Julia, but not the full extent of the connection. "What's her name, Gillian, no, Julia, right?" I was not sure that I was capable of formulating an understandable response, and before I could react in any suitable manner, Dan had already risen from his seat and was beckoning her over.

Julia, who had been walking back to her table, turned at the sound of her name and saw me in the same instant. Now it was her turn to register, and then suppress her surprise. She did so by freezing in her tracks, suspended in the moment, before she gathered her thoughts and walked toward our table.

"She's the woman who was at The Dove on Saturday, hon." I

heard Missy's voice from some distant place. "The one who wrote that song that Lee Ann Harris performed. You didn't mention that you knew her, no wonder you were staring at her that night, now it makes sense." I did not respond, as I had now adjusted my focus to include the fact that Julia's husband, Mike, had risen from his place at their table and was walking over toward Julia where she stood in the middle of the room. I was waiting for him to make some kind of move toward me, and I was hoping that I would be able to react accordingly.

"Really?" It was Dan, sounding incredulous. "You were at The Dove; you know Lee Ann Harris and you didn't invite me?"

"My friend knows her actually," Missy said. "Not this woman, Lee Ann Harris, he does her taxes."

"Wow, you've got to get me an introduction sometime. In the meantime, let me say hello to my fellow songwriter here. How good is this?" Dan was buzzing as Julia approached.

"There are no coincidences," Julia had told me on several occasions in the past. "We're always where we are supposed to be." Of course, she was right, as was reinforced for me, and as it will be for you as well, dear reader. At the time, however, I was more perplexed by how we had suddenly run into each other twice in rapid succession, after such a prolonged separation.

"Just relax," I recalled her telling me back at the beginning of things. "Sometimes the best way to hide something is to just leave it out in the open; people rarely suspect the obvious when it is left out there in front of them quite naturally."

Save for the brief view I had of her across the room from her at The Dove, this was the first time I had laid eyes on Julia in several months. She looked as sleek as ever, she walked as if she was gliding across the floor. I had taken great pleasure on many occasions watching her walk toward me, always taken aback by her beauty, and the fact that she was directing it toward me.

"This is the most amazing coincidence," Dan exclaimed, quite delighted with the way the evening had suddenly unfolded as he leaned forward and extended his hand in greeting, circumventing her approach to me, which all things considered, was probably a useful and natural distraction. "Julia, it's been quite a while since you did that photocopier ad for us, you probably don't even recall it. Dan Whittaker," he said, as Julia shook his hand.

"Yes, Dan, what a pleasant surprise."

"You know Josh of course." He continued.

"Of course, yes, I do remember."

She offered her hand to me and I touched her skin for the first time since that last good-bye. As my hand closed around hers, I felt her current shoot through me like lightning through my veins. I gave her hand a slight squeeze, and, with great effort on my part, I released it and set her free. Dan continued with the introductions, which was a good thing, because I had no idea what might come out of my mouth, had I attempted to speak at that moment.

"My wife, Amy, and this is Missy."

All the ladies exchanged smiles. I consciously averted my eyes from Julia, afraid that if I locked in on her, that there would be no turning away.

"How interesting to run into you both here tonight," Julia said to Dan and me, "and this is my husband, Mike."

Again, a round of handshakes and, yes, it did feel odd to be shaking the hand of the man who was married to my lover, or former lover, as it now appeared. I did notice that Julia's gaze lingered on Missy just that extra second. She turned to me.

"And how have you been since I saw you last? You made my grandmother and a few other relatives quite happy by giving them the opportunity to brag to their friends about that magazine ad."

"Always happy to help out a grandmother," I said. I could scarcely hear my voice; my pulse was pounding loudly in my ears. "Fine, fine, I've been fine," I said intentionally, knowing the distain we both held for that word. "It's been a bit of a crazy time I must admit." And before I could continue, Dan jumped in to control the conversation, for which I was thankful.

"It's a small world sometimes," Dan said, grabbing center stage. "You know, Julia, Josh and Missy were just saying that they saw you and heard your song debuted at The Dove Saturday night with Lee Ann Harris, now that must have been exciting."

Now it was Julia's turn to stumble.

"Really? You were there?" She turned to look at me, eyes

wide. "This is just turning out to be one big night of surprises, isn't it? You know, I think I recall you telling me during that photo shoot that you weren't much of a country music fan."

"Things change," was all I could manage.

"Julia, unlike our fickle friend here, I actually do like country music." Dan smiled at me teasingly. "In fact, I've tried my hand at writing some songs with varying degrees of success."

That would be degrees of slim and none, I thought.

"May I give you my card?" Dan asked, thrusting one into her hand. "I don't want to interfere with your dinner tonight, but if you could give me a call sometime, I'd really appreciate getting your take on some of the challenges of getting a song in front of the right people."

"That would be my pleasure." She smiled at Dan, and then gave me a quick look that said something like, "what the hell were you doing at The Dove?" "Dan, I'm just back home for another couple of days, so I'll likely just call you when I get back up to New York, if that's all right."

"Josh and I really enjoyed your song," Missy chimed in. I had all but forgotten about her. "Very heartfelt." She nodded and then gesturing to Mike she said, "I'll go out on a limb since you two are out for dinner tonight, and guess that it's not a song you wrote from personal experience. Where did you get the inspiration for it?"

Julia stared off at some faraway point and I wondered what she was picturing; was it the apartment that we had turned into our secret love nest? The hotel suite overlooking Rabat where we had been too exhausted from traveling to make love that night? For my part I pictured that black-and-white photograph I had taken of Julia's sleeping form, the one I kept in the Charlie Parker biography. It defined the tipping point in our relationship, as it was during that trip that I decided I would return to my children, and by default, to my marriage. I desperately wanted to crawl inside her head and know every thought she had created and entertained over the past almost year, and know where her heart truly was, and if her head was there as well.

"You know, Missy," Julia said, after a pause. "It is Missy,

isn't it?" She seemed to need those extra few seconds to organize her response. "The inspiration for a song comes from so many different sources, but I think that, as is the case in most creative fiction, that there is a thread of truth running through it, some seed from which the story can grow into its own."

Where was she going with this? I wondered. Were we all about to hear a grand testimonial that would finally expose the lie she had been living with Mike? Was this going to be the platform that we would finally stand together on? As far as I knew, Mike was not aware of my involvement with Julia; if he had been, he would have thrown a punch when he got within striking distance, instead of offering me his hand.

"The way I see it," Julia continued in her explanation to Missy, "every relationship has its moments when you're unsure of where you stand in it, what your role is, or what the other person perceives their role to be. You don't actually have to live out the details of what is described in the song, you can simply imagine how you would feel in a similar situation and you take it from there. In this instance, the song was inspired by someone I was close to, who was going through a troubling time in their marriage, they were at that point where it looked like it was all coming undone. They were confused about what they wanted and they hesitated and lost. Everyone in the song lost. Change was something the person was not ready to embrace, and when they hesitated, the world went on without them."

We were all strangely quiet for a moment and surprisingly it was Mike who broke the silence.

"I tell her when she writes some of these songs, that she lets herself get too caught up in other people's emotions. I've watched her sing that song in the living room, playing her guitar, and just crying her eyes out. Talk about suffering for your art." He chuckled, and the tension lifted.

"I'd like to be able to get to that place where I could feel a song as much as you do," Dan said, nodding sagely. "You obviously put a lot of yourself into it."

"Well, whether the song is something that you have lived, or some situation that you are projecting yourself into, it can take a lot out of you to really explore those emotions. I can tell you that as a songwriter, sometimes it's your truth, and sometimes you just make the whole thing up!" She laughed enthusiastically, and succinctly closed the door on the discussion. With that she and Mike excused themselves and returned to join the couple they were having dinner with. As they walked away, I saw Julia place Dan's business card in the side pocket of her purse.

The evening meandered through various wines and food courses. I could not tell you any details about what we ate or drank after the bombshell meeting with Julia. For my part, I needed every distraction I could find to keep my attention away from Julia and her torturous presence. I was probably overly animated as Missy and I told Dan and Amy the story of how we had finally begun dating these past couple of weeks, after doing our best to avoid it for the past twenty-five years or so.

All the while I really wanted only to be privy to the conversation at Julia's table. I willed her to look at me, to make eye contact, but I knew she wouldn't. I did my best not to look even in her general direction. I knew she was stronger than me at fighting off an urge like that; more determined to follow the rules and turn aside my silent entreaties to her. Turning her face once again to present her cheek to me instead of her mouth.

As I endeavored to detach myself from my desire, I drank a considerable amount of wine that night, with the intent of deadening my feelings. I was partially successful. At one point I got up from the table, a little unsteady on my feet for the first few seconds, and made my way to the restroom. When I emerged a few minutes later, I was face to face with Julia. She appeared to be lingering, as she fixed her hair while looking into the mirror in the small hallway. The encounter lasted only an instant, and she gave me three full seconds of undivided attention in the form of a penetrating gaze followed by a smile and the promise that she would be at my front door the next morning at 11, and that I should plan to be home. It was the most intimate moment we had shared in almost a year.

I knew full well that I should not have driven home that night, I would have surely ended up with a DUI had I been pulled over.

I must have been under the protection of Dionysus as I pulled out of the restaurant parking lot. I was sure I did not want to spend the night with Missy, which I knew would have happened had I accepted her offer to drive me home in her car. Not five minutes into my drive my phone rang and my heart jumped in anticipation of hearing Julia's voice. It was Missy. "Come over," she said, and in that moment I capitulated.

Later, as I lay beside Missy, her wine-tinged breath heavy on me as she pressed tightly against me, I could feel my attachment to her wilt. Missy was the beautiful flower that I had admired and desired from afar for so long. Now, having crossed over into the world of intimacy with her, I had cut the flower off at the stem. As much as I might caress this flower, I knew that I could not sustain its life. I had taken Missy from the fertile bed of my imagination where she had thrived and placed her in the harshness of my real world, where denied the water of desire, the dream was wilting and dying.

The next morning, after I returned home, I sat in my kitchen with my head slightly foggy and hung over. I had texted Dan to say I would work from home for the morning, due to a personal issue. I stared at the clock as it crawled toward eleven o'clock. It was taking forever.

Her text came around ten forty-five. Delayed. New meeting time was to be one pm and not at the house. Instead, she gave me the address of a coffee shop, the reasons, she said, would be explained later. What did that mean? I have learned several times over the years that anticipation did indeed often breed discontent.

CHAPTER TWENTY-TWO

How do you measure your love of a person? By how tightly you want to hold on to them, or by how willing you are to let them go? The trouble with hello was that it started the clock ticking toward the inevitable good-bye. Nothing ever lasted, nothing ever endured, or so it felt to me. Would it be easier, I wondered, knowing for certain that I would never see Julia again?

The last time I had spent any time with Julia, apart from our recent brief restaurant interlude, was when her child was about three months old. She had flown back to Nashville from New York and left baby John at her in-laws for a couple of hours so that she could detour to my house for a visit. It was the first time she had spent any time away from the child. That, coupled I'm sure with the emotional nature of our rendezvous, brought on another complication.

Julia had left some breast milk in a bottle for the grandparents to take care of John, however someone forgot to tell her breasts, and her milk started to let down. Her breasts quickly became engorged and painful. She was in such discomfort that she could not get to John in a timely manner in order to feed him, as her body was telling her to. She was about to go into the bathroom to try to express some milk into the sink to relieve the pressure, when I noticed a droplet of milk hanging from her nipple. I put my tongue out and tasted the sweet, warm, liquid. She did not say a word, but cupped her hand behind my head and lay on her side. I began to draw slowly on her breast and felt the warmth fill my mouth. I looked up at her and watched her close her eyes in relief as the pressure began to subside. After a few minutes she adjusted herself and brought her other breast to my mouth and I stayed nuzzled against her until she was at ease.

There are memories from your childhood that, given the chance, will float up to the surface of your consciousness with the vivacity of gas bubbles from a warm soda, spilling over the lip of the bottle in their frenzied desire to be free. The more complicated our lives became, the less willing those bubbles seemed to be to slip their bonds and, of late, I missed the feeling of fizzy tingles on my face.

Another thing I missed was the simple pleasure associated with eating cold watermelon on a hot summer day and spitting the seeds out as far as you could. It was my daughter Randi who reminded me that the things that make you happy as a young child are often the same things that make you happy as a grown-up, former child.

I had treated the kids to a tour de force performance of my expertise as a champion seed spitter a couple of summers before, and it had obviously made an impression. That was back when we all lived in that little Shangri-La, oblivious to the winds of war that were building around us. Grayson, as I recall, was so frustrated that he couldn't spit much beyond his chin, no doubt influenced by the two missing front teeth, that he didn't want to participate. Randi lost her interest rather dramatically after she swallowed more seeds than she spit out and started crying when Grayson told her how the watermelons would start growing in her stomach and split her gut open while she was sleeping. I thought they both hated that day, but later it turned out to be such a fond memory for them.

For me, that day took me back to a time when the biggest worries in my world could be dissipated by nothing more than a caring glance from my father. Like many who have suffered the loss of a parent, I did not realize how much I loved my father until he was taken away from me when we were both too young.

My father was an easy-going man, yet one who seemed to believe that a certain distance should be kept between two people; even father and son. I was never sure where he learned that lesson, but I wished on more than a few occasions that he had skipped class that day. My father, from the emotional bunker he inhabited, did however teach me many things in life that served me well; not the least of which was that the watermelon was a special treasure of the South and should be regarded as such, like any other southern delicacy, be it fried chicken, hush puppies, mint julep, or bourbon.

He was a Civil War aficionado who spent many quiet hours visiting a dusty and cramped old bookstore called Elder's, which ironically was located immediately behind the hospital that one day he would die in. Over the years he purchased dozens of books from that store, reflecting the national scar, written from the southern perspective, of course.

He taught me that my favorite childhood treat was brought to our shores courtesy of the slave ships who, along with their cargo of human misery and suffering, also brought with them sorghum and okra, and this beloved fruit of thick green skin, slick black seeds, and vibrant pink flesh. I could readily recall the late summer Sunday evenings from my childhood, when the sun had finally crawled away and left us with a hot humid night. My mother would put away the dinner and do the dishes while my father would sit with me in the backyard in the soft embrace of the deepening twilight. My father would take apart the melon with his pocketknife, telling stories of how during the Civil War the Confederate army split watermelons open and boiled them down for sweetener for their food. They called them August Hams because when they were harvested their size could rival that of a shank of ham. I remember reading in the *Tennessean*, long before a woman named Julia Moore wrote a travel column for the paper, about a guy in Arrington who had grown the largest watermelon anyone had ever heard of down our way, something in the neighborhood of two hundred and sixty pounds. I could imagine my father sharpening the blade of his knife on a whetstone, salivating at the thought of splitting that monster's rind.

Those Sundays were part of my summer's end routine, the premier bonding experience between my dad and I, until I hit my mid-teens and let it fall by the wayside much, I'm sure, to my father's disappointment, though he never spoke of it. We would spit seeds to see who could go the farthest, as long as the twilight allowed fair judging. When we were stuffed, faces sticky from the sweet juice and our cheeks sore from puckering up, we would sit in the darkness that had by then gathered around us, and enjoy the quiet of the night and each other's company.

My father was not a man given to physical demonstrations of fondness, though there were times on a few of those quiet nights, when I thought I could see a glimmer of affection welling up inside of him, wanting to slip free. So much of him seemed to live beneath the surface. These were also the times when I was aware of the emptiness and the sadness that lived in my father's eyes.

At the end of the evening, when the small scraps of our conversation had been awkwardly cleaned away, we would be left with a pile of watermelon rind and a ton of seeds scattered all over the yard for the birds and squirrels to go after at sunrise. The rind would be washed and scraped clean and then pickled so that it could be enjoyed in the months ahead. My father, as taught by his mother, claimed that watermelon was a great natural diuretic and wonderful for washing your insides clean.

When I was a kid, they would have to store the mason jars away on a top shelf to keep them from me because I would devour the contents like candy. It was a shame, I thought, that my kids had never tasted pickled watermelon rind, although they were both quite addicted to kosher dill pickles the way I was addicted to that rind. Just the thought of that little pop and hiss as the seal was cracked on the pickling jar would trigger a spurt of saliva in my mouth, and I could taste the salt and vinegar on my tongue all the way across the years.

There were many questions that I wished my father had asked me on those nights, and many more things I wish I had told him, but of course that is what hindsight is for. My father never met my children and that was something I would always regret, not that there was anything I could have done about it, but I regret that my father never saw his eyes looking back at him from a newborn a generation away. There were days when Grayson looked over the top of a book at me and I could swear that those were my daddy's eyes, locked in on me.

Grayson loved his books the way his grandpa did. I hoped that I had given him an environment where he would feel comfortable expressing himself on any level, and not follow too deeply down that path where he would lock his emotions away the way my father had. My own father kept so much locked up inside of him that sometimes I believed that it all just built up to the point where something had to give. Maybe, I wondered, if he had just laughed a little more, or even cried, that his heart wouldn't have attacked him as it did.

After my father died, one of the things I unearthed from the depository that was my parents' basement, was his pocketknife, the one that was used to carve all those watermelons and God knows what else.

CHAPTER TWENTY-THREE

Another text from Julia. "Can we make it three o'clock?" she asked. "Sorry for the change," she said. "Beyond my control, but we should be good for three. Same location."

When I had texted Dan earlier that morning and told him that I was a bit hung over and would be working from home, I did not tell him about my planned meeting with Julia. And now, with the random changes that Julia was texting me, I suddenly had even more time to occupy myself. I put on some music, it was Zoot Sims playing a languid tune called "The Trouble with Me Is You," totally apropos I thought, as I laid down on the sofa in the living room, my head racing with thoughts, and I really was a bit hungover. I really just needed to quiet everything down.

I've heard it said that you don't take the measure of a man when he is on top of the world and everything is going his way, because anyone can be brilliant and charming in that setting. Instead, the true nature of someone is usually revealed when they are flirting with the bottom of the bell curve and wondering which way was up.

At a time when I was heading south in a hurry to my own personal emotional bottom, it was a simple exercise prescribed to me by Hersch, which stopped me from actually hitting bottom and taking a nasty bounce. It involved building my own house, figuratively, inside my head, and populating the rooms with my hopes and fears. Each hope and fear had its own room with a door that could be either opened or closed firmly when required. When Hersch first proposed the concept to me I did not put a lot of faith in the idea. He explained to me that it was all about giving myself the power to choose which doors to open or close, and when. The more I put the plan into practice, the more, well, more often than not, it worked out. There was one specific time that I was particularly thankful that Hersch had empowered me to be able to open and close those doors.

Up to this moment I had never told anyone the details of that night; it had scared me so much that I dared not. I did not, could not, tell Hersch what I had experienced. I do suspect however, that he was smart enough to see through my words and go after that little stone I had hidden away. It was something that I had thought unthinkable, except for the brief moment where I actually thought it.

I had been sitting in the kitchen of the house where Amanda and the kids still lived. I can recall the moment vividly, sitting on a bar stool, gripping the granite countertop with my hand for stability while the walls of my own inner house began to collapse like some little Japanese stick dwelling shuddering beneath the tremors of a major quake. In that instant I stared into the darkest crevice of my being.

When I became a gun owner it was because I believed it would bring my family an additional degree of safety and security. I acquired the gun, permit and all, shortly after Amanda had become the regular weather anchor on the local TV affiliate. A viewer, we always assumed it was a guy, had taken more than a casual fancy to her and was sending letters to her. Never emails, too easy to track I'm sure, and the letters became more and more worrisome. We did talk to the cops, but there wasn't much they could do at that point, or so they told us. One of the cops, sensing my frustration, told me in an aside that if it were him, he'd be sure to have a gun in the house.

The mystery author never did make an actual appearance and when the letters finally abated, the gun, which I was never truly comfortable with in the house, was relegated to the trunk of my car, in a canvas bag beside the spare tire, held in place with a strip of Velcro. The Velcro was what saved my inner house from caving in completely that night.

It had been another of those times when a simple conversation had spiraled down into a senseless contest, where the two of us just went at each other with whatever we could pull out of thin air. In between our attacks on each other, while we refueled, we wallowed in those awkward gaps of silence that were as much a part of our arguments as the words themselves. It was in the midst of one of those islands of silence that something inside of me melted away, my filter collapsed, and my emotions began to churn like a giant undertow.

I recall feeling like I was in some kind of hypnotic state, like an out-of-body experience, before I had any idea of what one was. I watched as a part of me stepped outside of my consciousness. I don't remember getting up and walking out of the house, down the front steps to where my car was parked at the curb. I did not recall opening the trunk and pulling at the canvas bag. Luckily it stayed in place. It was not until I heard the crackling rip of the Velcro tabs as they released, that I was able to connect the dots of my intent, and snap out of my delusional state. There was something finite about the ripping sound that jarred me enough to realize that I had come face to face with my dark side.

It doesn't matter that people say that everyone has a dark side; until you see yourself, looking back at you, and you feel that coldest element of your being, you simply don't completely know yourself. The realization shocked me, and with all the energy I could muster I slammed the door of that emotional room shut.

I didn't know who to thank, so I thanked God, that the good side of me won out over the bad side. That was how I saw it; good and bad, black and white, right and wrong. I was just so thankful that the good side was able to out-scream the bad side, to be loud enough to convince me to leave the gun in place, to close the trunk, and just walk away.

I'm sure Amanda had no idea of how close I came to crossing over to the dark side that night. I don't think I fully realized it until much later that night, when I sat alone in the dark sunroom of my house, putting the frightening pieces of my broken puzzle back into place, recognizing the tragic picture that I had come so close to creating.

Later, when I allowed Hersch some small insight into the evening's events, I noted the concern that registered on his face. Hersch was a pretty good actor, but apparently not that good, and it was one of the rare times that he did not tap at the face of his watch as the end of the session approached. The significance was not lost on me.

I didn't actually tell Hersch how close I thought I might have come to truly carrying out the act, in that one microsecond when I felt the evil make its presence known. Had I physically taken the gun from the bag and held it in my hand, I may not have been able to stop myself from walking back into the house and changing my life, and the lives of everyone around me.

CHAPTER TWENTY-FOUR

"Everything happens for a reason," Julia had often reminded me. "There are no coincidences." Today would be a day that proved that to me beyond any doubt.

I had a regular session booked with Hersch for five pm. I was about to call Hersch's office to see if we could reschedule, since I wasn't sure how long my meeting with Julia would be, when he texted to say he had a cancellation and could I come in at one thirty? That seemed to line up perfectly with my new meeting time with Julia. If nothing else, the appointment gods were arranging things for me that day.

I met with Hersch at our new time and was recounting a dream to him toward the end of the session.

"I was in some large body of water, a lake, an ocean, I don't know, but I felt like I was drowning. I know there is something figurative about the idea of dreaming that you are drowning, but, Hersch, it felt so real."

He was quiet for a few moments before he answered me. When he did, it was in a voice that was both tender and firm.

"Figurative or not, Josh, you don't drown by falling into the water, you drown by staying there. You need to move on from these things that are causing you this distress. There are new experiences and new people that are out there for you. You need to learn to let go, just let go, accept and accelerate, remember?"

When I left his office, I felt the need to empty my head of everything before my three o'clock meet up with Julia at the coffee shop. My car was in a lot near Hersch's office and the coffee shop was less than a ten-minute walk away. I decided to leave the car in place since it might be difficult to find street parking with rush hour approaching. I was hopeful that the walk, and fresh air, would help me to be able to sit down with Julia with a clear and open mind, at least that was my desire.

Turning into the wind, I made my way from Hersch's office on Second Avenue over to Broadway. The warm gaze of the sun worked at finding its way through the mid-afternoon shadows cast by the buildings lining the street. The temperature had cooled slightly with a new weather front moving in and I could walk briskly today without breaking a sweat.

I looked up at the Batman building as it displayed a soft golden wash from the sun. The Batman building was at Commerce and Third, and was sometimes referred to as the Bell South building in any of the city guides. If you looked at it from the proper angle it looked like Batman's cowl, silhouetted against the Nashville skyline. Chicago had the Sears Tower, New York had the Empire State Building, and we had the Batman building. That, and a bunch of somewhat tacky souvenir shops around Broadway and Second, where you could stock up on t-shirts and decorated shot glasses. Then of course there was the Ernest Tubb record store, which I could readily confess to having never set foot in during the forty years I had been on earth, and in Nashville in particular.

I continued along Broadway, past the hockey arena at Fifth where the Predators played. I had been there a number of times with clients, and on occasion with Grayson, who wasn't much of a Predators fan, but if the Coyotes were coming through, he and I would make it a boy's night out.

Just past the Federal Building, which holds the US Courthouse at Ninth, is the Union Station Hotel. I had spent a good number of evenings there in the lobby bar, though not so much lately. It sits across from the *Tennessean* newspaper and there had been many late afternoons and early evenings during the time I had moved back into the house with Amanda, that I would meet Julia there for a quick drink and to dream of a future together as we tried to resuscitate our floundering relationship.

The big sign on the side of Baptist Hospital came into view and I felt my breath catch in my throat. I knew the sign was coming; I had only passed along this route about a thousand times since the day that Baptist became synonymous with the death of my father. To this day, and what a day it was to be, I had not yet become comfortable with seeing the collection of buildings that made up Baptist, even though they also represented happiness, in that it was also the place where my two children had entered this world.

As I made my way along the street, I pictured the area of the hospital, where my father had died on an operating table, having passed through those doors, never to get out alive. Back then all the cardiologists and all the King's Men could not put my daddy's damaged heart back together again, and he had slipped away through a chest cracked open to the air.

I was still several minutes early for my meeting with Julia, so I wandered over to the Vanderbilt campus and found a bench to rest on. My inner journey continued on its way, unencumbered.

Now it was my chest that felt like it had been cracked open, the rib spreader inserted into place, and my heart exposed to the cool air. I was aware of the empty place inside of me that used to house the warmth and love of Julia, when the dream of being with her breathed and responded with a life of its own. What precious lesson was I supposed to take away from losing her? And what about the dissolution of my family? How had I gained anything by losing them? I thought of something that Hersch has said to me in our first session. "Pain may be inevitable, but suffering is optional."

I thought of my children and the joy that they had brought into my life, and how sadly ironic it was that the woman I had conceived them with in love had become such a source of sadness in my life. I didn't know how to reconcile these things and so I continued to sit on the bench thinking, and then blissfully, not thinking. I felt that I was finally able to clear my mind of that jumble of thoughts that had been churning around in my head like a collection of dried leaves stirred up by a whirlwind of emotions. After a while the breeze began to settle and I watched the leaves cease their swirling dance, no longer held hostage in their spiral by the wind. They began to drift lazily downward, gently rocking back and forth, stem to stern, like little parachutes, making their way down to where they needed to rest.

The effect was very calming, very peaceful and relaxing. Their dance to the ground was their last function in that form, their swan song; they wanted to, they needed to, make their way to the ground so that they could perform their last useful deed and become part of the earth again and nourish the new growth that was promised to come forth.

As I sat motionless on the bench, ensconced in my own peacefulness, I heard the voice that lives inside each of us. It whispered to me that it was all right to want to remove the numbness that had come over me, that it was all right to begin to feel again. I knew that I must brush away the dust that had settled over my emotions, and I imagined my hands patting at the sleeves of my jacket, dispersing the fine residue that had gathered there. As I shook off the little particles, they danced in the air and resembled snowflakes that melted as they touched my warm skin. I looked up to the sky and saw the clouds hanging there bulge open to release a sparkling storm of snowflakes that swirled around me, soon obscuring my view until it seemed that earth and sky had melded into one misty landscape.

There was a feeling of being on water, and I saw that I rode the water on a ship, slowly gathering speed as I slipped along the surface, knowing that the key to moving forward was to simply let go of where I was. How could you leave the shoreline if you wouldn't let go of it? It seemed so obvious to me. Everything around me seemed so obvious to me. Cast off the lines, move away from the land. Watching the snowflakes stir around me, I was mesmerized as they kissed the surface of the water, silently dissolving into it, becoming one with it. Becoming one more drop of water that in its own small way meant so much to the structure of the ocean. I had lost sight of the land, and I was not at all concerned by it. I could feel the forward momentum but could not see, or care, where I was going. I had never been so close to this sense of peacefulness and I surrendered to this feeling of emptiness, of nothingness.

There was a sudden spark, a flash of insight that for a split-second breathed fire and enriched me with its message, and it was simply this: It is all right to let go.

It was all right to let go of Julia. It was all right to let go of the idea that I would not be with my children each and every day. It was all right for me to acknowledge that I could not fix everything in the world that I came in contact with, that some things that I perceived to be broken, someone else might look at as perfectly fine. Hersch was right, I could not carpet the entire world, sometimes it was indeed better to just get a comfortable pair of shoes for the journey.

As I floated effortlessly across the sea of images and emotions, I realized that I had been carrying the weight of so many things, for so long, that when the burden was removed from my shoulders as it was now, I actually felt like I was floating and rising upward into the sky.

I felt the warmth of Grayson and Miranda, feeding me with their love. I was aware of Amanda, close by but no longer close to me, and that was all right too. I could not see her yet, but I knew by her presence, growing brighter by the moment, that Julia was approaching.

She appeared as a pinpoint of light in the midst of the milkiness that surrounded me. I did not recall walking the final distance to meet with her at the coffee shop, but there she was before me, I could see her profile on the other side of the large window. Closer and closer, I moved toward the light that was Julia. I was almost upon her when I thought again of the very first time my eyes rested on her image, as I walked along Broadway, and I recognized the magic that had been in the air that day. The magic that had pulled me to her as surely as the ocean tide is pulled by the moon. I couldn't have resisted even if I had wanted to.

I knew as I walked toward her that very first day that I was meant to develop some kind of relationship with her, just as surely

171

as a seed knows that it will grow. Life is so simple, I thought; why do we complicate it?

I was so blissfully ensconced in the warm glow that enveloped me, that when at last I opened my eyes, I was caught off guard to discover that I was sitting in the sunroom of my house. Odd, I thought, I must have dozed off and fallen asleep in this chair. Was the idea that I was going to meet with Julia part of a dream I had just awakened from? I felt confused. Disoriented.

The gentle rhythm of the rain pulsed against the windowpane. Weren't there things I was supposed to do today? It felt early in the day, I envisioned the kids sleeping upstairs, wrapped in their blankets and their dreams. I hoped that the dreams running through their heads this drizzly morning brought them a good measure of comfort. They had been very good about the changes that their mother and I had put them through; at the very least they deserved nice dreams.

I thought of the dream I had just awakened from and wondered what it could possibly mean. The walk that had led me to the university grounds and that memory of being on a boat. The images were quite fresh in my mind as I sat here watching the shadowy entrance of morning. It was still more dark than light, beneath a blanket of cloud and the accompanying rain. My thoughts ran to Julia, as they always did, and of the mornings I had awoken beside her and would move my face close to hers so that I could feel her breath on my skin.

Here, in the lap of this misty morning, I sat and enjoyed the soft breathing of the house, this home, listening to its sounds and following its rhythms, feeling its pulse. I came to the conclusion that everything was indeed as it should be, that I had weathered a strong storm and had come out all right on the other side of it. I had finally stopped spinning inside.

From upstairs I heard a noise, someone was rustling about and a moment later I heard a toilet flush and feet padding along the hallway, back to a bedroom. I guessed it was Grayson because in the interval between the flush and the footsteps, there was not much time to wash hands. I knew that Randi would have taken the time to scrub. It made me smile.

Time was nature's way of making sure that everything didn't happen all at once, I reminded myself, as I found my thoughts wandering to Grayson and his approaching teen years. His growing body was getting ready for those long sleep-ins that would likely go well past noon, if allowed. I knew Grayson was likely already breathing heavily, having fallen back into his slumbers in a matter of seconds. Randi too was getting predictable in her routines. When she woke up, she was up for the day, no laying about for her. If it had been Randi just now, she would be on her way downstairs to root around and see if I was up yet. I was usually up before anyone else, and knowing this, she would be on her way downstairs to curl up in my lap and push her clean hands into my face saying, "Daddy, smell the soap, it smells like apples."

There were many things I wished I had done differently, if only I could turn back time. But surprisingly there were not as many items as I once thought there were. I got up from the chair that I had awoken in, pausing to see if the creaks it made would be echoed by noises from one of the kids upstairs beginning to stir. There was nothing; no sound, save for the rain pattering against the house.

I went into the living room to put on some music, and flicked the switch so that the speakers would only come on in the sunroom. On the coffee table by the records was the Charlie Parker book, *Bird: The Legend of Charlie Parker*. I checked inside to see if the picture I had taken of Julia, in that Rabat hotel room a million years ago, was still safely tucked between the pages. I loved this picture; looking at it I was transported back to that night, in spirit at least. I deftly slipped the photograph inside and put the book back on the shelf where it lived. I would enjoy it again another time.

I wanted something to match the mood of the day and moved over to the albums and my eyes settled on the "Sonny Meets Hawk" jacket and I placed the disc on the turntable and the moody opening notes of "Yesterdays" came slipping through the speakers in the sunroom. The first song was just Sonny and Hawk playing their tenors, with Paul Bley on piano keeping them company and adding his layer to their beautiful playing. I complimented myself on the choice of music, I was sure this was recorded with a day like this in mind. I checked the date of the recording on the back cover—July 1963, New York City. Well, perhaps they weren't thinking of a rainy day in Nashville when they moistened their reeds and someone counted the song in, but it worked for me here and now, and I decided that it was all that really mattered, the here and now.

I felt a light-headedness come over me and I was becoming aware of a growing pressure in my chest, the muscles in my arms and shoulders suddenly felt quite taut and I made a conscious effort to relax them. I was caught off guard by a feeling of tiredness, almost exhaustion, that overtook me. I looked around the sunroom and was surprised at how deeply the gray morning light had settled upon it. A feeble light contrasted this as it crept in from the kitchen and gave weak life to the shadows that were cast absently about the room.

Outside, the rain continued to fall as it swept over the windowpanes and ran into the corners of the glass where it gelled and then fell in thick rivulets. I focused on one drop as it grabbed onto the face of the glass and then slid into the mass of water that fell to the ground. I felt as languid as that raindrop. Then came the cloudburst and the rain peppered the windows and walls producing the sound of a drum tattoo. I felt wrapped within a womb, burrowed safe and warm in my hideaway, while I waited for the storm outside to subside. I could hear the swish of the water as it rushed like a river through the troughs and downspouts. The sound made me think of a heart pumping, and blood racing through the arteries of a body.

And then I noticed that the rain had ceased, and it was now silent around me. The windows were still coated with the heavy drops, which continued to drain lazily down the glass. I felt cleansed and refreshed, as if I had been standing in a warm shower of rain; washed by it, letting it run through my body and soul, filtering away the impurities that had accumulated over time; flushing my mind of the cobwebs that had formed over the years. Everything felt so fresh after the rain.

The illumination of the sunroom began to change as the light coming from the kitchen became brighter and brighter. With each passing moment it grew in intensity and it quickly chased away the shadows in the room where I sat, my elbow on the arm of the chair, my chin resting in the palm of my hand. My arm slipped from the armrest and the sudden jolt startled me, and when I looked toward the kitchen the light emanating from there grew in leaps and bounds until it became unbelievably brilliant. I stood up and began to make my way toward the shimmering kitchen.

PART THREE

Accept and Accelerate

CHAPTER TWENTY-FIVE

The scene that played out before me was cloaked in great intensity. I was aware of a number of things all at once, all of which were equally integral to what was going on around me.

I knew that I was in the ICU with Julia. I saw my body on the bed and I understood that I was standing outside of it. I was very mindful of the moments immediately previous to this scene, where I was in my house, walking toward the woman in the white dress.

A number of people had now entered this hospital room. One person was saying my name loudly as she busied herself with threading a plastic tube into the mouth and down the throat of my body on the bed. Someone else entered with a cart and other equipment. I understood that they were trying to get the body to breathe. I saw the chest rise and fall in compliance once the tube was hooked up to the ventilator.

"Call a code," a new person said, and a nurse slapped her hand against a large red button on the wall to the side of the bed.

Within a few seconds a voice emanated from the speaker in the ceiling, sounding quite indifferent to the tension I now felt in the room. "Code Blue, ICU. Code Blue, ICU."

I glanced across the room at Julia, who had been forgotten in the flurry of activity that was now occurring around us. She desperately tried to squeeze herself into a corner of the room.

"He's in fibrillation," a nurse was advising the group who were now stationed around my body which lay on the bed. "He's been intubated; we're at seventy seconds, no meds in yet," she said without looking up from her clipboard.

"Very erratic rhythm," someone I presumed to be a doctor said as he studied the monitors. "Let's try to get him back on track here. Paddles at 150 Joules."

I observed, rather calmly I thought, as gel was applied to the face of the plastic paddles of the defibrillator. A nurse pulled at the hospital gown and exposed the chest. The doctor placed the paddles against the bare skin. I remember thinking that this was exactly like watching my dad jump start the dead battery on his car. The top paddle represented the clamp over the negative terminal, the one on the side of the chest was the positive cable attached to the body frame.

"All right, everyone clear."

The electric shock pulsed through the body, causing it to budge slightly. I thought I might feel something physically at that point, but I felt nothing, not even a twinge. I looked over at Julia as she warily observed from her corner vantage point. She was staring at the body, willing it respond, I was sure. I looked up at the jagged white line that flowed across the face of the monitor screen. I didn't know what it meant, other than it didn't look good. The doctor stared along with me.

"Second charge is ready."

"Clear."

I saw Julia clutch at her stomach as if she was feeling the electrical current go through her. Out of the corner of my eye I saw the right arm of the body slide and then hang loosely, reaching forlornly toward the floor. A nurse placed it beside the body again.

I moved over to stand beside Julia, I stared intently at her, trying to get her to notice me. She was totally oblivious to my presence.

"Julia, please don't be frightened," I implored her as I looked into her reddened eyes. "There's nothing they can do, there's nothing I can do. I can't go back into that body again; I have to let go of it and everything around me. I don't know how it is that I know this, but you have to believe me. I've accepted it, you need to do the same."

This knowledge was like a powerful current running through my every thought as I looked around the room at the activity going on, and then I looked back at Julia. I locked my gaze onto her eyes while she stared straight through me, to the body that lay on the bed, receiving attention from the group of doctors and nurses gathered around it.

"What you're seeing is what was." I spoke the words softly to her, all the while sadly aware that she could not seem to benefit from my new insight. My words fell from her like stones.

"Let's get some adrenalin into him, one milligram." I turned toward the doctor's steady voice and watched as a syringe was inserted. "I'm going to defibrillate him again." I watched as the doctor took the paddles from the nurse once again. "Clear."

I heard the short dull thump as the electricity raced from the paddles to the body. Again, I felt nothing.

"Damn. Again," came the order.

Thump.

I turned away from the resuscitation efforts and focused again on Julia. I sensed that I may not have long to continue to talk with her.

"Julia, my love, please understand that I never meant to hurt you in any way. I would never do anything to hurt you."

"One hundred milligrams lidocaine right now, please." The doctor interrupted me, and I could now definitely detect an edge in his voice.

"Julia, do you see those monitors over there? The only reason they are showing even the slightest activity, is that I'm still here in this room with you, and there is a faint connection from me to that body on the bed over there. I don't know how it is that I know this, but I know it to be true.

"I know that if I concentrate on you, if I keep focused on you, then I can maintain some kind of connection, but I also know that I can't stay here beside you like this for too much longer. It's not that I don't want to, it's just that I know I have to leave, I have to move forward."

"We have asystole," someone said. I didn't know what that meant, but I could see that the jagged image on the heart monitor screen had collapsed into a flat line. What color that had remained drained from Julia's face and I watched, and felt, as her body began to shiver uncontrollably.

"Let's get some blood gases. Here, wait, I'll do it." The doctor who appeared to be leading the group took a large syringe from the tray and pushed it into the leg near the groin area. He had trouble inserting it, he was aiming for a vein, I was guessing. I felt no physical sensation as he stuck the needle in several times before he seems satisfied with his effort. "I need another amp of bi-carb and another milligram of adrenaline."

"Why is he not responding? I don't get why he suddenly crashed like this," another person in the room said, as she watched the meds going in.

I had assumed that by staying near the body that I could keep the connection with it, but that didn't appear to be the case any longer. I held out my hands in front of me and studied them. They seemed as real to me as ever. I did not share the same injuries as the body on the bed. What was very clear to me was that the body on the bed was in obvious physical distress, while the body I felt myself in now was brimming with strength and vitality. I felt absolutely euphoric, there was such an influx of energy flowing into me that I kept thinking that at any moment I might just explode right out of the room.

"Two milligrams of atropine. Is he getting any air in that left side?"

I heard Julia's voice behind me; as I turned to respond I realized that she was not actually speaking out loud. I was able to hear what she was saying, in her thoughts. Her mouth was not moving, except for a slight quiver, but I heard her words as though she was addressing me directly, out loud.

"Oh God, Josh, I am so scared. Please, please, don't die. I don't know what to say; I don't know what to do. You mean so much to me; I don't want you out of my life. Please, be all right; please, don't let it be over."

I stood by, impotently, as the scene unfolded in the room around me. I could see how this was torturing Julia, and I knew there was nothing I could do to alleviate the agony I had created for her, and the sadness that my children would soon know. I listened as Julia continued on, feeling as though I was eavesdropping on a private moment, yet unable to turn away.

I looked forlornly at Julia, sensing that my time remaining with her was fleeting. I noticed a glow that had begun to emanate from the deepest recesses of the corner where Julia huddled and I understood that it was the woman. She stepped out from behind Julia, rather she simply appeared to pass through her, and she stood before me. It felt like she and I were standing in a bubble, floating in the room, we were aware of what was going on, and yet we were isolated from being able to interact with anyone. We did not speak; it just didn't seem necessary.

She returned my look with a gentle smile. I felt a pull, discreet at first, which radiated from her. It wasn't a physical pull, like she was yanking on a string attached to me, it was more like a magnetic draw that grabbed hold of something deep inside of me and simultaneously pulled at every part of me at once.

"Julia, if there is any way you can hear me, if you can feel me near you, know that I love you, I have always loved you. You need to know that you mean more to me that any woman in my life and that you were the only woman who ever owned my heart." I did not know whether she could hear me or not, still I felt compelled to say these words to her.

"He may have a pericardial tamponade. Let me have a needle, I'm going to see if there is any blood in the pericardial sac."

I glanced over my shoulder at the sound of the doctor's voice and watched as he positioned his fingers on the ribcage and located the spot between two ribs where he was going to insert the needle. I watched him force the long point into the flesh between the bones and he drew on the plunger.

"Damn, there's nothing. Give him another amp of bi-carb and a milligram of adrenaline. Get a new bag up there and start an isuprel drip."

I watched the bag being hung on the IV stand and the liquid was started on its way. I was aware that the room had gone eerily quiet at this point. Several seconds passed as everyone waited for a reaction that did not come.

"We've done everything we can; I've run out of procedures." The voice sounded fatigued. "If this doesn't work, we're out of options."

"No response from the isuprel," a nurse said after a short while, as she continued to make notations on the chart she was holding.

"I've got to call it. Resuscitation stopped at eighteen fifty-one."

"Julia," I said, turning to face her for what I feared would be the final time. "Don't forget me. I love you, don't forget me." I lingered as close to her as I could, I felt the magnetic draw continue to exert its pull at me as I persisted in the hope of staying just a little longer.

"I'm sorry, I had no idea you were still here in the room." I spun about at the sound of the voice and realized it was one of the doctors speaking with Julia. "I'm sorry, you shouldn't have experienced that. We did everything we could, sometimes our best efforts are not enough."

I watched helplessly as Julia half leaned, half fell, against the man.

"Come with me, let's get you away from here, you don't need

to be here anymore." Julia allowed the man to lead her away, but as they reached the doorway, she stopped short.

"I have to say good-bye," she whispered. "I haven't said good-bye to him yet." She turned back into the room just as one of the nurses was beginning to remove tubes and electrodes from the body. The woman discreetly placed the tube she was holding on the cart beside the bed and covered it with a small towel. Julia stepped toward the bed, and the nurse quietly excused herself.

We're alone together, I thought, as I stood beside Julia and I felt the ache and sadness that engulfed her as she stared down at the empty body.

"There was so much I wanted for us, Josh, so much," she whispered, but then I realized that she was not actually speaking. Once again, I was somehow able to be privy to her thoughts.

"I know it didn't always seem that way, I know I was difficult at times, but I had my own way of dealing with things. I don't know what I'm going to do without you in my life, I really don't. I can't believe I've lost you, I always believed that no matter what, you would always be there, ready for me when I was finally ready for you, for us, to be together. I can't believe this is really happening."

Her body began to tremble, as if she was suddenly very cold. She bent over the body on the bed and placed her hand on the head, running her fingers through the hair as I had felt her do so many times before, only now I could not feel her touch. Slowly she lowered her mouth to the face and kissed the forehead. A tear slipped free from her reddened eyes and dropped onto the face, rolling down the crease to the neck where it pooled in the crevice of the Adams apple. She rose stiffly and stood immobile for a few more seconds before she turned to go.

"I'm sorry for your loss," the doctor said as he led her gently out of the room. "I'm sorry that you witnessed his final moments, that is not supposed to happen."

"It's all right," she said quietly. "Somehow it feels right to me that I was with him right up to the very end."

I followed them down the hallway, but they were oblivious to my presence.

"The entire time we spoke his focus was on comforting me, that's the kind of person he is. It's hard for me to gather my thoughts, I feel like I'm stuck in a fog bank inside my head."

"It's a natural feeling after suffering a loss like this," the doctor said to Julia.

"He said a lot of things to me," she continued. "He said he had seen his father, who passed on many years ago. He kept trying to tell me about the meaning in our lives. It's funny because he's not the slightest bit religious but he said that our purpose was to share love and seek the truth, which didn't sound like anything he would have normally said. He wanted me to know that there was something beyond, I don't know, something beyond this life."

"Sometimes people who have been through some sort of trauma, or who have been resuscitated, have mentioned experiences like that. Some are more religious, some more metaphysical. Sometimes people who have been in a near-death situation feel they have been given some special gift or insight; sometimes it changes their life quite dramatically, sometimes not. Sometimes they feel they have been given a message to bring back from the other side, if you believe in the other side, Heaven, or whatever you believe."

I watched as they reached the doorway to the waiting room area and the doctor shook her hand and Julia turned to go. I followed her along the last stretch of hallway, I was just drifting along beside her, floating in fact, as I managed to keep up alongside of her. She reached the double doors that led into the waiting area and placed her hands on the metal bar, pausing to draw in a deep breath. As she exhaled, she pushed the doors open and walked toward Dan, who stood rigid in the middle of the room. Until last night she had never actually spoken with him, and now she walked over to him and put her head against his chest and began to sob.

"He's gone, Dan," she said, almost inaudibly, her voice depleted. "I can't believe it; I can't believe any of this is happening."

Dan said something to her, I did not hear the words, it seemed I did not have access to what he was thinking, the way I did with

CHAPTER TWENTY-FIVE

Julia.

I instinctively stepped forward to Julia, but quickly realized that my effort was an empty gesture. I could do nothing for her of significance. I stood watching from my lonely post as Dan placed his arm around her shoulder and led her toward the next set of doors, which they passed through and stepped into the embrace of the other side of the world. The door closed behind them, and I stood staring as they walked away and disappeared from view. I was very much aware of the symbolism.

A cluster of miniature fragments began to gather in front of my eyes, similar to what I had experienced as I sat on the bench on the university grounds. There were thousands of these illuminated particles; it made me think of a massive flock of starlings in a murmuration high above in the sky, swirling about in fanciful patterns that were absolutely mesmerizing.

Each fragment glowed with its own source of light as they danced in front of my eyes until the glow began to come together in a soft build. The lights coalesced into a glowing radiant ball. I looked into the center of it, and I saw the woman in white, standing silently smiling, her hand extended in welcome to me. I reached toward her and was swallowed up in the maelstrom.

CHAPTER TWENTY-SIX

As I touched her hand we were immediately fused together in some kind of chemical- or physics-related reaction. I recall having an image appear in my head, of a sperm fusing with an egg at the moment of conception. And then I was aware of sudden movement, at great velocity. I could not tell you which direction I was going in. There was no left, or right, no up or down. The point of reference for me was the center of my being, and so it felt like I was moving in every direction at once. It was a massive expansion of every part of me; I envisioned myself stretching across the vastness of the universe. The sun, the moon, planets, stars, entire constellations, all streaked past me as I looked on in wonderment, all the while ensconced in my radiant cocoon.

At some point the expansion reached a plateau. I did not experience the sensation of slowing down, it was simply that the feeling of movement suddenly ceased. Somewhere in my mind's eye I saw a small stone flung into the center of a pond. I was not the stone; I was the effect of the stone upon the smooth face of the water. I became the first ripple, and as the strength of the ripples intensified, they began to sparkle and dance as they were reflected into the air above and down to the floor of the pond below. I was the ripple as it pulsed through the air, the ground, and the water. I was resonating with everything around me.

My body felt like it had become part of the universe, mingling with the thousands, or millions, of stars and pinpoints of light that I felt connected to on some intimate level. Every cell in my body felt refreshed and energized. I envisioned someone standing in the inky darkness of a countryside somewhere, staring up at the illuminated canvas of the night sky above them, marveling at the multitude of stars hanging overhead and all the while never having the slightest awareness that they were staring up at me, Joshua Davidson, high above them, gazing back at them as they gazed up at me.

As I lay at rest, enjoying the host of sensations running through my body, I embraced a concept; perhaps each star, each bit of light in this universe that I inhabited, was in fact a part of me and was represented by a cell or some other unit of measure in my body. I felt quite at ease with the notion that if I could somehow be laid bare across a canvas of the night sky, that a cellular or DNA map of my body would mirror a map of the universe.

I wondered, when an astrologer studied the star chart of a person's birth-time and place, were they actually studying the cellular makeup of that person at the time they emerged into the physical world? Was the cellular makeup of a person continually in flux as the planets and other heavenly bodies moved about in their orbits? At the moment they were born, at that exact moment, were the cells within their body synced up with the position of every star and planet and moon? Is this how their universal astrology chart was mapped out?

I had to stop thinking about the concept, as all I really did was overwhelm myself with an insurmountable number of questions and loose ends. But then, as I tried to switch gears, another interesting concept came to me. Instead of me, Joshua Davidson, being a body that was made up of these millions of cells, what if my complete being was just one cell, and that my one cell was part of the millions and billions of cells that made up another body, or another consciousness? What if every cell had its own layer of millions of cells that made up another, and another, and another layer of consciousness?

I could not make head nor tails of it. I tried to empty my mind because, frankly, I was beginning to confuse myself.

As I lay stretched across the infinite sky, the glow of the lights around me seeped into every pore of my skin and filled me with a comforting warmth. I felt myself drift into the welcoming embrace that flowed into me with every breath I took. I closed my eyes, turned out the stars, and turned off my mind.

When I awoke from my, well, I'll call it my sleep, I felt refreshed and very much at ease. I had no idea of how long I slept, for all I knew it could just as easily have been an hour as it could have been an entire day or more.

As I looked around me, there were lush groupings of flowers, resplendent in their vibrant colors, sown among the splendor of the greenery all around me. I heard the soft rustling of the wind in the hedgerows and trees that stood at the perimeter of this garden. From somewhere near me, the sound of birds spilled into the air.

Slowly I began to put together pieces of memory that took me through those last moments in the hospital room. I saw Julia's face, and then those of my children, and I felt an overwhelming longing for them.

"Gray and Randi, I miss you," I said, the first words I had spoken aloud in ages. Where were they? How could I get to them, how could I communicate with them? I began to question my actions. How did I allow myself to slip away to this place and leave them, and Julia, behind? I felt a great sense of loss and failure. I hung my head despondently, not sure of what to do next.

"There is no failure, Josh. Every thought, every action has a purpose and within it, something to be learned. You'll see that soon enough."

I raised my head at the sound of my father's voice.

"Dad," I blurted out happily. In that moment I was peering out from the eyes of a six-year-old with all the naïve wonder that was the gift of that age. "Dad, here we are again in this dream." I beamed at my father, who smiled back at me in greeting, his face alive with a radiance that I don't think I had ever seen come from him before. My father held out his hand and beckoned me, and in that moment I wanted nothing more than to run into his arms, which I did, luxuriating in my connection at last.

"Come and walk with me, Sport." I enjoyed hearing the old

nickname from my childhood. "There is so much for us to talk about and catch up on, you must have so many questions."

Yes, I had many questions. As I slipped my hand into my father's hand, not the least of my questions was why I felt like I was in the mind and body of a six-year-old.

"So, Sport, it's good to be with you, to be able to see and talk with you. Are you up to speed on all that's been going on with you?"

I began to talk with him about what transpired at the hospital, about my interactions with Julia and how much I wanted to be with my kids. When I mentioned the woman in white and the visits I had with her, my father nodded encouragingly.

"The sensations I felt when I was outside of my body, if that is the right description, it seemed to me that I fully stepped away from my physical body," I said to him. "If I am to believe what I think I believe, then I think I died in that hospital room, and that everything I experienced, no matter how fascinating and unreal it might have seemed, really happened.

"I still don't understand how everything came together, how I am now without my children, your grandchildren, that you never met. And Julia, why was it that she and I had those random meet ups, and the final one, why is it now over, just like that?"

"It's not over, Josh." My father's voice was joyful in contrast to mine. "It's not over at all; in fact, this is just a pause along the way, a pause in your journey. It's the same journey that you were on, you're still on it, and you will engage with it again. What you see as an end, is really just a way of creating a beginning. And those kids of yours, beautiful children that they are ..." He laughed and gazed off as though he might actually be looking at them. "And Julia, truly the great love of that lifetime for you, and several others before that as well, in one way or another, at least as I understand it. For now, I wouldn't worry about the kids or Julia. They have people looking out for them, and whether they are actually aware of it, they are well taken care of and they will survive this and carry on. For now, it's more important for you to think about you a bit more, so that you can gain a better understanding of all the aspects of your life; who you are, where you are in the grander scheme of things. You're in a safe and good place here, it's okay to just let your guard down and relax."

As my father spoke of Julia, the image of her floated into my thoughts and I could smell her scent around me.

"Julia will be all right," my father said, giving my hand a squeeze.

"Oh my God," I responded. "You can read my mind just like the woman." I paused. "And, just like me!" I exclaimed, recalling how I was able to hear what Julia was thinking in those last moments, in those dying moments, in the hospital room. Then a new thought entered my head. "Is it all right to say 'Oh God' here?" Not really knowing where "here" was.

"Of course, it is." He chuckled. "You can say it here or wherever you want and you can say whatever you want, whenever. This will all become clear to you soon enough. And, by the way, I can't read your mind; it's just that when you push out a thought as strongly as you just did, I can't help but be aware of it. It's like you've turned on a projector and your thoughts are playing out like a movie. I can't see every nuance of your thoughts, but I can sometimes understand the essence of what you are projecting. There are many, many things for you to learn about your new awareness, but for now we need to move on."

"Move on from where? And to where?" I asked.

"Right now, you are free of that broken body that you were in, and you are also free of the day-to-day concerns of that lifetime; that in and of itself is a precious gift," my father said.

"I think I understand that," I said. "A couple of times now I have thought that I should be feeling very guilty about leaving my children. How will they react to their dad being gone? How will their lives evolve now? At the same time, I also feel that, somehow, everything is under control, but I don't understand why I feel that way. Does that make sense?"

"Of course, it makes sense to me, Josh, and it is a very healthy approach." He placed his hand on my shoulder and we began to walk along together. "I'm not the one to give you the full insight into what happened to you, and why. I would like to, but that's better left to someone with a deeper knowledge of you; they can do it better than I could. I do know that there are so many different ways that people handle the transition away from an earth lifetime and from what I can see, whether it's a conscious effort on your part or not, you are melding with this new segment of your life quite splendidly. In terms of feeling guilty about your kids, don't. At this point your life path has seemingly veered fully away from theirs but really, it's something that the three of you are connected to and it did not happen by chance.

"As special as that lifetime was, now is an equally special time and this place, well, this place and what it offers to you is an opportunity for you to really explore who you are and why you have chosen the paths that led you to now. There is a saying that I'm sure you've heard before 'when the student is ready, the teacher will appear' and while I'm not the person to be your teacher, I do know that they are waiting for you. The person I'm referring to as your teacher is probably better described as your spiritual guide. They will guide you through your experiences and try to help you understand how everything around you is related to you."

"Did you go through the same thing as I did?" I asked my father. "What happened to you when you died? I was so sad, you meant so much to me and I felt totally lost." We both paused in our walking and faced each other. I embraced my father, still not quite believing that I could hold him close and actually feel his arms offering me the comfort I sought out.

"It's different for everyone, Josh," he said softly and patted my back. "It's dependent on so many factors, but at the same time there are familiar scenarios that many people share in. To a large degree, what happens at the moment of your death is based on how you lived your life up to that point. It depends on what type of energies you surrounded yourself with and what expectations might have existed in your belief system. You create the reality that you experience both during that lifetime, and at the point of transition to what you call death. That's why everyone's experience is different. It is exclusive to them, because as much as we share in certain things, each of us is a unique being with our own unique story, our own set of dreams and fears and goals and with that, our own self-imposed limitations.

"You know, Josh, so many people, at the end of their lives, simply refuse to see the gift, the opportunity that the experience of a life really is. They either don't want to or they simply can't see beyond their own nose, so to speak. You, on the other hand, you seem to be willing to embrace what was going on around you. I was nearby you, offering whatever comforting thoughts I could while you were in the hospital. That was when you were able to sense my presence."

"I saw you by the water's edge," I said, recalling the image so clearly. "Then we were separated by a small bridge over the water and you told me not to approach the bridge and I still tried but the distance kept increasing."

"That's correct," my father said. "The bridge was an image that you created, one that you could relate to. Crossing that bridge symbolized you cutting the ties to your earth body, which would have resulted in your death at that moment. It was you, or rather a portion of your consciousness, that required the timing to be different."

Sometime later that day, well, it could have been a matter of moments later, I couldn't determine how long anything took to transpire, I was sitting with my father in a room not unlike the sunroom that had been at the rear of my house in Nashville. We were across from each other, separated by a long low-slung table that held plates of cheeses and olives, some grilled strips of eggplant and zucchini; it was a very nice presentation of Mediterranean-style foods. My father sipped from his glass and then placed it on the table in front of him.

"What is that, bourbon?" I asked as I sniffed the air. "Where did you get that?"

"Want some?" he smiled.

"Well, I'll have one with you, for old times' sake, if you like."

"It's whatever you like, Josh."

"I'd rather have a Lagavulin if I have a choice in the matter, with all respect."

My father chuckled.

"I don't know how you drink that stuff, but you're welcome

to it." He gestured to the table and my glass of Lag was sitting there on the heavy wood top. I reached for it and as I brought it near to me the familiar scent filled my nose, and chest, with warmth.

There was music playing in the background and I recognized the gentle touch of Bill Evans playing his rendition of a wonderful old standard that I liked called "If You Could See Me Now." I smiled at the appropriateness of the title.

"I've learned to appreciate jazz, you'll be happy to know," my father said. "Good choice of music by the way, I quite like this, I'm quite fond of certain styles of jazz it seems."

"I'm happy to hear that, I'm happy for you. You just complimented my choice of music, but I don't remember putting it on." I looked around the room for the source of the music.

"Well, you didn't physically put the music on, but it's what you were thinking that you'd like to hear, and so that is what we're enjoying."

I suppose my confusion was readily apparent to him.

"Same as the scotch, you wanted it, you created it."

"I created the scotch?"

"That's right. You created the scotch, so you could enjoy it. Same as the music, same as the food in front of you, same as the surroundings, same as you and I enjoying each other's company. I'm happy to share in it all with you. You see, Josh, everything is made up of energy and here you, we all, have the ability to one degree or another, to influence or manipulate that energy to a much greater extent than we ever knew in our earth life. The energy is more fluid here, not as dense, and so when you create a thought it flows quite readily into what you perceive as a physical manifestation of what your desire was. You attract to you the things, the feelings, that you desire."

"Really? Is that how things work here? I'll have to be careful what I wish for!" I took another sip of the Lagavulin; it certainly smelled and tasted like the real thing. "Tell me, Dad, when did you turn the corner and begin to like jazz?"

"Remember Otis? The mechanic?"

"Of course, I do, he was the guy who turned me onto jazz in

the first place. I forgot that you two were sort of friends."

"We were, but I have to admit that I was somewhat selectively friends with Otis at the outset. I had a number of underlying issues with bigotry and he helped me work through those during our lifetime, whether he was aware of it or not at the time. Otis died before I did, he got sick with cancer, and as it turned out he was one of the people who helped me with my transition. We were more alike than we knew. With his help, and then with the assistance of my spirit guide, I came to understand some of my very deep-rooted feelings, and what was needed for me to move beyond them. It helped me to grow and initially Otis was a big part of it. I don't know if the music had anything to do with it, but he always liked it to be there in the background as we talked and shared ideas and it just kind of grew on me, I suppose."

The visits with my father began to settle into a comfortable routine. I only had to think of him, and the next thing I knew I would see him strolling up the front path to the house that I now occupied. Our conversation would pick up at the point we had left off at, as if one of us had simply gone into the other room for a moment and then returned.

"You know, I don't think Mom would like this place at all," I said to him, after I had welcomed him into the house.

My father laughed. "Why do you say that?"

"Well, she is expecting to see angels and the pearly gates when she passes."

"Then she might," he said, surprising me. "Remember I told you early on that the passing over experience is different for everyone. Her experience would no doubt be very different from yours."

"I understand that," I told him. "I've been here, well, I don't know exactly how long, but for a while anyway. I'm beginning to get a feel for it, but wouldn't we all share at least some common ground with our experience? If there were pearly gates for some, wouldn't I have felt something about it? And, for that matter, if there are no pearly gates, even though I heard about them all the time from her and those Sunday sermons I went to, what else doesn't exist that we all took for granted?"

I watched my father rub his chin in that way he did when he was being contemplative.

"What you have to consider, Josh, is that you are the creator of your reality, and so is every other person who is on par with you at that particular level of awareness. You are in this house because this is where you want to be. These surroundings feel safe and comfortable to you, and so you envisioned this image of how you would like to be accommodated. I am here with you because I am very strongly in your thoughts, and of course I want to be here to help you to acclimatize yourself to this new existence. At some point I will move on, and then you will meet up with your guide because they have the ability to help you on levels that I can't."

"But how can someone I've never met know me better than my own father?" I could not help asking.

"Ah, Josh, there is so much more to our completeness than what we experience on a day-to-day basis. Our connection, you and I, is from our last lifetime. What I know of you, I know from that lifetime, but I don't have access to any information beyond that, and there is so much more beyond that. I can't know what lifetimes you have already experienced, and how they have influenced who you are and why certain events occurred the way they did. Your guide has known you through many different stages of your lifetimes, I am more of a greeter to you, they will have much greater insight to offer you."

"And did I create the guide?" I wondered aloud.

"The guides exist regardless; however, they exist in the form you will see them in because you created that particular setting or framework. A guide is a highly advanced entity, they can take on virtually any appearance, they can appear as a person, but also as a shape, a color, a light, or simply as an awareness that you can't even begin to imagine.

"As a matter of fact, I need to share with you the information that our time together is drawing to a close, for now at least. There are other things I need to deal with for my own personal growth, and of course there are many things for you to consider and perhaps involve yourself with."

"Does that mean I'll have to leave this place? Am I only here because you are here?"

"Not necessarily, Josh, actually I'm here primarily because you are here. The thing is, you don't change places so much as you change your perception of where you are. It's not that you'll travel to a new place geographically, it's more like a migration to a different level of perception or understanding." He paused and I waited as he seemed to be wrestling with his explanation. "I don't want to confuse you with my way of describing things, these are items that your guide will share with you, and in a way that will be compatible with your level of understanding. The one thing I do want to share with you, the thing that I have finally understood myself, is that it is all about desire. Whether you are here on this particular level of reality, or back on the earth plane, what you experience is all based on what you desire. What you project outward from yourself is what is reflected back at you and that becomes a significant part of what you experience as your reality.

"Going back to your mother and what she might experience when she passes over, think of how comfortable you are with this particular setting that you created, understand that your desire was manifested around you. Each person, when they shed the skin of their earth life, sees and feels things according to their own creation. Believe me, not everyone creates such a pleasant setting as you have."

"Dad, I understand that you have to go, but before we part company, please what can you tell me about my children? How are they dealing with my death, how are they doing without me? And, what about Julia, how is she doing? What has happened to all of them in light of what has happened to me?" The three of them were often on my mind here in this place; it seemed to me that almost every time I slept, I dreamed about one or all of them.

"From my perspective, from what I understand of it, the children are doing fine, well, as fine as can be expected when their father has passed on. They are not in any danger and they appear to be dealing with it very well, considering. I don't actually know this, as I don't have any connection with them; this is information that has been shared with me by others who have knowledge of the situation. I can't be aware of their actual thoughts, or even the day-to-day aspects of your children's lives, or anyone else for that matter. To do that requires a type of permission or ability that I don't have. This is part of the reason why it is important for you to meet up with your guide, as a more advanced soul they can pass freely between here and the earth plane, and of course other planes as well. You and I can interact at this level of consciousness, but I can't tie the different levels together for you in the way that they will.

"It's pretty much time for you and I to go our separate ways, Josh, for now at least. You have your own path to follow and I have mine. Even though you and I share a great love and many other things between us, we are each still on our own journey. What we shared is, of course, very special to each of us, but other souls also wish to share in experiences with us and that requires our focus and attention elsewhere. That's not to say we won't share things again, it's just that I don't know when or in what context that might be. The fact that we shared a lifetime together tells me that we will always share that connection and we will always be a part of each other's consciousness."

And with that, my father and I embraced warmly, and I wished him well as he made his way down the path from my house. I watched as his sauntered toward a large hedge that ran beside the pathway and then he was gone from my view.

CHAPTER TWENTY-SEVEN

I tried to meditate on several occasions in the past, my most recent past, generally to no avail. I could never quite empty my head of thoughts, a phone would ring, a child would call out to me, something would move in my peripheral vision. But now it was different. Somehow, I had learned to not hear the silence; I had discovered, quite by chance, that if you could hear the silence, then your head was not empty, you were still busy listening.

I had been relaxing with my eyes barely closed, in that beautiful cocoon of being, just being, until something caused me to bring myself out of my self-imposed meditative state. I opened my eyes, looking straight ahead through the window, my gaze traveling down the pathway which led to the house, and I saw her standing there.

"Hello, Joshua, I hope I didn't disturb you. May I join you?"

I heard her voice as clearly as if she had been standing beside me, instead of where she beckoned to me from a good fifty feet away from the house. I rose to my feet to greet her as she walked toward the house. I opened the front door and offered my hand to her in greeting. I was half expecting the touch of her skin to send me off on another cosmic journey like the last time I had reached out toward her hand. I was pleased when that was not the case.

"It's so enjoyable to be seeing you in this relaxed setting," she said, as she entered the house. "Please tell me how you are doing; I hope that you are pleased with your surroundings and that you are comfortable."

"Yes, yes, I am; I mean, all things considered." Since I had those several meetings with my father, I had become quite at ease with what I had gone through, I now felt settled and grounded with my situation. "Every time I have seen you, up to now, it has been a precursor to something new about to happen to me, what should I be expecting this time?" She radiated a sense of calm that I welcomed. "Are you the spirit guide that my father mentioned to me?"

"I am." She smiled, and I felt a new level of calm surround me. "I think I owe you an explanation of some of the experiences that you and I have shared recently. May I sit down with you?" She gestured toward the pair of brown leather chairs.

"Of course, of course, I'm sorry, I should have offered. I'm a little, well, my father said I should be expecting to meet my guide but I wasn't sure what or who to expect although I thought that you might be involved somehow."

"Yes, I understand what you've been through, and the adjustments you've had to make in your thinking. I'm sure it's been challenging at times, and when you saw me just now at the end of your walkway you could be forgiven for expecting some new upheaval to your day."

"Well, based on my past experiences, you certainly know how to make an entrance." I chuckled.

"We might yet end up with some monumental change, but I promise that it will be change that you will be ready for and will welcome." She sat in the chair, crossed her ankles, and sat with her chin against her hand, studying me. "You look well, you've been resting quite a long time since you and your father parted company. I think that rest was exactly the thing you needed."

Really? Had it been quite a long time? I had no idea of how to measure time here. As far as I was concerned, after my father and I had warmly parted company, I had sat down to meditate and then I opened my eyes to see the woman. Here she was suggesting that a considerable amount of time had passed between the two events. I was in no position to contest her comment.

"Our first few meetings were rather intense," the woman acknowledged. "There are reasons for that, which we will talk about, but before we do that perhaps a fresh introduction might be in order."

"Absolutely," I agreed. "A fresh start and a new understanding of what is going on."

"Excellent. Hello, Joshua, my name is Sophia." She extended her hand to me, and I took it. "When you and I first established our bond that was the name you knew me by."

As she said that to me, I felt a current of electricity run through my body. I felt a resonance with her words, I felt that her words were true, and that I was, in fact, absolutely safe in accepting her at her word. I felt that I was in good hands with her, that I could trust her. She smiled at me as though she knew exactly what I was thinking.

"Before I begin to tell you some of the things that I think you might like to know, why don't we start with you, and what you would like to talk about."

I had to think for a moment before I answered. It was like the genie offering you three wishes and suddenly you're not sure what to ask for, or what you truly want. Where to begin?

"Well," I said, after some consideration, "could we begin by getting me up to speed on the sequence of events that I have gone through? I'm having difficulty with the chronology of that. What I remember first, was standing in the sunroom at my house, holding a photo of Julia that I had taken on our trip to Morocco. Then, I was in the hospital room, with Julia and I felt that I died there but at the same time I started reliving many elements of my life, everything from memories of my children, to how I felt about certain events and people from my life, including my first meeting with Julia. I even went through my relationship with Amanda and how I felt about that. Then I found myself back in the hospital again. It was like I was watching a movie of my life as an audience member, but I also was starring in it, and then it took me all the way through to the end of my life."

"And then to a fresh beginning," Sophia added, smiling. "That was quite the journey, wouldn't you say? We have a lot to talk about, and your question is as good a place as any to begin. So, yes, I am what you can call your spirit guide; I am the teacher that your father referred to and, yes, I am the same person you met by the river."

"I recognize you from that, and from the hospital room, but you look a bit different. I mean, you're dressed differently now." I was picturing the diaphanous robe or gown that she had worn by the river. Now as we sat in the comfort of this house, she wore what I would call contemporary clothes, something that Julia might wear; jeans with a white cotton blouse and a short jacket, she wore some sort of stylish sandals.

"Let me try to paint this picture for you in such a way that you can take in the entire view. My appearance, my looks, and in particular the clothing you saw me wearing by the river, was what you remembered me wearing from our initial connection, many lifetimes ago.

"I am an entity made up of the energy and awareness that has been cultivated through many incarnations and subsequent spiritual development. Because of that, I have the ability to pass between various levels of reality and this enables me to function in my role as your spirit guide. You and I are alike in many ways; however, I have refined my awareness to a level that is beyond yours, at least for now.

"I have been with you through many lifetimes since our first bonding, offering whatever direction and assistance that you would allow. We have gone through many experiences together. There were times when your actions were very much at odds with your ability to advance spiritually, but by and large you have managed to continue to develop and grow in the ways that will lead you to the higher awareness that you seek. I look forward to the many conversations ahead with you.

"Joshua, it's important to understand that there are no coincidences. The people you have met in your life, the events that played a significant role in your life, they were all there for a reason. You may choose to ignore or abuse the reason, you may choose to embrace it or shun it, but in time you will understand that there is a plan, a plan that is orchestrated by you. And in the event that there is a change in the plan, that too is sanctioned by you.

"I have always been in close proximity to you, our energy has always interacted, sometimes in ways so seemingly insignificant that you may have felt nothing more than a nudge in a certain direction, or experienced a fleeting thought about a particular idea. When major events were coming together in this most recent lifetime, culminating with the end of that particular life, you allowed me to move from the background to the forefront of your awareness, so that I could assist you through the transition period."

As time went on, an interesting development occurred as my interactions with Sophia evolved; I could not lie to myself or distract myself away from the truth of a situation that dealt with an event from my most recent lifetime. I felt compelled to determine when a thought or action was a positive influence in my spiritual growth, or when it was not. From my perspective there was a natural gravitation toward the warmth and pleasure that I associated with the positive events and a distinct revulsion from the negative.

I instinctively knew when something fell into one category or the other, there was no need for debate or justification. The gray area just disappeared and the simple acknowledgment of the clarity of the event was impossible to ignore.

At the moment of my death, my life didn't quite "flash before my eyes," it was more like I was reliving certain episodes of that life in real time, and yet I realized now that it had all taken place in the blink of an eye.

It happened in those few precious moments just after Julia had been allowed to visit with me in the ICU. I remembered the point where I suddenly realized that I was not breathing, and within that short time frame when I fell into Julia's arms, to the point where I felt myself step out of my body, it seemed to me that I reviewed all the key elements of my lifetime.

As this was going on, I was somehow sorting the events of that life into camps of positive and negative, good and bad. The emotions and sensations I experienced were not just memories; I tasted every flavor, felt every bit of grit, every aspect of pain and pleasure associated with them. Sights, sounds, scent, the raw energy that I recognized in each of them was not like any dream I had ever known. By the time I began my first conversation with Sophia in this house, I had a pretty clear understanding of what I felt good about from that lifetime, and also what left me feeling lacking.

"First of all, let me tell you that what you went through, what you felt, what you saw, your entire experience, was totally normal from your perspective. It's good to be curious, but you should not be concerned."

On this occasion, Sophia was helping me to peel back some of the layers of my actual transition from that lifetime, to what was now, this new reality. I was able to follow her presentation relatively easily, and I'm pleased that I am able to share it with you here, dear reader.

"It's important to understand that there is no right or wrong way to cross from one level of consciousness to another. Remember that the closing of a lifetime is unique to the entity undergoing it. Some individuals may examine every second of their lifetime in minute detail, others only feel the need to focus on certain events, major or not, to allow them the insight that is required to truthfully review their lifetime, to have an understanding of the accomplishments or shortfalls of their spiritual growth.

"There are some, initially at least, who may actually refuse to acknowledge what they are going through; they pretend things didn't happen, even to the point where they refuse to recognize that they have crossed a physical barrier with their death. Of course, they will realize, in time, what has occurred, and they will begin the process of acceptance."

"When you spoke earlier about the idea of judgment, of judging myself, how was I supposed to know what I was supposed to be judging?" I asked Sophia. "How was I supposed to know what lessons were to be learned, without really knowing what the parameters were, or how to measure these things?"

She regarded me for a moment and then I saw the glint of an idea come to her.

"If it helps, think of it in terms of something that your therapist Hersch told you. Do you remember when he said that he would try to teach you to swim, rather than worry about being there to pull you out of the water every time you fell in?"

The reference to Hersch caught me completely off guard, but it made me smile. She was obviously more aware of my experiences than I had previously considered.

"In much the same way as Hersch was helping you to self-direct your coping ability, I want to help you to understand that process of judgment is also self-directed. It is very important that you understand and accept how the judgment is exercised; otherwise, how can you retain the lesson from it?

"There is something else that you should be aware of," Sophia continued. "I can't make you learn or believe anything that you do not accept to be truth. Every entity makes their way along the journey toward truth at their own pace and I cannot speed up or slow down your progress, that can only be done by you. However, once you are aware of something, once you are aware of truth, it becomes part of your overall makeup and then we can build from there.

"Imagine that we are building a road through a forest, clearing a few feet of brush and then laying down a foundation for the road as we go. We can't accomplish our goal or get to our destination in one day. In fact, at the start of that project we can't see where that road will end or what it will look like. However, we move forward in the knowledge that we are exercising our plan. We advance a bit more every day until we do finally get to where 'there' is. If you look at the construction of the road all at once, in its entirety, of course the project can seem overwhelming, even insurmountable. My purpose with you, right now, is to accompany you and help you to understand that every thought, action, and intention you have or have had, is the layout for the next few feet of road on your way to the completion. Along the way you can ask as many questions as you like. We have time to sort through everything, all the time you could possibly want."

I knew from our conversations that Sophia had assisted many people as they slipped the bonds of their earthly lives, and had welcomed them to this level of awareness. She was there to help them, and in this case, me; to adjust, adapt, and when it was appropriate, to help them move beyond. I was aware of the fact that Sophia, while she presented herself to me as a friendly companion who was able to converse with me in a comfortable way, was also a highly evolved entity whose abilities far exceeded anything I could currently envision. I felt an innate trust in her and her words. It was not that I felt I needed to believe her, I truly felt that I wanted to, and that I could very much trust my teacher, my spirit guide.

"While you are actively immersed in your reality within the earth plane it is quite normal, and expected of you, that you be in sync with your surroundings so that you, and all the others occupying that level, relate to everything from a common platform of understanding.

"When your consciousness is preparing for release from a lifetime on the earth plane, it begins to function on a much higher frequency than that which you are generally familiar with. This transformation begins without you being aware of it, it is happening behind a screen, so to speak, and when the timing is appropriate the curtain is pulled back and voilà, a new scene in your play is presented to you.

"As you are now aware, there are other levels of reality beyond that of the earth plane. Occasionally you may have gained brief insights into these other levels, but for the most part the cells, molecules, and energy that make up your physical mind, body, and surroundings, are all subject to the vibrational frequency that is specifically attuned to the earth plane."

Everything was so simple, and yet complex, at the same time. Sophia's answers to my myriad of questions were always presented to me in an easy-to-understand manner. She made every effort to not overcomplicate matters with layers of explanation, and thankfully she did not employ quantum physics or anything of that nature to prove her points, although I'm sure she could have, had I pressed for it. Her way was indeed the simple way, and I was appreciative of that.

"The explanation can be as simple or as difficult as you wish it to be," Sophia reminded me, after a short discussion. She let her words rest with me before continuing. "When I look at the difference in the vibration of the various levels of consciousness, I see them as shades of colors, or I can hear them as blends of sounds, I can also feel the vibration itself course through me. They are a simple extension of everything around me, they are as much a part of me as I am of them, and I can move between the levels by simply melding with them.

"This is not possible for you just yet," she reminded me. "But of course, it can be. Within the confines of the earth plane, it is generally not possible for someone in that lower level of consciousness to experience the grandeur of the higher levels; however, there are those people who are able to understand much more about the makeup of the universe. Even though they may have this insight, it is often difficult for them to attempt to describe the bridge that exists between the levels of awareness. Often, it is necessary for them to develop mathematical formulas that would almost fill the sky, to describe something that I may see as pink changing to mauve and even then, they may not grasp the full meaning of what they are trying to understand and explain.

"It is natural to observe everything through the physical reality of the earth plane, that is the thread that holds that world together. It is the prevalent force in your mind and in the collective consciousness of everyone around you. It is an illusion, but a necessary one in order to operate effectively in that environment.

"Time is part of that illusion. If we look at the concept of time, the amount of physical time that elapsed in the second or two from when your heart stopped, to your death, you were able to experience all the key moments and emotions from your entire lifetime. You experienced those events in what you would call 'real time.' To do that would involve spanning years and years, and that is what it felt like to you, but it all occurred in that second between your heart stopping and you, the energy which is you, stepping away from your physical body.

"Everything that you experienced in that lifetime, including the intention behind all of your actions, every thought, sight, taste, emotion, every life experience was included in your review. It was, of course, very real to you, the only illusion was that of space and time."

Sophia spoke with me about the uniqueness of every entity. She explained that while some progressed at a very advanced rate, many were content to simply know that there was some kind of existence that followed the earth life they had just completed. They did not wish to explore anything beyond that point, and instead fell back on comforting themselves with elements of their religious or social backgrounds that they were familiar with, rather than allowing their consciousness to expand to take in the greater picture. She taught me that, while there was nothing patently wrong with their choice, it meant that they had placed a ceiling, at least temporarily, on their ability to access what Sophia referred to as the truth. When this occurred, a number of possible scenarios were presented to the entity for their consideration. The conversations with their spirit guide would pause, and the person would fall into a deep-sleep state, while plans for their future development were finalized on another level of consciousness.

In the case of these particular entities, they would reenter the earth plane at some point in order to experience another lifetime. Their search for the truth would continue at a rate that was more conducive to their abilities and desires. It was all there to be had, but it had to be wanted. Freedom of choice was a powerful freedom to have.

A key lesson for me from these sessions was the recurring theme that every thought, and therefore every intention, is a living thing in the sense that it vibrates with its own consciousness. If you were to match your vibration with that of the thought, or desire, you would be able to attract those things to you. It could be a person, a situation, or a possession. It was a law of attraction, like a physics equation, that brought two vibrations of the same frequency into one.

"There are many ways that someone on the earth plane might utilize this law of attraction," Sophia told me. "When someone prays intently, what they are doing is creating a thought, which takes on a vibration at a particular frequency. The universe then brings that vibration together and pairs it with similar sources, and when these elements are joined, the vibration of the thought is able to manifest into that person's reality. You can do this with prayer, with meditation, or simply by creating the thought as you are walking down the street. It has nothing to do specifically with religion, with any religion. There is no prerequisite manner to achieve this, you simply focus your energy on creating the appropriate vibrational force, and the attraction will happen of its own accord. You must take ownership and responsibility for your thoughts and intentions, because ultimately you will judge yourself based on them, but you can attract anything you desire to you. Many, many people do this on a regular basis without even being aware. They think it is fate, or that some deity has presented them with a favorable gift or punishment. Really, it is themselves, bringing either positive or negative energy into their life, as they desire."

Knowing that I could have whatever I wanted actually made me feel all the more content with what I currently had. I appreciated this private country house where we enjoyed our conversations, without distraction from the surroundings or other people.

"I find it interesting how very relaxed I feel around you," I told Sophia during one of our meetings. "In fact, I felt very much at ease around you from the moment I first saw you by the river, you felt familiar to me even back then. It's like I've known you for a long time."

"Oh, we certainly have created many connections between us." Sophia smiled. "There is a lot for you to learn about yourself, and as we go down that path, you'll better understand how you and I share certain commonalities. Remember what I said about the information coming to you at the appropriate pace, there's no need for us to rush things.

"With that in mind, today I would like to talk with you about the moment when your higher self recognized that you had come to a pivotal point in your evolution. The next step was for you to shed your earthly body. It's not unlike an animal shedding a skin; they are still the same animal in virtually every way, just as you were the same person in virtually every way, but as you shed that skin, you do have to peel yourself away from earthly ties. As you do this, you have greater access to the realms of higher awareness, again, if you so choose.

"Of course, it's very common for someone to feel a series of conflicts similar to the ones you experienced as you realized that the shedding of the skin also meant the shedding of your connection to certain elements of that lifetime, more specifically, your children, Julia, and everything else that you had cared so deeply for.

"The desire you felt to remain with them is something to celebrate, not something to be sad about. Loving deeply was something that you needed to experience and to retain from that lifetime. As souls evolve, they are continually shedding the skins of earth lives. Learning to surrender, learning to understand that letting go is a necessary part of moving forward, is such a key part of growth.

"Think about this: a tree sheds its leaves as winter approaches in order for the leaves to nourish the ground that the tree inhabits. Then, when the leaves are ready to be reborn on the branches in the spring, the tree is ready to draw on the rest it has had, and on the nutrients which it has helped create in the soil, to develop the new leaves. This then leads to a new segment of its lifetime. In theory and in practice, the life cycles of a tree and the life cycles of a soul are comparable. Everything and everyone evolve, it is simply a matter of to what degree and at what pace."

On another occasion, when we met in the bucolic setting of my house, I wanted to learn more about the events that appeared to be hidden away from me, behind the scenes, so to speak, as I used to go about my day-to-day activities.

"I understand what you have told me about the astral body, the one I inhabit now, being more aware than the temporal body, the physical one that I left behind. Does that mean that my astral body knew ahead of time that I was going to be involved in that accident that took my life?" This was not a subject I had delved into very much before now. "What I'm trying to ask is, are you saying that I was supposed to be in that accident, that I was supposed to die suddenly and leave my children without a father, and leave everyone else in my life behind?" I had hesitated to ask Sophia this question up to now. I was having difficulty accepting that I could have possibly considered and agreed to something like that.

Sophia sat quietly across from me. I assumed she was doing this for my benefit, letting me sift through my thoughts, as I was sure she would be direct with her answer.

"Yes, is the short answer to that," she said, following the pause. "Yes, you were aware that you were supposed to be in that situation. In fact, you created it so that you could fulfill your mandate for that lifetime. The astral body is always connected to your higher self. It receives a stream of energy and information that your temporal body could not possibly comprehend if it were exposed to it. So, yes, on the astral level it was very much understood and accepted.

"Joshua, I understand how knowing you were involved in the planning of your death, your exit from that lifetime, would be disturbing to you, but remember that physical death is totally in keeping with the concept of physical life. It is as natural for a life cycle to end as it is for one to begin. The important part is what happens in the middle, in between those two significant events. Over the course of our visits, I will show you how you were the architect of your life. You'll see how it then stands to reason that you were the architect of the end of that life as well, closing the circle, completing the cycle of that one of many lifetimes. The 'why' of it may seem a bit perplexing right now, but as you raise your energy and increase your vibration to a purer level, the mystery of it will evaporate like a morning mist.

"I've told you that here, in this environment, you can create almost any situation you desire; you can live in any house, be around any type of person you wish, enjoy any food or other stimulus. The fact is, you had that ability during each of your lifetimes. Here, you merely have to desire it; there you had to create layer upon layer of situations to accomplish the same goal. All you are doing is influencing energy, the energy all around you. The universe wants to match its energy to your energy, its desire to your desire. It wants to become in sync with you, and here on the astral plane it can interact much more easily with you. On the earth plane, the vibration is so much slower and therefore so much denser, so that the energy cannot flow as effortlessly, this makes it more difficult to complete your desire. Energy is energy, desire is desire; combine those two and you can create anything ultimately."

CHAPTER TWENTY-EIGHT

Please let me take a moment to say to you, my dear reader, that I hope that I have been able to convey to you a somewhat clear understanding of the manner in which Sophia and I conducted our conversations. This was how I gained insight into the lessons that she was offering to me, which I am now happy to be sharing with you. I am sure that each and every interaction between a newly arrived entity and their spirit guide would have its own personal characteristics, but these were mine.

It was at this point that I wondered how religion, geographical location, culture, and philosophy fit into the equation of how an entity's awareness developed on the earth plane, and then beyond.

"I'd like to relate this to the earth plane for the purpose of my question," I said to Sophia, as we relaxed in the comfort of the living room. "I can't help but wonder, with so many different religions in the world, with so many dramatic differences between countries and cultures, how are we all supposed to make progress together on this journey?"

I detected a twinkle in her eyes as I formed my question, as if she had been waiting patiently for me to get to this particular area.

"Well, Joshua, here we get to a very important topic as it relates to the earth plane and indeed how that level of reality affects an entity's development and growth.

"It is very important to understand that the earth plane is

one very small speck in the wholeness of what we will call the universe. It is a grain of sand in a world of beaches.

"While the entities who inhabit this plane tend to believe that they are the only intelligent life force in existence, they are an incredibly small component of all that is. They occupy a small portion of the greater consciousness of the universe, but many believe they are the only important part of it. Perception influences their reality, whether they are actually right or wrong means very little to them.

"These unenlightened entities are so entwined within the physical vibration of the earth plane that they cannot, and in many cases, will not, allow anything to disrupt their belief system. This system is based on wanting to control and influence everything around them, to take on what they perceive to be power and influence over others. If they were to admit that they were on the same journey as every other entity, they would surely perceive this to be a weakness. Of course, they are quite out of sync with the vibration of the universe, but their focus on the physical plane is such that they cannot see the obvious, they refuse to see the truth.

"Love and fear are two great forces of the earth plane, and they are often at odds with each other. If your belief or adherence to a religion or culture is based on fear, you are living your life in a way that is fueled by trying to avoid punishment or retribution. It doesn't mean you are acting based on your true feelings. If you believe in doing things based on love, you will gain a much better insight into your true nature.

"Religion, any religion, is a man-made creation. What began as a basic understanding of truth and love was manipulated to confer power and control to a very few, over the very many. Stories were verbally told, and later written down, in a way to reinforce the idea that if you did not adhere to the various tenets of that particular religion, or cult, if you will, you would suffer immensely at the hand of some god, not just in that lifetime, but for all of time to come. Every religion, or tribe, wrote its own version of how it would control the thought process for those who followed it, whether by choice or by force. What began as an embrace of truth and love, became a fictional rendition of a story, designed to control the people of that group. Then, each group had to find ways to define their teachings as different from the next group, and the next, in order to proclaim that theirs was the one true religion and that the 'god' figure smiled favorably only on their group. In doing so, the 'god' would abandon all the other groups, all those other entities, and condemn them to a life in hell, or whatever horrible fate they proclaimed awaited the nonbelievers.

"If this 'god' were to do that, then the power associated with this belief would be fueled by fear. If this 'god' were to be motivated by love, then there would be no preference of one group over another. All would be equal, as all are equal. There is no 'ONE' religion for the people on the earth plane. All religions are patently false. You can see this by their very nature of exclusion, in particular. They were created by people who wished to control and condemn other people. In this manner they sought to achieve their 'exclusive' relationship with what they called their 'creator.' No religion and no leader of any religion has ever been any closer to the 'creator' than any other person. This is because there is not a single creator, but rather the creation of the universe was formed by a universal, and all-inclusive, process of creation.

"The stories in the various books and teachings of these religions, of all religions whether they claim to be thousands of years old or whether they were formed in recent history, are fables and falsehoods. They were fashioned to create a fear of the unknown, and the unknown was only to be known by those who claimed to be the leaders of these groups. Religion is the great lie of humankind, and it will continue to occupy that position until all entities within the earth plane are awakened to the truth and love of the universe. In the meantime, these so-called leaders have attempted to keep people ignorant of the truth. They take their strength from the ignorance and fear of the people. It is parasitic in its nature, and abhorrent in its practice."

"But why," I asked, "are religions so powerful and impactful on the earth plane? How is it that they are able to proclaim that their way is the only true way and that God blesses and embraces them and no one else? Why is this allowed to happen?"

"It happens because there are so few on that plane who truly understand the meaning of truth and love. That is why it is the primary underlying desire of every entity on that plane to seek out truth and love. You don't need to write a thousand laws and create a thousand restrictions, you only need to embrace the vibration of truth and love, in order to experience the type of life that will allow you to gravitate toward a higher, more refined vibration. That in turn allows your soul to progress to higher levels of awareness, ultimately leading to the goal of oneness.

"Before I continue, let me be clear that obtaining a higher level of awareness can be compared to becoming more spiritual. However, becoming more spiritual and being religious are not comparable situations. To be a practicing member of a religion does not make you more spiritual, in fact it can often be a hinderance. While many religions appear to promote love as part of their mandate, they are primarily built on fear.

"As their self-created mandates were written and rewritten over the hundreds, and indeed, thousands of years, their primary role was to maintain more power and control over physical possessions, as well as people, ideologies, countries, or wealth. They did this by not allowing people to think for themselves, or even to know that they had the ability to follow their natural desire to seek out truth and love.

"For those who have evolved spiritually, they are often able, at the point of their transformation, to immediately enter into the higher levels of vibration and begin to thrive within the energy of their new reality. For them it can be, figuratively, as easy as stepping out of one garment and into another. The issue, often, is when one is weighed down by clutching onto religious teachings and traditions that keep the entity from opening themselves up to the truth. Rather than progressing forward, they remain a prisoner to their past.

"The goal of each soul, as it progresses through each successive lifetime, is the pursuit of truth and love. Most religious teachings tell their followers how a person, having lived a life tied to their religion, will find themselves at the side of this 'god' they talk about when they die. This is not the truth of the universe. This is a manipulation of the truth, and nothing more."

The following day we met up once again at the house. I had now reached the point where I realized that I did not require food and drink on a daily basis in order to be nourished, and I rarely engaged in the formality of eating meals. Initially I had felt the need, the comfort perhaps, of sitting down to enjoy a meal, the routine that I had long ago established.

"Today let's talk about the apparent coincidences that occur during a lifetime on the earth plane," Sophia announced as we sat comfortably once again in the living room. "I'd like to begin by telling you that there are no coincidences. There are no random collisions between you and other people and events." She laughed.

"As you think back on your lifetime, you will recall that along the way certain people came into your life at a particular time and place to assist you through a situation, or to introduce you to a new one. Let me give you some small, but significant examples, of how the idea of a want or need and a solution came together.

"Do you remember the apartment that you rented for that short period of time when you and your wife, Amanda, lived apart?"

"Yes, of course," I readily answered.

"Did you think that was just luck or coincidence that you found it at that time?"

"Yes, I suppose I did. If I hadn't mentioned the situation that I was in to our client, and him telling me about his friend, I never would have come across that opportunity. The fact that it was so close to my office, furnished, a short-term rental arrangement, it was everything that I needed at the time; of course I felt fortunate to have access to it."

"Was it out of character for you to be explaining your personal life to a client the way you did?" Sophia asked.

I suspected that it was a rhetorical question.

"I'm sure you already know the answer to that," I said. "No, I would not usually talk about my personal life with a client, it just wasn't appropriate, and I was a bit surprised that it came out of me in that way. Where are you going with this?"

"Here's where I'm going with this, Joshua. Ask yourself why, in that moment, confronted by the situation you faced, why did circumstances flow the way they did? If you recall, the client you met with was someone you had not expected to see at the time, his request for a meeting came as a surprise to you. It was, in fact, something that you orchestrated. You see, when you focus on something, consciously or unconsciously, your thoughts and desires stir up particles of energy that act as a beacon to attract that thing, that person, that situation, that you desire."

"But how random is that?" I said. "Wouldn't that be so complex to arrange all the bits and pieces of information and timing and availability and everything? Who keeps track of all the requests, and who determines which one is worthy and in what order they get fulfilled, if at all?"

"You keep track of them, and you decide, if it is in your best interests. And remember, Joshua, not every entreaty that the universe grants you is a life-and-death situation, sometimes it is merely something that is a convenient request, conveniently granted," Sophia said, simply.

"I decide if my wishes come true?" I'm sure I snorted as I said it.

"Why is that so unbelievable? Remember that you are in control of what you experience. It is your higher self that guides you. It is you, bringing your desires to fulfillment. The lens you view a picture through will determine the picture you will see. Your lens, your view, is based on many criteria, such as what is your karmic plan in this lifetime? What are your desires? What are you willing to do in order to achieve them? The laws that govern attraction mean that once you are in the appropriate vibrational mode, you and the universe will begin to attract and direct those desires to you. You can only operate within the frequency that you have allowed yourself to rise to; once there, all the possibilities of that frequency, are available to you.

"Remember, Joshua, that a thought is energy, and when this energy seeks to interact with a like source of energy, then certain connections begin to form. This happens at a level of awareness that you might currently have difficulty understanding; however, this awareness still exists, and fulfills its role.

"Back to the apartment and the client; a lot went on that you were unaware of, consciously, in order for you and the client, and his friend, to complete the desire that you created. You attracted this energy to you, and in turn you created the interaction with the person and your desire and the accompanying offer was facilitated. This is not magic, it is not luck, and there was no coincidence involved."

I pondered this for a moment.

"Does that mean that everything I do is part of a master plan? Is there someone overseeing everything in my life? Isn't that what god is supposed to be?"

Sophia chuckled. "Ah, we're digging a little deeper now! There is a lot to talk about regarding the god concept. Let's continue to talk about plans that you have made and what you have done to attract the response to your plans. The important lesson for you to take away from this, is that moments of significance in your lifetime, and what develops from them, are not random or strange, they are quite deliberate. There are no coincidences and that is a powerful truth to understand.

"Here's another example; your involvement with Missy after all those years of being apart was set in motion not simply because you suddenly longed for her, but because she would become the conduit for you to reconnect with Julia."

I felt a surge of emotion rise in me.

"The last time I was to meet with Julia was what led to the accident which led to my death."

"That's exactly right," she told me. "Be patient with me as I walk this road with you. Let me give you a preview and tell you that it was just as important for Julia to be the reason you were walking toward that coffee shop when your incident occurred, as it was that you were subject of the events that day. Along the lines of no coincidences, it is right to refer to that situation as an accident, as it is common vernacular to describe it that way; however, there was nothing accidental about it."

"I'm beginning to get that part now, about the coincidence,

or lack of," I told Sophia. "But Missy called me, I didn't initiate anything with her. I hadn't talked with her in years, so how did I set anything in motion?"

"Ah, but you did initiate. You may not have understood what you were doing, but you sent out a call, a request, and it was answered in a way that utilized your past involvement with Missy, who, when she became part of your circle again briefly, would lead you to see Julia during that performance in that club. Missy became the facilitator of some of the events that would bring you back into contact to Julia.

"That night when you saw Julia at the music venue, your reaction created a burst of energy that you sent out into the universe, which then impacted Julia and her husband to select the particular restaurant where you and Missy were planning to have dinner with your partner Dan and his wife, Amy.

"You should also know that your very first meeting with Julia, when you saw her talking with her husband on the street in Nashville, was the first time you met her in that lifetime, but it was not the first time you met her. A relationship as intense and as involved as the one you recently shared with Julia did not simply happen based on a first-time meeting. That relationship was part of a cycle that has brought together the components of several lifetimes for each of you."

I sat there, quiet, and more or less astonished. I was trying to distill the information that Sophia had just shared with me. I had become so distracted by all the reasons that something couldn't or shouldn't make sense, that I forgot to focus on the reasons why it could and should make sense. Part of my learning curve with Sophia had been to remember to remove my self-imposed limits on the ways I perceived things. I needed to stop using old methods of looking at a situation, and to realize that a new perspective would bring me to new realizations.

"Since we're talking about some of the women I was involved with in my life, you explained why Missy came back into my life, but let me ask you about Laura. What about my affair with her? How did that play into the rest of the circumstances, what was the connection?"

"The connection was her desire and your willingness to facilitate that desire," she replied.

"That sounds a little clinical," I laughed. "I thought we were a little more connected than that."

Sophia smiled.

"Joshua, not every person you meet or interact with in a lifetime is meant to be connected with you going forward, not every new relationship is tied to your past. There are many people and situations that are there to assist one or both parties in their particular goal. This is something that is created between the individuals, and it is based on mutual intent and agreement. As long as one does not harm or take advantage of the other, or cause any reason for karmic debt, it can be a simple and temporary contract. Once it is fulfilled, it is over, like a transaction.

"In the case of Laura, you and she were like-minded about certain elements of your lives, and you recognized this in each other. There are those times when you feel a particular attraction to someone and you might wonder, what is it based on? Depending on the circumstance you might consider whether this might be a past-life connection. Perhaps it is, but sometimes it is just that two people recognize each other as kindred spirits, so to speak, and understand that they can join together to create or facilitate a situation and they work together to that end.

"Now, as a situation develops it is possible that it could lead to something more involved, possibly on a more complex platform, but that is the nature of free will. You can take a situation and grow it into something that may have a profound effect on your life or on your karmic balance, but it can also be that you wish to experience something together and then to simply move along, separately.

"In the case of Laura, she had a need, a desire, to step away from her marriage situation, and her 'request' went out into the universe and you were in a position to play the role that was required. It was a mutual involvement, but it was primarily geared to her request."

"I seem to recall that I got something out of the arrangement as well," I said, with what might have been a twinge of guilt.

"Of course, of course." Sophia smiled. "The situation helped you to deal with some of your emotional and physical needs, but as you saw as things developed, it was not a relationship with deep roots."

"True, I remember feeling that way, but was it wrong for me to have been involved with someone who was married?" I asked.

"I don't know, you tell me," Sophia said.

"When you marry someone, aren't you supposed to be faithful to them?" I responded.

"Once again, you tell me. There is no right or wrong answer to your question. What there is, is your own self-judgment of the intent or motivation behind the action. Marriage is an agreement between two people. It does not mean that they are bound together for that lifetime, or for all time. The laws and beliefs that govern marriage are something that was created on the earth plane, by men, literally. Like the majority of the teachings in religious books, and various laws and customs created by men, they are not the laws of the universe. They are not a mandate based on the god concept that is embraced by many on the earth plane. They are man-made rules, to govern a man-made situation.

"In the case of you and Laura, it was a personal decision, and self-judgment will play a role in how you determine whether it is what you declare to be right or wrong, for you. Your relationship with Laura was not what you would call a sin, using a religious term. If someone willfully and intentionally hurts another through their actions, then that will be judged a certain way, but the relationship you had with Laura could not be called sinful or wrong necessarily.

"No one owns you; you do not own anyone else. The fact that two people are in any sort of relationship, whether it has a written contract or a verbal acknowledgment, you are still free to act as you see fit. Relationship infidelity, as you might define it, breaks no rules or laws except those that are man-made. You may have broken a promise to someone with your actions, but that is something between the two of you. There is no need for any involvement from any other person or group. You must understand that every action has its own set of potential consequences, but seeking happiness or pleasure or comfort, by whatever means, is not a bad thing as long as you do not victimize anyone. When two parties are in agreement, then there is no conflict."

"So, what becomes of that situation for Laura?" I had to ask. "Do she and Doug work through things and live happily ever after?"

"It's not something you have to concern yourself with, Joshua. It was an incident in that lifetime that, while important to you at the time, was really only meant to exist as long as it was necessary that it be shared between you two. It's part of Laura's journey of discovery, you were a helpful stop along the way."

CHAPTER TWENTY-NINE

I think it was the casual setting of our discussions that was a key factor in helping me to take in the, at times, esoteric teachings that Sophia offered me. The trust factor had long been established, and while I still had to take things at my own pace, Sophia saw to it that my growth was steady and incremental.

The day arrived when the topic of reincarnation, an idea that we had flirted with over many discussions, came fully into focus.

"You have lived many lives, Joshua, and from those lifetimes you have retained a substantial amount of spiritual knowledge. It was because of those efforts that you are now at the stage where you have the opportunity to further broaden your awareness. Together we now have the opportunity of helping you to understand where you are on your journey along the path to your enlightenment."

From what I was beginning to understand, the lifetime I had just lived, and what had preceded it, and what was to happen beyond it, were circles operating within circles, and it was all linked to some huge interconnected design. At least that was how I was picturing it in my mind.

"You seem to be feeling quite comfortable in the astral body that you now occupy," Sophia commented to me one afternoon, as she relaxed in the armchair across from me. "Even though I know you are concerned with certain items from your recent lifetime, such as why your children lost their father when they were both at such a young age, and why you could not fulfill more of your dreams with Julia, I see that you are more accepting of it now. You are slowly learning to let go of the physical emotions and desires, and instead you are becoming more aware of the energy that is around you and how you can better understand and utilize it.

"One of the most important lessons to be taken from a lifetime on the earth plane, is to understand how it was that you chose to live that life. It is best when you understand the manner in which you lived, how you chose to love, and, not to be overlooked, how well you learned to let go.

"The more you hold on to something, the less you really possess it. Physical items, whether they are an object, a place, or even a desire, are illusions. Letting go of these things is the key to freedom, freedom to step away from the cycle of rebirth so that you can progress to a higher level of awareness and being.

"Understanding that love is a form of energy allows you to rejoice and be nourished by that energy regardless of where, how, or to whom it is directed or, for that matter, how it is received. On the physical plane, when we direct that energy toward a person or other living thing, it is a process that actually nurtures you in return. When it is directed toward an object, power, or possessions, it is another matter. When you attempt to use the energy to feed the physical manifestation of your ego, an interesting thing happens; rather than nourishing you, it actually begins to feed on you and depletes you in a spiritual sense, which in turn, depletes you in the physical sense.

"There are those entities who are sometimes so consumed by the idea of not wanting to accept their situation, and not wanting to let go of the physical trappings of that lifetime, that they become increasingly earth bound, clinging relentlessly to the illusion of the physical plane. Even though they have reached the end of that particular lifetime, they keep going about their daily routines, creating the settings and interactions that they crave. They fool themselves for as long as they can, and in the process sometimes end up upsetting others with their crude manipulations of the energy around them."

"You mean ghosts?" I sat forward abruptly. "Are there really such things?"

Sophia laughed.

"No, no, not in the sense like the Halloween concept or any of those movies you might have seen that include ghosts and other creatures created by a writer's imagination; but, yes, in the sense that these are entities that have temporarily lost their way.

"All life forms are simply energy; in the case of the earth plane they are encapsuled in a physical body. These entities that are temporarily lost are not able to make the full transition to their astral body, and they try to cling onto what they have known, instead of what is. In doing so they can sometimes be responsible for some seemingly unexplained physical acts as they crudely attempt to manipulate the energy around them.

"While we're on this topic, I should also tell you that sometimes acts of physical manipulation come from entities you may have been close to, and they are looking for some way of letting you know that they continue to exist. Things like a set of keys going missing for a short time, or a piece of jewelry or something that you have a particular affinity toward, suddenly ending up in an unexpected place. Again, these are not what someone might call ghosts, their intention is not to frighten you. Often, they are just those close to you, friends or family, who want to reach out to you in a caring way to let you know that they are still around you, just in another form.

"So, yes, energy exists in the form of what some people would call ghosts, when really it is just the astral projection of an entity trying to communicate with you. When you exist within the earth plane, you occupy three bodies. The physical body, which is governed by physical laws; it is how health and joy and pain and pleasure and disease and so on are made relevant to you. There is the etheric body; this serves as a connector between your higher self and your physical body, it is like a transformer that takes the raw energy that makes us the universe, and steps it down a multitude of levels so that the physical body and brain can interact with it. Then we have the astral body, which is a purer form of energy that allows you to dwell in the astral consciousness."

"The holy trinity," I said casually, and surprised myself with the clarity I saw within my statement. Of course, what I had heard in my Sunday School teachings was that the term referred to the Father, the Son, and the Holy Ghost. What Sophia had presented to me, and what I had made of it, was a very different concept. On cue, Sophia picked up on my insight and continued along the path.

"Yes," Sophia nodded enthusiastically. "This is the type of symbolism that religions have used in their teachings. The holy trinity is the whole you: the physical body, the etheric body, and the astral body. Each body represents a reality which serves a specific purpose.

"As we have discussed, during this life review in the moments that the physical body and mind approach and embrace death, you create a frame of reference for judging your lifetime. Was it a life well intentioned and well lived? Did you give more than you took? Did you create more love than pain? At the end, how well were you able to accept the letting go of the physical in order to embrace the astral and spiritual reality? All of these elements are combined and in this manner your growth or progress is measured.

"Many religions refer to the 'judgment day,' and while it is a day of judgment, it is not an examination by a god concept, it is not a final judgment. It is not a matter of being judged according to a religious concept or practice. You are not judged forever based on this event; you are simply recognizing the thoughts and actions of that lifetime. You can correct anything that you wish, either through deep introspection, or as is often the case, by reincarnating and dealing with those issues in a new life. It is something that is experienced by everyone at the end of every lifetime. This is how an entity grows toward oneness."

The conversations that I had with Sophia were like a balm to me, in that they soothed but also enlightened me. Her words would settle on me like a fine mist that would gently seep into my consciousness, providing me with a deep understanding of the teachings that she was sharing with me.

"I'm hoping you can share more insight into the concept of Heaven," I said to her during one occasion. "I know you said to me that Heaven is not a place, but what about the role that Heaven plays in our lives, on the earth plane at the very least? I guess I'm speaking from the perspective of what follows after we die and reach this place where we are now. Is there another level of awareness that we would consider to be Heaven?"

I did not think for a minute that wherever I was, was Heaven. At least, it could not be the Heaven that had been promised, or threatened, to me those times I had attended a church service with my mother. Even without the church reference, the idea of a Heaven of some sort had been entrenched in my mind from so many sources, that I simply couldn't ignore asking about the obvious. I wondered how the concept of Heaven and the self-judgment that Sophia had already spoken about were connected.

"When we go through this process of self-judgment, how does a person weigh the contents of their life to determine if they are allowed into Heaven? How advanced does a soul have to be to get into that place?"

Sophia smiled at me.

"Do you remember that I told you that you don't have to physically travel from one place to another?"

"Yes, I do," I responded. "But everything is in a place at some point, somewhere, isn't it? When I was in Nashville I was living in a place, here at this nice house where we're sitting right now, even in this astral body, I am still in a place. Wouldn't Heaven have to be a place somewhere?"

"If that is how you wish to perceive it, then, yes, everything has its place, some place. And so, if Heaven is a place, is there a place called Hell?"

"Yes, I guess from everything I was taught, if there is a Heaven, then it stands that there is a Hell, and we're also told that there is Purgatory," I said hesitantly.

"Joshua, what I am trying to have you grasp is that rather than Heaven being in a geographic or otherwise measurable location where you have to travel to it, the idea of Heaven is more of a state of being. First of all, there is no Heaven, and there is no Hell, except that which you create. You create your own reality; therefore, you create your own Heaven or Hell.

"The concept of Heaven and Hell, as presented by the various religions that you are familiar with, is a fantasy created to control others, through fear and reward. That is not to say that a soul does not suffer or celebrate the contents of a lifetime, but there is no actual place where they go to, or are sent to. No one person or thing judges you, except for you. In the clear light of knowledge, of truth, you will review your lifetimes and you will be subject to the laws of cause and effect, the law of karma, and you will experience the consequences of your actions. This is your Heaven or Hell."

Sophia paused as if to consider something. I wasn't sure I was able to fully embrace this particular lesson, and she seemed to sense that.

"Here," she said after a short time. "I was looking through some of the events of your most recent lifetime, looking to take something that you are familiar with, and to then see if we can apply it to some of the more abstract thoughts that I am asking you to consider. Do you recall when you were in university at Vanderbilt in Nashville, you became interested for a short time in the concept of Buddhism?"

I told her that I did recall that. I had pretty much forgotten my brief dalliance with it, but as she asked me about it now, a very clear picture formed in my mind about a discussion I had attended. A guest lecturer presented an overview of Buddhism as part of a series of talks put together by a student group. For the most part I had steered clear of any involvement with traditional religions, once I had broken the Sunday tradition of attending my mother's Baptist church. Still, something had drawn my attention to this particular meeting.

"At that lecture," Sophia continued, "do you recall the story that was told of the Samurai and the Zen Master regarding Heaven and Hell?"

"I do," I acknowledged, and I pictured myself in the sparsely filled auditorium. I let my mind wander back to the story of a Zen Master who encountered a heavily armed Samurai as he walked along a path toward a village. I could hear the strong voice emanating from the diminutive elderly man standing alone at the front of the stage, and I was struck by how real it felt. I could actually place myself at that time and place, and for all intents and purposes, I felt that I was physically back in that room, hearing the man narrate his story.

"I'd like to inquire about something, Master," the Samurai had exclaimed. "I'd like to know if there really is such a place as Heaven, and if there is such a place as Hell."

The speaker continued, describing the situation in some detail, and told us how the Master had regarded the warrior for several breaths; letting his gaze run over the powerful man from head to toe, he then pulled his head back in condescension and snorted.

"Who do you think you are to have the nerve to speak to someone like me about such a question?"

"I am a Samurai of the Imperial Guard, that's who I am!" the warrior responded aggressively.

The Master laughed at him disdainfully.

"Impossible. Obviously, the Emperor has never laid eyes on you; he would never allow such a shameful individual as you to represent the Imperial Guard!"

"What did you say?" the Samurai exclaimed loudly as his temper rose at the Master's response. "How dare you offend me! I will avenge my honor!"

With that, he drew his sword, raising it high over his head and advanced menacingly toward the Master. The Master, not flinching, raised his hand, smiled at the warrior, and said calmly, "You have just opened the gates of Hell."

The Samurai halted in mid-attack, realizing how close he had come to fulfilling his intention to harm the Master. He lowered his sword and put it safely away. He bowed to the Master, who then quietly said to the warrior, "The gates of Heaven have now been opened."

The image of the stage and the auditorium faded away, and I was sitting with Sophia once again.

"Yes, I remember that now. It had totally slipped my mind, but I do recall it now quite clearly." As I spoke to her, I felt a chill run through my body as another memory came back to me. I pictured myself at Amanda's house, standing in front of the open trunk of my car, the rip of the Velcro strap holding the gun in place had just punctuated the night air. I had wavered between the gates to my own Heaven and Hell. I shuddered at the memory of that moment, when I had thought the unthinkable, and almost created it.

I took a deep breath and composed myself, thankful now for the opportunity to have heard that lecture and wondering to what degree it may have, subconsciously at least, sparked the response that resulted in my decision to turn away from the dark action that had been waiting for my acceptance or denial of it. I may well have saved two lives that night. One that would have been taken, and one that would have been destroyed.

"After attending that lecture, I meant to learn more about the Buddhist way of life, but I got caught up in everything else going on in my world and I never followed up on it," I mumbled to Sophia. I was sure that she had specifically chosen that page of my life to present to me. Again, she inherently knew what I was thinking and feeling and she spoke gently to me.

"Joshua, you should not view your action as a failure, but rather as a success. Thanks in part to that lecture you attended, you changed the cycle that you had been on, and I will explain that to you in greater detail shortly. You'll see that it is part of a cycle that needed to be broken if you were to move forward. And, do not feel guilt that you did not embrace Buddhism, or any other religion. The fact is, Buddhism would not have all the answers for you in that lifetime. No religion can make that claim. However, that day, you did gain an insight, that stayed living within you, for the time when you needed it.

"Whether you choose to follow a particular religion or not is of no consequence; karma and the laws of the universe, the laws of truth and love, ultimately are the only laws that matter. The choices you make will determine your accountability for your actions and intentions. You cannot blame anyone else for your situation, since you are the creator of your reality. Your actions and intentions mark who you are. Even to choose to do nothing is still a decision that has been made. We choose to follow our desires. When your desire is strong enough, you will create the result. You are the creator of your lifetime, and ultimately you will be the judge of the contents of that lifetime, as we have discussed.

"Regardless of what any religion says to you, you will be born, you will live your life, and at the end of that lifetime, as we are doing now, you will review that lifetime and hopefully accept what had been learned. Your vibration will evolve in concert with what you have embraced, and then, as the situation dictates, you will be born again, into another lifetime. This is the law of karma and reincarnation, and it supersedes any teachings that a man-made religion might suggest.

"The truth exists whether or not you believe it. When the truth is presented to you, you have free will to accept it or deny it. However, if you deny it, the truth still exists, you are just not a part of it, and this will become an impediment to your growth.

"Everything you have ever needed to know is within your grasp, as it always has been, you need only to adjust your vibration to that which you wish to be a part of. This is how you create your Heaven, or your Hell."

I began to understand the concept that Heaven lived within our consciousness, and that neither it nor Hell was a physical place that we could be assigned to. I still had difficulty coming to grips with the idea that huge masses of people, much of the world in fact, could be so misled in their beliefs. I had to pose the question to Sophia.

"Remember, Joshua, that you create your own reality. Reality is shaped by what you choose to embrace. If you desire to embrace an illusion, that is what your reality becomes. There is truth in the universe. Once you know it, you cannot deny it. Free will, which we will talk about in greater detail as we move forward, free will is a very powerful force. It is this concept that has allowed for the creation of various religions, political groups, militaries, and so on. These groups, religious or not, but often they are, have taken a universal truth, and subverted it in order to create an illusionary power or focus to fulfill their own agenda.

"All roads eventually lead to spiritual development and advancement, it's just that some roads are a long and circuitous path, where the journey is lengthy and tiring, and other roads are quicker and a comparative pleasure to travel.

"When a group requires that you follow their rules and their way of doing things, ask yourself if your road truly matches the path that they want to lead you down. You must be true to yourself. The choice of the road to take is yours alone, but there will always be those people and groups who wish to influence your decisions. Ask yourself if they are friends who wish to assist you, or if they are simply mining your energy and essence for their own gain."

On the earth plane, much like food and drink, sleep was a necessary requirement for the physical body. I had begun to understand lately that while it was not specifically a need for the astral body, sleep, or the act of sleep, could be an important part of our connection with our higher self and so while the astral body did not require sleep in order to function, I did find that I was using the routine of sleep as a means of meditation.

When the mood struck, I would lay myself down and close my eyes, focusing on a particular sensation or event. I would enter a state of consciousness which was not unlike the dream state of the earth plane, except that everything I experienced was enhanced to a much greater degree.

Recently I had experienced an entire series of these dreams that revolved around my ex-wife, Amanda. I am referring to these episodes as "dreams" because it is the most convenient way for me to describe them to you, but you have to understand that the experience is so much more involved than what you and I have known as our dreams.

When I dreamed of a person, such as Amanda, I felt as though I was actually visiting with them. It was like we had agreed on a time and location, and we both showed up there and interacted with each other. We did not travel to a physical location; we were simply together in our heads and in our hearts.

At first, I was not sure how to relate to Amanda. I felt in conflict with the emotions I associated with her: love, apathy, anger, sadness. I felt very strongly that we needed to resolve something between us, and that appeared to be the purpose of these visits.

Another thing about these dreams was that I felt that each of us had the ability, I certainly felt that way for myself, to direct the events to some degree and not simply experience things, the way you might in a traditional dream where things seemed to happen without your input. It was an interactive experience, like being inside of a painting and acting out as a player within it, rather than just staring at a piece of art in a gallery. I felt that we were going through this process in order to influence or redefine the nature of the relationship she and I had shared. I felt I had been given the choice to decide if I wanted to remain angry with her and stay hurt over the acrimonious ending to our relationship, or to choose to move past it. It was not that I could erase the past, but I did feel strongly that I could repurpose the emotions and energy that were associated with it.

As we went through the series of visits, I found that my anger, my negative feelings in general toward Amanda, had dissipated. I'm sure it could well have gone another way, but now I felt that it was possible to write a new ending to my story with Amanda. Once I chose this realization, I felt quite emotional about it, in a very good way. The openness of our communication with each other transcended the negatives that had shadowed the last few years of our marriage. It was quite a cathartic experience, and I at once began to feel more at peace as I let go of the negative energy that had surrounded the latter years of our relationship.

For all that I felt I had resolved with Amanda, I found my interactions with my mother to be quite curious, at the very least. During the visits I had with her, I found the same feelings that had been a part of my lifetime with her were still very present now. There was a distance, a zone of non-connect between us that continued to be, honestly, a bit of a frustration to me. She was flighty, easily allowing herself to be distracted away from any meaningful contact with me. When I would approach her in these visits, she would back away. Not run away, but simply edge away as though she was anxious about being in close proximity to me. I tried to interact with her on several occasions, but over time I had to accept her reluctance to engage, and in time my dreams about her gradually faded. I had since learned, from my discussions with Sophia, that while we may have desires to resolve certain situations with those people we have been involved with, it was a requirement that both parties had to share those desires. We could never coerce someone to do something against their will.

The time I spent with Randi and Grayson was incredibly nourishing and enjoyable to me. I would "awaken" from these sessions feeling enriched and at peace with fond memories of most everything that we had shared. Of course, there was some sadness, even some regret with regard to certain events, but these were easily overshadowed by the wave of positive energy that surrounded us. The dreams with them took place in a variety of settings; sometimes it would just be me with one of them, often it was the three of us together. At times we were together at the family home, sometimes it was in a garden or meadow where we would meet up, walking toward each other in what would become a sprint, ending in a big hug as we embraced and shared in our happiness at being together.

I was grateful that the dream visits provided me with the opportunity to be with my children. In our initial meetings I had expressed my concern about how they were dealing with their lives without me. I was comforted to know that they had made it through the difficult days following my death, surrounded by an immense amount of love and attention. I was aware that they still missed me, as I did them, but I was pleased to know that they were managing reasonably well.

One other unique factor of these dreams was that unlike the dreams where the memory of that dream would vanish in a puff of smoke within seconds of opening my eyes, these dreams remained set in place. Once the dream had been experienced, it remained a part of my active memory and I could call upon it at any time, the entire story ready to be laid out before me for further review.

"These dreams, as you refer to them, Joshua, are often tied to when you reach out to others that you share a bond with. It's an opportunity to enjoy each other's company and to offer and receive love, energy, and other expressions. It's also an opportunity to revisit any negative experiences, and work through them in order to bring them to a conclusion that you are happy with. In this way you can reevaluate your past actions and intentions, in order to create a new energy for your present," Sophia explained as we sat in the living room of the house.

"Situations that were not fully worked out on the earth plane can be addressed in this way. Sometimes it is an opportunity to make plans for other lifetimes, or it can simply be to resolve an issue, in order that it is no longer a concern. No door is ever truly closed. While physical death appears to those on the earth plane to be an ending, you are now aware that it is just the opening of another door, to another part of your journey. You will reach a point where you no longer feel the need to put yourself into this dream state, but for now, it is quite a useful process for you."

"Sophia, when I awaken from these dreams, I can remember them completely, they stay with me. Do the people who are in my dreams remember them the same way that I do? Is it a two-way street? By that I mean, I am aware that they are in my dream but are they aware of what transpired in the dream?"

"The people who share your dream with you are willing participants. You invite them, and they accept or decline. They have a say in whether they will be in the dream, as evidenced by the difficulty you had in communicating with your mother. Here's the thing to understand, right now we are referring to these events as dreams, because this is how they are perceived to be, but in truth these are actual events that occur on another level of consciousness.

"The simple answer to your question is, yes, they are aware of the dream, but to them it is strictly a dream and they have difficulty in translating the contents of their dream to their day-to-day understanding of life. As the dream filters through the slower frequency of their physical consciousness, their understanding of the content is often dissipated, and sometimes entirely lost. The issue is that their physical system cannot fully process the immensity of the experience. That is why people are sometimes confused by the happenings within their dreams and they would wake up thinking that it didn't make sense, or that it was simply an impossible situation.

"There are certainly those people on the earth plane who, because of their level of awareness, are able to enter into something similar to the dream state while still awake and you may be able to communicate with them.

"Many advanced souls, they might be musicians, writers, scientists, or just very curious individuals, regularly go into a meditative state and experience contact with their higher self. They are able to tap into the knowledge that is there to be taken in. Many medical and technological advances, many beautiful pieces of music and works of art, also many new views of consciousness, have been experienced on a higher plane and then brought back, more or less intact, to the level of physical reality. In this way knowledge is shared with the intention of raising the overall vibration of the earth plane."

CHAPTER THIRTY

The early morning air still contained a hint of dampness from the rain that I had enjoyed listening to as it fell softly throughout the night. I still enjoyed the idea of a routine. I had not yet reached the point where I was able to discard all of the familiar activities that I had become so used to. I liked my day to have a certain amount of structure to it including having a beginning and an end. In the evening the sky would darken at my request, and I would enter my sleep mode as I went off on my nightly journeys.

Today, upon awakening, I felt the desire to step outside the safe harbor of the house, to venture out to sit on the front porch. The plants and grasses looked as if they were smoldering, the warming sun coaxed the moisture on them into a hazy mist. Just as before, I found solace in the aftermath of the rain. I breathed in deeply and caught the scent of freshly wet soil, and my thoughts were nudged back to the sunroom of the house in Nashville. I was thinking specifically of the day when, beneath a more aggressive canopy of rain, I had walked toward the light that was emanating from my kitchen, where I had encountered Sophia and reached out to take her hand.

Sitting here now on the front porch of this house, I felt that there was some sort of significance that revolved around the overnight rain. I felt refreshed and ready to take on new challenges, whatever they might be. And, right on cue, as I looked up, I saw

Sophia making her way along the path to the house.

"Good morning," Sophia said, waving to me. I raised my hand in welcome and stood up to greet her, as always. I looked forward to her visits; they always brought me comfort and insight. "It's such a beautiful day, I thought that we might take a walk and find a place to sit outside and have our conversation under this amazing sky. What do you think of that?"

What did I think of that indeed? I had begun to wonder why it was that we had not taken more walks around the property. I simply had never felt the desire to do so, but today, today felt different, and I happily embraced her suggestion. Sophia waited at the end of the walkway for me to join her, and we made our way toward a low growth of trees a short distance away. I could see the trees from the house and I had often wondered what lay out there beyond them, here in the middle of this idyllic pasture, or meadow, or whatever it was.

The distance was deceiving, it didn't seem to take many steps to reach our destination, but when I turned to look back at the house it seemed like a small dot on the horizon. Definitely a curiosity, I thought, as we entered the clump of trees. There were a few large stones in a semicircle that would easily function as seating, and they faced a small glen with a stream that trickled through. Sophia sat down and gestured for me to join her.

"Today I want to talk with you about opening yourself up in a more substantial way to the knowledge that is surrounding you. I'd like to help you to find ways to free yourself to accept more of what the universe is keen to present to you.

"This is an exciting time for you, Joshua. You see, up until now you have been in what you might call a transitory state. A transition from the consciousness that you have known, to the higher awareness that you are now ready to engage with. It has been a slow but necessary process to help you to get to this point; however, I think it is something that you will find quite rewarding. The fact that you readily agreed to travel away from the house today signifies to me your readiness and willingness to begin this new phase of your journey."

"Really?" I responded. "Why is it so significant? We're just out walking." Initially I didn't see that my leaving the house could make that much difference. Sophia smiled at me, giving me one of those looks that I had become accustomed to over the course of our talks.

"Well, yes, we are just out walking, but this is the first time that we have left the immediate area of the house. Remember that symbolism is often used as a means of communicating a shift in your awareness. I can't teach you anything that you are not willing to, or able to, take in. I can't take you to any level that you don't desire to strive for. It's up to you to manifest your surroundings as you see fit, and your desire to travel this distance away from the house sends its own signals. On the physical plane you were near the top of your ladder of awareness; here on the astral plane you are beginning again at the bottom of the rungs, on your way to greater awareness on a whole new level. It's a very normal and natural reaction, but trust me, the fact that we are sitting here away from the house is a very good and welcome sign of your development."

"Okay," I said. "I can understand that. I didn't think I still needed to crutch on the physical concept, but I suppose I do."

"It's like you're learning a new culture and language. There are going to be times when you blend a bit of the previous language with the new one. It's a natural process, not to worry."

"I appreciate your patience with me," I told Sophia. "Sometimes I still feel like I'm not fully grasping the situation, even though on many levels I really feel that I am understanding more and more."

"Let me help you appreciate that," Sophia said, as always in a kind and caring way. "Do you recall the incidents that you experienced while you were in the hospital? Seeing yourself hovering near the ceiling, looking down at the doctors and nurses working on your body?"

I nodded. I saw it quite clearly in my mind.

"Then later you were walking in the hallways, you saw your friends, although they were unaware of you. You then visited with your father and then with me, and in those instances, you saw yourself near a body of water."

"Of course, I remember that," I told her.

"Well, those were your first conscious excursions taken in your astral body. Your consciousness stepped outside of your physical body, into your astral body. Now, here, you are residing exclusively in your astral body, yet you still relate many things to physical terms, which is normal, since until recently you were so familiar with that structure.

"You created the house that you are currently residing in as your safe environment as you went through the transition away from the world of physical manifestation. Since then, you have been growing and opening up to what is around you at your own pace, and remember, there is no right or wrong pace. For you now to allow yourself to be out here in the open, away from the house, is the signaling of your acceptance of the greater energy around you, and your acknowledgment that you are ready to expand your consciousness once again, to a new level. The fact that you are still using physical references is just your way of getting used to the new language of communication. The physical will bump up against the astral the same way as you might insert an English word into a French phrase and say something a bit awkwardly. We still understand each other, but the language is not yet perfect. It will all join together, when you are ready. Trust me on that.

"There are many occasions when an entity, even when they have begun to understand that the physical plane is just one particular stage of development, is so focused on returning to that reality that they shy away from gaining the necessary understanding of the astral body and what it offers. These entities simply get stuck in a circular routine of being born, living, dying, and then wishing only to be reborn again on the earth plane, they are so attracted to its particular vibrational level. You, on the other hand, have embraced awareness on a greater level."

"I have, that is very much true," I told Sophia. "I am a little hesitant at times, but I very much want to continue to move forward and grow. To me it feels like the natural thing to do. It took me forever to consider actually stepping outside of the house, for example. I could be making faster progress, I'm sure."

"All in your own good time," Sophia assured me. "When you

did project the idea of sitting on the porch this morning, you were projecting your image outward and testing your comfort limits. The house and the garden are, of course, an illusion; but it is one that worked in concert with your familiar perception of physical reality. The walk we just took away from the house was you allowing your consciousness, giving yourself permission if you will, to move to a higher level of awareness."

"Everything seems to be a matter of interpretation," I said to Sophia. "It's all very symbolic and I'm sometimes confused by what I should be taking at face value."

"Symbolism is a very large part of what makes up the physical reality. It is pervasive in all the religions on the earth plane, it is quite ingrained in the DNA of that level of reality. Many entities leaving the earth plane are still so attached to the concept, it stays with them until they can finally understand that they have been sitting in the equivalent of a movie theater. They have been experiencing their life on a projected landscape, and that when that life, that movie, is over they can step outside into the greater world. Many like to stay inside the theater rather than face the wholeness of the universe."

I nodded in agreement with Sophia, feeling quite relaxed and comfortable with the level of our conversation. "For some reason when I awoke today I felt more alert, more aware. All that time I spent in the house, I felt fine, but sometimes I would be sleepy, sluggish, not really lazy but just kind of a lazy Sunday afternoon feeling. Now, today, I literally feel like I've stepped out into a crisp new morning, full of energy and I'm ready to go. Not sure to where, but I feel ready for something new. You know, I came up with this analogy while you were talking with me, can I share it with you?"

"Of course, please do."

"Around about the time I turned forty years old I ended up getting a pair of reading glasses. Up to that point I thought I was seeing everything perfectly fine and that images got a little blurry only when I was tired, of course that wasn't the case at all. When I got behind that contraption in the optometrist's office and they began dialing in the different strength lenses, I was amazed at how much I had been missing things that were right in front of me! If I relate that to what you and I have been discussing, I am beginning to realize the clarity that you have brought to me. The same words, the same ideas, suddenly have a much deeper meaning."

"I like that, it's a good example," Sophia told me. "Now that you have left the comfortable setting that you have been functioning in since your transition, you will indeed dial up the strong lenses that you referenced, and you will see deeper and farther than you ever have."

"There is something else I would like to ask you about," I said to Sophia. We had walked on a little farther and found a new spot. There always seemed to be a rock or fallen tree conveniently placed for us to sit on and continue our talk.

"You often mention the slower vibration of the earth plane and it makes me wonder if something should be avoided if it involves enjoyment, pleasure, or desire?"

"No, no, Joshua. I don't want you to come away with that observation. Avoiding physical reality, and certainly avoiding pleasurable things, is not the message I was trying to present; it is more a matter of not allowing earthbound influences to control your desires. There is that which you need, and that which you want, it is in that space between where your desire lives. It is that desire that determines what enriches you and what bankrupts you, so to speak.

"It is absolutely appropriate and encouraged for all to enjoy what we will call pleasures of the physical reality; after all, it is the primary reality of that plane. It is also appropriate that you create a balance between your wants and needs, it is your desires that will determine where you stand on the ladder of growth and development. You should not steer clear of pleasure any more than you should go out of your way to experience pain and suffering. Each has its own place and purpose in someone's existence. A person with many possessions is no less a good person than the one who has nothing, the equation does not function that way. It is more about what those possessions, the perceived ownership of possessions, or lack of ownership, means to the person. How do they allow the situation to shape and characterize them? If they define themselves by their possessions, or their titles, they will be in for a surprise, because these things are ultimately an illusion.

"The person who consciously denies themselves any pleasure during their lifetime is not necessarily any further ahead spiritually than the one who overindulges in everything. So many of the influences of the earth plane are borne of either love or fear. If you avoid something only out of fear of repercussions, have you really advanced your development? Ultimately you have the ability to choose what it is you wish to be and how you will interact with those choices. This is free will—a very powerful gift.

"You see, Joshua, when you have the ability to understand that what you desire is what you attract to yourself, it will help you appreciate why certain people and events become a part of your experience. You will find that you will be drawn to those of a similar nature, and them to you. As you desire something, your vibration becomes attuned to the vibration of that desire and you join together in harmony."

"Birds of a feather," I mused aloud.

"Precisely," Sophia responded. "Every thought you create, every action you initiate, is a function of your desire and an expression of your free will. Everything that you transmit is a form of energy that has an effect not just on you, but also on everyone and everything around you. What you do is deliberate, there are no accidents or coincidences. In this way you attract the same energy that you project outward."

I was keenly focused on Sophia, absorbing the images that she presented to me. I did my best to keep up with her. Gradually I noticed that she had stopped speaking directly to me and I was no longer actually hearing her words. We had moved into that mode where her communications with me were transferred in complete blocks to me. Her eyes looked directly at me; the contents of her thoughts flowed to me like a stream of consciousness. I don't know how long we had been engaged in this form of communication; however, something she said made me realize that we must have been here for what I considered to be the entire day.

"Enjoy the last bit of light from this day, Joshua," she said to me. Her voice was audible once more, no longer just in my head, and it soothingly penetrated the silence that I had been so warmly ensconced in. In speaking aloud now, she refocused my attention. "Let the rays of the sun wash over you and pacify any tension or tiredness that you may feel. Imagine yourself, your entire being, as a body of water. Feel the ebb and flow; and now picture your consciousness as the sunlight, as it dances joyfully on the water, bringing you peace and enlightenment. Now, let it all go out of you, let yourself be empty and let the soft light relax your thoughts until they too are empty. The communications that you have had with your children, and family, and friends, let that go, too. Those conversations have run their course.

"In order for you to grow, you must now turn your attention to other matters. As you focus on the images that will be presented to you shortly, as you hear and feel my words, as they take form and shape inside of you, you will know that you are ready to enter a new level as you open yourself.

"You have experienced a great amount of insight since you passed from the physical body to your astral body. With your permission I will accompany you on an inner journey of your many lives lived. I give you my word that I will speak only the truth to you, and that everything I present to you will be for your benefit and growth."

As Sophia's words nestled in me, I felt nourished by their energy. I was suffused in the serenity of many pleasing layers of stimulation, in an almost narcotic-like level of relaxation. You'll have to forgive me somewhat as I try to describe this bliss that I was experiencing, it was unlike anything I had known. I'm not sure I could ever truly describe it adequately; I don't think I could ever do it justice.

I pictured myself sitting, half reclining, on a chair somewhere outdoors, I wasn't sure of the exact location. I turned my face to the softening rays of what I perceived to be the late-day sun. I lovingly embraced the sensation of it warming my skin and soaking in deeper and deeper. I gave myself over to the feeling, surrendering to the bliss, knowing inherently that it was what I both wanted, and needed, to do.

The shapes and colors of Sophia's words began to flow through me in a slow spiral that wound its way deeper and deeper into my being. From behind my closed eyes, I could tell that the light from the sun had now all but fully faded away, and it was replaced by a new glowing light source that originated inside of me and was projecting outward.

CHAPTER THIRTY-ONE

"Joshua, you have lived many lives and you have experienced many incarnations." Sophia's voice emanated from somewhere very deep in my mind. I felt her words, her energy actually, flow out to the far reaches of my consciousness, the way a rising tide sought out equilibrium with the shoreline around it. I felt that I was housed in a body again, but I could not determine the size or shape of it, or whether it was physical or not.

I felt that I was floating, that my body or perhaps it was my consciousness, lay upon some vast area of water. There I was, floating at ease, enjoying the sensation of being safely ensconced in a sea of warm water, carried along in a gentle current, the motion and direction of which was somehow influenced by Sophia's energy.

"The person that you know yourself to be from your most recent lifetime is the sum total of all of your lives and experiences. To reach this point you have gone through many situations where you have had to make choices based on the desires that you wished to gravitate toward."

Previously when Sophia had spoken to me of past lives, it had been from a more generic standpoint. Now, I understood that we would deal with specific instances.

"You are at a level of development where you and I can communicate without the need of filters. The truth that I will share with you will come in the way of thought forms of energy. I encourage you to translate whatever I share with you into whatever words, symbols, and physical images you are most comfortable with, in order for you to best understand and take in what is being presented.

"Essentially, I am going to introduce you to several of your lifetimes that have had a direct influence on your present status. I will help you to understand how events in one lifetime have affected other lifetimes, including your most recent one. It isn't necessary for you to be aware of every breath and every thought of every life lived; however, we do have that possibility if you wish. At any point you wish to delve deeper into an event or lifetime, we can do so. Some of your lifetimes did not lead to any particularly significant milestones; some were in fact almost exact repeats of previous lives where you needed to be exposed to similar lessons several times before you embraced the learning that was required. These lifetimes, while certainly not purposeless, did not enhance your growth in a direct way and you would likely not gain much insight from them. Still, they did play a role, no matter how small, in your chain of lives. With your permission I will leave the particulars of those lifetimes out of this discussion. Please remember that at any time you may ask any questions or challenge anything that I share with you.

"Within us all is the energy that is the life force. Think of this as pure energy, something that can never be diminished or destroyed. Within this life force is a consciousness, which is the essence of your being. This consciousness inhabits many different levels of reality and has been a constant in the lifetimes you have experienced. The life force is the spark within you that is your soul; this is your direct and omnipresent connection to the oneness.

"Each lifetime has been chosen by you to fulfill a particular purpose or group of goals. In your self-judgment, you felt this was necessary to advance your understanding and acceptance of truth. In this way you were following your natural desire to evolve to the awareness of the higher vibrations."

Already I felt the need to reach out to her with a question, one that I had been considering since our early conversations. I did not speak the question to her aloud, I simply formed the thought in my head, and she read it as if I had sent her an electronic message.

"Sophia, what is there to stop me from reviewing the events of any one particular lifetime and decide that everything I did in that lifetime was good? What if I was also able to justify everything I did as something that was necessary? In other words, if it is self-judgment, what is there to stop me from self-defining good from bad, right from wrong?"

I detected something that I'll describe as a playful tone in her response.

"I'd like to tell you that you are the first one to pose that question, but here is a simple truth: Once you know and accept the truth, you cannot deny it. You can choose to ignore it, temporarily; you can wander from the path, but you cannot deny that which you know to be true.

"For every thought and action, there is the automatic generation of a reaction. This is the truth of karma; karma is the law of cause and effect; it is an immutable law of the universe. You function within the law of karma; it doesn't function within you. Even if you deny the truth of karma, it still exists and will still exert its influence.

"For example, this is where sayings such as 'an eye for an eye' come from in various books attached to religions. It is not a literal interpretation, and it is described in different ways; however, it remains a karmic truth that 'as you sow, so shall you reap,' which is another one of these writings. Karmic balance does not mean that if you cut off someone's finger, that your finger will be cut off in another lifetime, but it does mean that you will come to face the result of your action with a similar action that will help you to understand the lesson you are meant to take from that event.

"You, and every other soul, have spirit guides at every level of your growth and as you make your way from lesson to lesson, lifetime to lifetime, you are helped, taught, and informed. When a guide sees you straying from the true path that you have set out on, they will attempt to lead you back toward the path, to the truth. The fact is, the actual decision to stay on the path, or to wander, is yours. The 'inner voice' that you have heard, or sensed, at different times in your life, is often one of these guides assisting you in one manner or another. We can guide you, but we cannot lead you. That remains your responsibility.

"The idea is not to achieve perfection in one lifetime; this is extremely difficult. However, it is possible to master many of the intricacies of the physical plane, which then places you in a better position to advance to the next level of consciousness, to the point where one day you will fully step away from physical rebirth, to exist exclusively on the astral plane.

"The teachings of all of the religious books were written by men, to establish a code of rules and commands, but remember that the content of these books and teachings were man-made and have nothing to do with the universal truth. Various social procedures, what foods you are allowed to eat, and when. How you should treat those around you. These are the rules of a particular group, they are not a guide for you from some heavenly hand. Many of these commands were simply made up to meet that person's or that particular group's desire to control or manipulate their environment. Many of these books and supposed teachings have gone through so many alterations, literally made up on the spot, to serve the wants or expectations of different generations and monarchs, priests, and other self-professed leaders. None of these people, none of these books, is the true and unadulterated word of a god, or a prophet. Much of what they contain was written hundreds of years after the events were allegedly first spoken of. In almost every case they are simply made up, man-made projections, of how that person or group wanted to exert their control over others. Karma cares only about your thoughts, your intentions, and your actions as they pertain to your lifetime. Karma will never punish you for eating a particular food, or loving a particular person, or accepting or denying a particular religion. Over the centuries the method to enforce these teachings has always been to threaten with the fear of an eternity in hell, or some terrible physical punishment if you ignored the threats made to you. So many people were literally executed simply for questioning the truth within those teachings. The laws of karma are the laws of the universe. Anything else is a self-serving edict created by those wishing to influence and control others.

"At the point of physical death, the shroud that filters the information available to you is lifted away. As you accept the truth, the vibration of your consciousness increases in order to allow you even greater access to the higher teachings. The other side of this truth is that as you ignore what you are now aware of, you may become even more embroiled in the ongoing cycle of earth lives. This, sadly, explains so much of the suffering that exists on the earth plane and within that reality.

"So, Joshua, I hope that I have answered your question as to whether you can decide to contradict your truth with regard to karma. I will say that you can turn your face away from the view, but that doesn't mean the view will cease to exist."

I withdrew briefly from the conversation in order to let this stream of information settle into place for me. I did believe and embrace her words; it was a lot to take in and I wanted to be sure that it became a proper part of how I saw myself and all else around me.

This had become a somewhat predictable custom whenever Sophia and I engaged in these types of deep exchanges. There were times when I felt somewhat overwhelmed with the intensity of the lessons. At face value they didn't always seem so deep, but as I would begin to apply them to scenarios that I had known, I became aware of the massive number of connections between myself and my action or intention, and the people and situations around me. There often seemed to be an almost infinite number of possibilities that developed from a single, simple thought. I remember thinking of a statement made by a physics professor that a single drop of water contained more energy than a hydrogen bomb, if only we understood how to harness it. All these lessons encapsulated in these little drops of water could be quite overwhelming if I allowed them free rein.

"Sophia, I'm curious to know how a person develops through various lifetimes. As they take in the lessons of a particular lifetime, and then of course during the period between lives, which I am now experiencing, is it a continual learning or growth cycle or can it be interrupted?"

"Do you recall our conversations about free will?" Sophia asked. "That is a key factor in your development because, even if a person knows the truth, they can attempt to forsake it. They can choose to ignore it. Of course, if they choose that path, they must also accept the ramifications associated with that choice. Do what you wish, but wish carefully, because what you desire, you will ultimately create. This is where karma comes into play. You can fall as well as rise with each lifetime."

CHAPTER THIRTY-TWO

There was one constant that I remained acutely aware of with regard to my new state of consciousness. It was the ongoing presence of one person in my thoughts; that person, not surprisingly to me, was Julia. By presence, I mean that she was somehow always a part of what I was involved with. I would experience something new or learn a different perspective on how to understand an event, and my first thought was that I wanted to tell her about it. In my moments of meditation, I would often spend time recreating the shared times and situations I had known with her. It felt so real to me that I swore I could smell her skin and feel her warm breath on the back of my neck.

"Sophia, I need to ask you again about Julia," I said to her at the end of one of our many exchanges.

"Of course," she responded, and there seemed to be a bit of a twinkle in her voice, if I can describe it that way, as though she had been anticipating my question. "What would you like to know about Julia?"

"Well, I am aware of how strongly I still feel about her. I think of her all the time, it seems. From the moment I first saw her I was aware of a strong desire to be with her, and when I finally was with her, it felt like the most natural thing I could imagine. You've talked with me about how we progress through successive lifetimes, working through various situations. I can't help but wonder to what degree Julia and I have been together before this last lifetime. Is that the case?"

"Oh, it is very much the case," Sophia told me enthusiastically. "Joshua, when you meet someone who has this kind of impact on your emotions, indeed on your life, there is often a connection to a past life. Of course, that doesn't mean that every person you met or shared a meaningful conversation with is connected to you through past-life involvements. However, in the case of you and Julia, yes, there is a strong karmic and past-life connection."

"Is this the reason why I dream about her so often?" I asked. "I almost feel as though my connection to her has remained constant, despite the changes I have been through."

"Joshua, you and Julia are like dance partners. Even when you are apart, you are still connected by the music that is continuously in both your backgrounds. You perform your dance even when you are not together in the physical sense. You both hear the same song; you dance to it as though you were in each other's arms. That is why she is continually in your thoughts, as you are in hers."

"Even now?"

"Even now, Joshua, especially now. The relationship you share with Julia is like a twin flame. A flame that has been separated into two and longs to be joined back together as one flame. This has been the basis of your relationships with her through many lifetimes. When you knew that you were about to leave your physical reality, when you knew you were about to die, you were able to accept it on one level, since you knew you had been through it with her on many past occasions. At the same time, your ego did not want to let go of her yet again. Such an amazing conflict, no wonder it had such an impact on your transition experience."

"So, when did this begin?" I asked, quite intrigued and hungry to know more. "And what does it mean for my future?"

I sensed that this was a moment for which Sophia had been patiently waiting. I knew that even though knowledge and truth had always been there for me to take in, I had to be ready to receive it and understand it. I recognized that Sophia had been gradually leading me down this road, building a foundation of acceptance and understanding, before she was ready to allow the knowledge to flow to me at this greater rate.

"Your connection to Julia, as you know her most recently, originally goes back to a life you led around the mid-fourth century BC." Sophia began, and I felt myself become enraptured by her words. "I'm giving you that date reference simply to help you understand the chronological progression of the lifetimes. This is how a physical mind would interpret this flow of time.

"As I have mentioned to you, the entity does not always incarnate in the same sex as the previous lifetime, in fact it is quite natural to experience many lives as either male or female. The soul is truly androgynous, and the sex chosen for a particular lifetime is a matter of what role or situation would best serve the primary purpose of that lifetime. Are you following me so far?"

"I am following you." I reassured Sophia. "Please go on, I'm quite enthralled."

"In the lifetime we are discussing, you were in the role of a male student of the Hippocratic Convention, as they were referred to. You were learning and practicing the art of medicine, along the lines that had been set out by Hippocrates, who was a prominent figure for many in that lifetime. During that time, Julia was a young girl attending a school that was established by a woman who took in certain female students and trained them in the art of being companions to some of the elite members of the society who influenced the development of the city-state of Athens.

"This was a lifetime where your primary intention was to gain understanding of the new teachings of medicine because you felt a yearning to assist those less fortunate around you. In addition, you wished to have a stronger understanding of the relationship between body, mind, and spirit. That lifetime had the markings of a period of great karmic and spiritual growth for you.

"You, and others who studied alongside you, were part of a select inner circle and from time to time you were invited to attend to the children and other relatives of the luminaries of the city of Athens. At one of these sessions, you met the entity that you know as Julia, and you were instantly attracted to her, and she to you. One of the first things you noticed about her was the scent that she was wearing; it was Nardos, a scent taken from the spikenard plant. You could say you fell in love with her before you even laid eyes on her, such was the intensity of the connection you felt toward her before you ever turned your head to look at her.

"Do you recall our discussion in the hospital room of the scent you were noticing all around you?"

"Yes, yes, of course I do. I associated it with you, I thought you were the one wearing it as you were the only person around me."

"The reason for that, Joshua, was because of the combination of energy that was present in that room, in part due to my presence, in part due to yours, and of course Julia was influencing the balance in the room with her energy. I served as a catalyst for your higher self to connect points of contact between you and Julia, and for you there was a focus on that first meeting between you two, you were reliving that initial meeting with her."

"So, part of my consciousness was trying to alert me to the connection I had with Julia, but I couldn't quite translate the full meaning. Was that it?"

"It is often difficult for the earthbound consciousness to take the information that is available to it from higher levels, and, as you say, to translate it. This is why, when you awaken from a dream, events and situations seem difficult to decipher once you awake; it's like you are trying to input two different languages, and the result can be very confusing in the least, or sometimes impossible to comprehend at all.

"So, let me take you back to the original story," Sophia continued. "You did immediately recognize the attraction you felt to Julia, but there was a problem in that she had already been promised to one of the statesmen of Athens, and despite your best efforts to convince her to leave her situation, to run away with you, she denied your request since she had taken a vow to become the companion, the mistress, of the statesman.

"It was during that time that Athens was caught in a great sickness, a plague, and you and your fellow practitioners were called upon to treat those who were infected. Here's where things took a turn for you. You were so heartbroken and angry by Julia's refusal to leave her vow, that you veered dramatically away from the virtues you had cultivated in that lifetime, and in doing so you created a series of karmic events that you would be held accountable to.

"The man who Julia was promised to told you that he believed that if he wore an article of clothing that had been worn by someone who had died from the sickness that it would serve as an amulet to protect him. Despite the fact that you knew the belief to be false, you did not warn him against it. This was fueled by your desire to be with Julia and you simply waited for the sickness to take over this man's life, thereby removing Julia from her vow. Not only did he succumb to the sickness, he also infected a number of his household, including his lover, who of course is the entity that you know as Julia. Your action, or intentional inaction in this case, helped contribute to the deaths of many, including your beloved.

"You did survive the ravages of the plague, but not the ravages of living with the truth of your actions, and what had been the promise of an enlightened incarnation, was turned instead into a series of karmic challenges. Joshua, do you recall when you asked whether a growth cycle could be continuous through each lifetime? My answer to you was that you could just as easily rise or fall in a particular lifetime. The events of that lifetime ended in a fall, and it caused you to enter a new cycle of earth lives in order to present you with the opportunity to seek balance once again."

As Sophia related the events of the Athens life, and several subsequent lifetimes following that, I was able to visualize the events in such a manner that entire portions of a life were contained in a single burst of energy. This flash of awareness seemed to take only a second to experience but within that moment I was presented with the entire chronology of that lifetime. I have no idea how I was able to take in that volume of information in such a brief segment of time, but my comprehension of the events, and the subsequent impact it had on me, was very clear to me.

The method of reviewing these lifetimes with Sophia became

a regular part of each of our meetings. As we went through the process, I became more aware of how the passive administration of karma was administered within the situations I experienced. I now understood that I could not deny a failing on my part any more than I could not help but feel joy and contentment in the positive influences I exerted during these lifetimes. I was firmly cognizant of what Sophia had meant when she had told me that you could not unduly influence the outcome of self-judgment; you saw and you judged yourself in the clear light of day; there was simply no way around it.

I found that I was able to encapsulate the contents of each of those lifetimes into a single element. It was as if one word, one sound or picture, could capture the overall experience of a particular lifetime. I felt I could look at a drop of water and, figuratively speaking, be able to comprehend the completeness of the ocean. I saw it, I felt it, I knew it. I asked Sophia to explain it to me further.

"Joshua, every soul exists on several levels of reality," she reminded me, "although you are generally only aware of your current perspective. If you are involved with the earth plane, you will likely experience life in a 'time' setting, meaning there is a past, a present, and a future to events. This 'time' setting presents the illusion of time continually marching forward, with one moment unable to occur until the previous moment has had its space within that sequence. That is how the physical mind is able to translate what it is perceiving. There are higher levels of awareness where time, as you know it, does not exist. There is no past, present, or future. There simply *is*."

I had to ask a couple of questions at this point. "The part that is still difficult for me to fully grasp, is why we have to go through so many incarnations. Why can't I just take the knowledge, the awareness that you have shared with me, and progress to the higher levels?"

"I understand your confusion, Joshua, I truly do," Sophia said, and I felt her sincerity. "The truth that you have been exposed to needs to become a part of you on every level. It is one thing to be told something, it is entirely different to use that information to guide your life. Once you are born again into the essence of physical reality, it's up to you, and each entity, to set your own pace of progress. Existing within physical reality is the opportunity for you to take the knowledge that you have gained and put it into practice in such a manner that it describes who you are. What happens, in so many cases, is that you enter that lifetime with a view of what you wish to accomplish, and along the way you change those plans. You might revert to the very behavior you were trying to overcome, or you might find yourself reacting to a stimulus in such a way that causes a distinct change in how you have been experiencing that lifetime.

"Remember that whatever you desire, you will receive. Life is meant to be embraced; it is not meant to be avoided. However, if you deviate from the plan that you set out with, there may well be consequences. It is up to you to follow the path that embraces the truth and love that you are aware of. When you veer from that path, your life changes and lessons that were meant to be learned may fall by the wayside, to be encountered again, later in that life, or perhaps in another lifetime. Your best intentions for that lifetime need to be put into practice, they need to become a part of your reality if you are to truly learn from them.

"Be aware of the truth of your intentions and actions. If you act out of love, you will receive out of love. The rule of karma is the rule of truth."

As Sophia said this to me, a light went off in my mind, and I found myself again staring into that age-old teaching of "as you sow, so shall you reap." I heard a voice from my childhood of an old preacher talking about "an eye for an eye."

"Cause and effect," I said to Sophia. "These teachings that I remember from the Bible were just talking about karma."

"Indeed, as is the case with other teachings such as those in the Koran, the Torah, the I Ching, and so on. The original teachers were not tied into any religion or sect; what these teachers were trying to do was to pass down the truth of the universe and put it into a language that could be easily understood, particularly by those who could neither read nor write, which was almost everyone at that time.

"That one truth was meant to be the basis for living one's life in such a way that it would allow the gift of advancing to the higher levels, without having to necessarily go through so many successive lifetimes.

"Of course, what happened was that the ego took over. Certain people began to draw others around them and they formed tribes, which later became religions. These 'leaders' then began to recite their own made-up truths in order to exert greater control over those around them, and to strike out at those who were not like them.

"Others, seeing what was happening around them, formed their own tribes, and later religions. They each, in turn, began to explore their desires and they added their own interpretations of the basic truth in order to further their own desire for the illusion of power and control. This was the beginning of the fractured structure of religions throughout the earth plane. Religion has always been about ignorance and fear. These so-called leaders of the religions used this fear and ignorance as a method to increase their greed and lust and sense of self-importance over the masses."

I interrupted her at this point. "How can you have so many different religions that all claim to have the one and only connection to 'god'? How can they also claim that theirs is the one and only road to this 'god'? Which one do we believe, if any?"

"Remember, Joshua, I have said it before, all religions were created by men, for men. They created illusions of power and knowledge, and a unique connection to what they called god. In this way, they created a hierarchy in which they claimed dominion over everything that fell under their influence.

"Each of the religions on the earth plane exist for their own purposes, none of them are any more connected to anything resembling the god energy than their competitor is. Their buildings are homages to themselves; their teachings and rituals are based on self-serving principals. They are not based on the truth and love that is the ultimate essence of the universe.

"All we are, anything that you perceive, is energy. Some take energy and envision it in ways that create illusions of power and grandeur. Others take their interpretation of that same energy and project it through their own filters as expressions of painting, dance, sound, texture, building, and so on. Many great artistic works have been based on that person's desire to take what they perceive the energy of the universe to be and project it through their own prism of insight. The end result we experience is perceived in their painting, their song, their symphony, or some other artistic creation. Others fashion their insight of energy to create medicine and technology-based platforms. They develop procedures and programs that will enhance the living experience of those around them. There is no limit to how the energy of the universe can be interpreted and presented. The important factor in this is the free will to form the energy into a positive or a negative force. As you are aware, this intention will be used by you in self-judgment at the appropriate time. Choice is all important.

"The philosophers and teachers, the great leaders of any era, have heard and understood at least part of the message of truth and love that reverberates throughout the universe and they too, in their own way, have attempted to translate that message into the words and ways of that time.

"Some were thought odd, or even accused of being insane, or possessed, for suggesting things that flew in the face of popular teachings or beliefs of the day. Many were persecuted by the religious authorities for attempting to present the truth. They became a threat to the stranglehold of fear and ignorance that those in their positions of power lusted after in their unenlightened state.

"So much of the conflict revolving around the various religions of the world is based on two simple elements. First, that all religions are man-made, and second, that the distortions that these religions project outward are created intentionally by a desire based on greed, egotism, and fear. They do not desire to share the truth and the love of the universe, because to do so would diminish their ability to feed the physical manifestations of their existence. They would have to give up their position of power, of riches, and control, over the day-to-day activities of their followers. This would be an anathema to them.

"The reasons why so many entities require so many lifetimes to experience the lessons they need to learn are all but infinite, Joshua, but many of the reasons relate back to the religious teachings that they have been subjected to, and in many cases, embraced. This is the reason why there is the period following your physical lifetime where as much awareness of the truth is presented to you as you can reasonably take in. This is to help break the cult bond that religions fuel on the physical plane of reality.

"Joshua, you are aware that you are connected to the entirety of the energy of the universe, as are all. It is this energy that is the concept on which the god belief is based on by those within the religions. They gave the energy a male image, then claimed that they were the only one who could communicate with this male deity. They abandoned the truth when they decided to give the god concept a name and a face, one that only they could see and talk to. God is not a person; it is not a place or thing. It is the sum of all things that you can imagine, and all things that you cannot. There is no god, there is only that which is. God is a name that has been applied to the energy of the universe. There is no person to appeal to, no one to reach out to, except to appeal to all and reach out to all. Whether the name applied to this energy is Buddha, or Christ, Allah, Adonai, or Heavenly Father, it is simply a name given to a man-made concept. Most often this belief is based on fear."

"And why is god a man?" I asked Sophia. I remember having this thought as a young boy during those few times I had been coerced into attending a Sunday church service.

"Simply put, Joshua, when these stories were being created, they wished to shape the stories to a narrative that suited their particular goals. To do this they used the dominant fears and beliefs of the day. Of course, god would be a man, a heavenly father, the patriarch of the family of mankind. They were simply making it up as they went along, as long as it fit the narrative they were cultivating. Do this through thousands of years, through multiple generations, torture and burn people alive who doubted your teachings, and you form a seemingly very solid belief system. Accept or suffer the consequences. Believe our lie, or die, can be a very convincing argument over time.

"In truth, when an entity within the physical reality refers to god, whether they are fully aware or not, they are simply referencing the energy that flows throughout every portion of the universe. It is not someone or something that can be worshiped, or paid allegiance to. Within the earth plane this energy is the essence of every person, mammal, reptile, fish, insect, the smallest microbe, every drop of water, every grain of sand, every color viewed, every sound heard, every tree, mountain, and beyond every thought, every action, and every single thing. It is all. It is one. When you finally understand this and become one with all that is … then you have reached at-one-ment, or as some religions call it, atonement. They demand that you atone for your sins, but truly, it is just the acceptance that we are one and one is all, that is the true meaning of atonement or of being at one with the moment.

"When someone prays, in a formal setting within a building, or while they are walking down the street; when someone meditates and asks for something to be altered or created, they are sending out a vibration in the form of a thought. This vibration is naturally attracted to, and interacts with, like-vibrations. Though they may like to think so, they are not talking to a person, or any type of entity.

"When an athlete or performer thanks god for the prize which they have just been awarded, they speak as though they are thanking some deity for assisting them to receive this award. Even if the false concept of god were true, you have to wonder with all the things going on in the world, why this great force would care or even be aware of who won a particular game or received an award for a song or a movie. It is their delusion that they are feeding when the say these things, as they thank this imaginary benefactor.

"The god concept does not grant you wishes, because there is no god entity to grant you, or anyone else, anything. Tribes, and then religions, created the man-made image of this god, and then they created many hundreds, even thousands, of other gods. Look at the various mythologies of the earth plane, there are gods for every conceivable situation. Religion is the big lie of the human race.

"How can energy be cruel or kind? And yet this is what religions teach about the god concept. God is angry, "he" will smite you, and punish you. Energy cannot decide to punish or reward you.

"The earth plane is the only level of reality where the god concept exists. On the earth plane, in truth, god is the sunrise and the sunset, the flash of lightning as it delights the night sky and then scorches the earth and destroys forests. It is the gentle rain that soothes and nourishes the seed; it is also the flood that drowns entire groups of people. It is the instinct within an animal and the force that holds both the pebble and the mountain together. It is every star in the universe and every planet, moon, and galaxy. It is the fury of the wind and the gentle touch of a hand. It is found in every emotion you create and every thought you imagine. When you speak of god, you are speaking of yourself and your place within the Whole. When you search for god, you search for yourself.

"In order for the mind to be open to the state of oneness, the ego must be empty of desire. There is a Buddhist saying that you may recall from your brief indulgence in that philosophy, that states, 'At the end of your lifetime on earth you must burn yourself up completely and obliterate the ego.' This doesn't mean that you must burn the body physically on a funeral pyre, although many have believed this, hence more traditions. It means simply that you must remove and destroy the ego and in doing so you surrender yourself to your true self, not the manifestation of the self on the physical plane.

"All living things die in their physical body, whether it is a leaf, an animal or micro-organism, or a human being. How and when one embraces this change can have a profound impact of what grows from this event. The stick or stone does not concern itself with this change, it simply accepts the change, unlike its human counterpart who often has to battle ego in order to be free, so that they too can accept the change, and move onward.

"Because of ego and free will, a human is the only element present within the earth plane that actually fights the natural flow of change and evolvement. If you want to move higher, the only thing stopping you is that you have to let go of the current ladder rung you're holding in order to grab the one above. Humans have an incredibly difficult time with this concept.

"Learning to let go, to free yourself from attachments, whether they are traditions or people, is important in order to facilitate your progress. One of the best examples I can provide to you deals with the insight into your relationship with the woman who was your wife in your most recent lifetime, the mother of your children, Amanda.

"As with many significant relationships within a lifetime, there is often a strong possibility of a previous life connection, and that was certainly the case with you and Amanda.

"For you it was the lifetime before your most recent one. In that incarnation you inhabited the body of a woman; Amanda was your male partner. It was not a healthy relationship, the two of you were often at odds with each other and your lifestyle predicaments. At times the relationship was quite violent, particularly against you. After one evening where there was heavy drinking of alcohol involved by your mate, there was a severe altercation where you were physically assaulted, and you felt that your limit had finally been reached. You waited until your partner fell asleep in a drunken haze, and you took an axe from the pile of firewood and clubbed him with the blunt end, and he died.

"The taking of a life will create a strong karmic reaction. While there are instances where the degree of this reaction can be mitigated by circumstances such as soldiers in battle, self-defense, and the protection of others from harm, there will be some degree of consequence to the action.

"As I've said to you before, souls will often incarnate together as a family or a group, in order to accomplish a joint goal. They choose to connect with others whom they wish to work through their karma with. In taking the life of your partner, you took the life of the father of the two children whom you had with this man. These were the same entities that incarnated with you and

Amanda this lifetime, as Miranda and Grayson. They were your children in each of the last two lifetimes, though in different circumstances."

I want to jump in at this point to tell you, my reader, that as much as I was shocked by this revelation from Sophia, I knew, intrinsically, that it was the truth. As she relayed the information to me, I was able to see it, to feel it, I could smell the sweat and the wood smoke of the small cabin that we had inhabited. In the blink of an eye, I relived that entire lifetime she had described, and in doing so I was aware of what I had learned or, as was the case, not learned from it.

"Joshua, this is in part why you felt such a strong connection to your children. It was also why you felt such heartache for not only yourself, but also for them, at the failure of your marriage and the subsequent feelings of helplessness in your ability to affect the outcome. The animosity that you and Amanda felt toward each other was borne of the seeds sown in that previous life. She needed to deal with the way she treated you in that lifetime and so she presented herself to you once again, this time as your wife. One of the goals you each had set out for this lifetime was to forgive the other for their actions.

"Your past acts, combined with the needs of the other people that existed within your circle, required the orchestration of your death in the manner that it came about. In this way everyone drew from their karmic account and they applied it to their development and their growth. There are no random acts, Joshua, but of course that is not always apparent to those experiencing the events at the time. People call it god's will, but as you are now aware, there is no god who wishes to apply a will to anything. This god concept did not decide to take anyone away with the death of someone. The god concept did not 'call anyone home' or punish them in any way. It was a decision made by those most intimately involved with the situation. Your death within the context of that lifetime not only facilitated fulfillment of your karma, but it also allowed karmic debts to be balanced by all the entities that had connections with you."

I acknowledged to myself, truly for the first time, why it had been so difficult to cultivate love with Amanda. I saw now how she could look at my broken heart and see nothing. I now knew how it was, that even though she could see me clinging to the idea of our family and my desire to preserve it, that she could only respond with what appeared to be indifference. I also understood that it was not her fault; she was simply playing the role that we had agreed upon, that was determined in large part through our past involvement. We had been the ones to set the wheels in motion, the question had been whether we would replay the same scenario over and over again, or whether we would see our way clear to break the cycle. I felt a glow of optimism with the realization that, finally, we had broken that cycle, that karmic debts had been repaid, and possibly, that forgiveness had been achieved.

Randi and Grayson weighed heavily on my thoughts; they were such beautiful souls. Despite the grief I had caused them in a life now long past, I understood how I had needed to experience the sting of the broken family, and the anguish I felt at leaving them at my death. The knowledge that Sophia had shared with me allowed me to see why I had chosen the particular paths I had traveled, and in turn, how those paths were connected to the paths of other wants, needs, and desires.

In taking responsibility for all that I was, I acknowledged that I was, in fact, the master of my destiny. My desire became my reality. My reality would in turn influence my desires. It was yin and yang; love and fear; want and need. It all grew from the same seed.

CHAPTER THIRTY-THREE

The pleasing glow of a soft light was present around me on a continuous basis. Whether my eyes were open or closed, whether I felt asleep or awake, the line between my awake state and my sleep state had become substantially blurred and I simply accepted that my dreams were as real as my awake time, and vice versa.

I had the overriding sense that I existed more in a thought form than a physical or even metaphysical state. I pictured myself, my form, as a cluster of energy and light which merged with the consciousness of what I knew to be my basic personality. I could feel that it was me, still, but the lines that defined who I was had been dramatically altered.

"When you pray, meditate, or just sit and think about a particular person, place, or event, you are focusing your intention. As your consciousness enters the earth plane as a newborn it becomes encoded, as does your brain, with the natural laws that govern the physical plane of reality. A building or a mountain feels very real and substantial. The rain feels wet, running across a field brings a feeling of exertion and the perception of covering a physical distance. A touch can be comforting or hurtful, a word or gesture can initiate love or fear. Eating, breathing, living, dying, every function that occurs on the earth plane occurs through this remarkable illusion that is held together by the collective consciousness of the earth plane.

"While you inhabit the earth plane you remain connected to the universe through your soul. The physical mind and body are the brush, the physical reality is your canvas, and your desires are the paint with which you create your self-portrait. You are the artist, as such you cannot blame others for how you perceive yourself, or what particular landscape or other settings you place yourself in. You choose the content of the picture, you surround yourself with the people, places, and situations that you desire. You are the creator of you and your experience.

"Each painting that you create ultimately represents the totality of a lifetime, and the gallery that houses our paintings is known as the Akashic record of your soul. These astral, or Akashic records are the in-depth exploration of every element of every lifetime. They are the record of every thought and intention, every action and interaction on every level, experienced by the entity. It is through the review of these 'paintings' that you are given the true ability, and responsibility, to study and review these Akashic records so that you can judge yourself in the pure light of truth and love. They serve as an evolving blueprint of who you are, what structures you have created, and what opportunities are at hand for you to attract and develop as you desire."

Hearing these words, feeling their deep intention, I flashed back to the night in Amanda's kitchen where at the peak of my frustration with our situation I had tasted, and then thankfully overcome, the desire to harm her. As I relived that experience now, I was aware of every stimulus that had impacted me. From the cool night air that I had drawn so sharply into my lungs as I strode down the pathway to where my car was parked; to the vision of popping open the trunk and the ripping sound of the Velcro as I released the handgun from its hiding place by the car jack. I could feel the heaviness of it in my hand, I could smell the faintly oily metallic scent of the gun. Somehow in that moment I had managed to break the cycle that had found its beginning in our previous lifetime. I had created the opportunity once again to be confronted with the rawness of my emotions with Amanda, but this time I had created a new outcome. The past would not repeat itself.

"Free will is one of the greatest influences you possess," Sophia said, as she continued her communication with me. "It can enrich your experience, or it can bankrupt you, depending on how you choose to apply it. Free will is how you determine what your experience will be; the result is entirely within your control.

"Many entities learn through their observations of the experiences of others. Some, like you in this particular case, require the experience of actually taking part in the event. Again, how you react to the experience you create will determine your future experiences.

"You have lived many lives, Joshua. Some were lived in periods of great darkness and suffering. The lifetime in the city-state of Athens, where you first met the person you know as Julia, was where you first began to accumulate some of this karmic debt. There was another lifetime that you need to be aware of, where you lived the role of a religious leader who so enjoyed the trappings of power, that you chose to promote fear as a means of achieving your desires. Under the guise of leading people along a spiritual path you instead enslaved them through fear. The events of that lifetime reached their peak in the late fifteen hundreds.

"In 1592 you were a priest of the Catholic faith in France. This was the time that was known as the massacre of St. Bartholomew. You combined the teachings of your church, along with your craving for power and domination of others, to fulfill your painful desires. You urged your followers to take part in the killing of the Huguenots and other followers of the Protestant faith. At the end of a matter of weeks, because of you and others like you, fifty thousand lay dead and countless more were left scarred physically and emotionally. Pope Gregory, your leader, had a medal struck to celebrate the event and thanked and rewarded you personally for your involvement.

"At the end of that lifetime, there was a large gap before your next incarnation on the earth plane. During that lifetime the severity of your actions against others, against what you intrinsically knew to be a crime against the truth and love of the universe, was such that you entered what you might best understand as a state of suspended animation. Your actions were so heinous that your soul could not interact with any but the vilest intentioned entities. It took the prolonged involvement of many guides, myself included, until we could bring you out of this self-induced exile so that we could help you once again prepare for a rebirth.

"At this point, you went through several short lifetimes where you fulfilled the role of a facilitator to assist others as they worked through their karmic needs. This was a suitable method that allowed you to acclimatize yourself once again to the earth plane. In each of these lifetimes you did not live long, often dying as a young child, or during the birth process. This was done to enable others to go through the particular experience that was necessary for them, in order that they could meet their needs with regard to learning and growth. By making yourself of service to others you were able to gradually extricate yourself from the extremely negative cycle you had immersed yourself in during that time in France.

"You are now well past the experiences of that lifetime, and others that were similar. There is no need to present each and all of the details to you, as it would now be a difficult thing for you to experience, having removed yourself from the negativity of that vibration level. It is enough to say that you have repaid a substantial portion of your karmic debt and come away from it with many valuable lessons, that hopefully you choose to retain as you prepare for rebirth.

"To be reborn means to be born once again into a physical body, and nothing more than that. You cannot be reborn in the middle of an existing lifetime. That is simply a man-made concept involved in a man-made religious belief. In order to experience the benefits and opportunities of successive lifetimes, you must physically die in order to be physically reborn, reincarnated, into a new lifetime.

"The next time that you and Julia shared portions of a lifetime together, she occupied the body of a male who was a guard overseeing the dungeons where those judged guilty of religious heresy were held. Here they awaited their inquisition, torture, and eventual death for the crime, in this instance, of not pledging their allegiance to the Church of Rome. Once again you were in France during this particular lifetime. This lifetime was in the 1600s and you and Julia were lovers. You in the body of a woman and she in the body of a male.

"You and Julia met through a series of seemingly nonrelated circumstances, but of course you know better about the idea of these so-called chance occurrences. After the persecution that you had brought to bear on so many in your earlier lifetime, it was only fitting that you would need to have an understanding of the fate you had perpetrated upon others. As you will continue to see, karma has an interesting way of working, and in doing so, maintaining balance.

"You and Julia carried on your relationship over a period of several months. The day arrived when you were arrested, along with a group of people that you had been associating with. You were accused of being a heretic and ordered to trial. Following the trial, which was a sham event by any standard, you were sent to the dungeons to await your fate. It was not a coincidence that one of your guards was your lover, whom you would later know as Julia.

"Within a matter of days, you were sentenced to torture and death, this was carried out in the underground cells where the prisoners were held. As your lover listened to your horrific screams while you were burned alive over a blistering bed of coals, he went out of his mind in his own internal agony. He endured your screams as long as he could, knowing there was nothing he could do to save you from the group around you, that he would have been struck down before getting within arm's length of you, that he literally fell on his sword and took his own life, believing that he would be with you in death."

Sophia's voice was a gentle vibration that flowed through my consciousness like an ocean current, steady and with strong intention. I was acutely aware of the images that she had brought forth in describing my death in that lifetime. While it was a terrifying scene to contemplate, I was able to accept and process the information in such a way that I was not traumatized by it. I was very much at peace as I considered the roads I had traveled, the host of lifetimes that Sophia had accompanied me through. Despite the content of some of the experiences, I was thankful for the ability to view those events in an honest and candid way. I was able to look deeply into the mirror of my being, and I now felt at ease.

Sophia had become my constant companion by this point. It was rare that we were not in each other's company. I still had my moments where I would consciously enter a sleep state, as I still referred to it, and through this method I was the beneficiary of many very vibrant interactions.

"Tell me more about Julia," I asked Sophia, upon waking from a particularly engaging dream. "Lately I have been feeling her around me in a way that I can't explain, but it feels as though my connection to her, strong as it has always been, has intensified. She has often been in my dreams, but now she is essentially always a part of them."

"You have been spending a lot of time with her, Joshua, that is true," Sophia said. "For you, and particularly for Julia, this contact occurs in your sleep state."

"Does she remember these conversations, these dreams, the same way I do?" I wondered.

"She is aware of them," Sophia replied. "But not to the same degree that you are. Remember that in her dream state, when she is in a deep enough sleep, her astral body is able to extend far enough from her physical body that she is able to interact with your astral body. Her difficulty lies in translating the actual content of your conversations into a context that she could readily explain with words. Her interpretation is hindered by her conscious mind. How are you enjoying these interactions?"

"They're wonderful," I replied enthusiastically. "I've said before that being with her feels so natural to me. I think that we have unfinished business with each other from that last lifetime. I am sure, given the chance, that there would be so much more for us to experience together and learn from."

"Quite so," Sophia replied. "Let me ask you this, Joshua, if you could be with her again, would you?"

I felt a surge of exhilaration race through me.

"What do you mean, if I could be with her again? Is that possible? Am I able to go back and pick up where I left off? Can I go back to that street and choose not to step off the sidewalk into the path of that truck? Can I choose not to die in that way at that time? Can I choose to change the outcome of that day and be with Julia and my children again?"

There was a notable pause between us.

"No, Joshua, you would not be able to do those things. The events of that day, of that lifetime, were constructed to meet specific needs and objectives that were necessary for your growth, and the growth of all the others connected to you. It would not serve anyone well to alter the outcome."

"Sophia, if it is not possible for me to go back to that time, could you at least tell me how long it has been since I was with her? I really have no idea of how much time has passed since that day."

"Well, measured by time on the earth plane, approximately three years has elapsed since the last time you were physically present with Julia."

I thought for a moment about what options might be available to me, based on the many lessons that Sophia had presented to me during our time together. If it had only been three years, how was it possible for me to pick up again with Julia? Would it be in the guise of a new relationship? Sophia had explained the idea of a "walk-in" scenario; this was when an entity literally walked in to an existing person's body, and life. The soul of the existing body would vacate the body in order to allow another to occupy it to facilitate new opportunities for all involved. The way she had explained it to me, sometimes after a traumatic experience, a physical or psychological injury perhaps, the soul within the affected body recognized that all of its goals in that lifetime had been realized, and that rather than allowing the physical body to die, it was possible for another soul, with its own unique set of goals, to "walk in" to that physical body and continue on with that particular lifetime.

"What would I have to do in order to be with Julia again, Sophia?" I asked excitedly. "Would I be a walk-in? How would we make that happen? And how would I plan to end up meeting with her? How would she know me? For that matter, how would I know her?"

"That would require a very intricate set of circumstances, Joshua," Sophia told me, and I could immediately sense that it was likely not a viable option. "There must be a specific set of needs in place, and of course there must be absolute agreement and permission from all involved for that event to occur. A 'walk-in' situation, as we have discussed, is reserved for a unique set of conditions, your situation does not meet the requirement. No, Joshua, in this case you would play a different role. Are you still interested?"

"Of course, I am," I told Sophia. "But if I'm not to be a walk-in, then how would we arrange for me to be with her? By the time I was born again, until I could reach adulthood, the age difference would be, well, it doesn't make sense to me," I said, confused by her apparent offer.

"Let me share some information with you," Sophia began to explain. "Recently, Julia became pregnant again, this is the catalyst that has caused the increased communication between you two. You are still very much tied into seeing things as they were, as you knew them in your last lifetime. You're still trying to capture what has gone, you must learn to let go. I want you to remember how we discussed the idea of love, being love, in whatever form it takes. Love is energy, and you and Julia have shared this energy a number of times in many different scenarios. When we talked recently, you told me that you felt you had come to know Julia on a higher level, that you felt the two of you had, on occasion, become so close that you almost felt like you had melded into one. Do you recall?"

"Yes, yes, I do," I said.

"When these feelings began to intensify, you used the word melded; this is significant. At the point of conception, when a sperm and egg fuse together, there is a release of a very strong burst of energy. This moment is like an enormous calling out to all souls that are connected in any way to those two entities who have created this joining of cells, especially those who have a karmic interest.

"A birth represents opportunities for all concerned, not just the mother and father, and not just the soul about to reincarnate, but also all who will come into contact with that entity. When you are reborn you choose your parents, but they also invite you to choose them. There is a fantastic amount of activity that occurs on multiple platforms at once. It is instantaneous, and quite complex, if you are attempting to relate to it from a physical perspective. For the higher self of those souls involved, however, it is a very natural selection process that can take place quite effortlessly and efficiently.

"The communication going on between you and Julia, and all those others who are connected to each of you in one way or another, is on such a very grand scale that you could not hope to comprehend it fully, even at your current level of awareness.

"Right now, the child developing inside of Julia exists only as an extension of the mother, it is a clump of cells unable to live outside of the mother's body. It requires a soul, a life force, to actually inhabit the body, if it is to survive. It is possible that the soul that ends up residing in that body could be you."

Looking back on the situation I could see that, as Sophia had reminded me, I was often predisposed to embrace the familiarity of my most recent lifetime. I continued to see Julia as my lover. To go from that to then embrace the idea of being involved with her as her child was, I'm sure you can imagine, a considerable leap for me to entertain. Sophia continued to discuss details of the situation with me. The more I listened to her, the more fascinated I became by the idea she was presenting to me.

"There are pregnancies that end before the mother is even aware that she has become pregnant," she explained to me. "There are times when one or both parents need to experience what you would call a lost pregnancy, where no soul inhabits the body. Sometimes it is the soul that wishes to reincarnate that requires the experience of loss. There are circumstances where the soul meant to inhabit the body will decide that it is not the right set of circumstances for it, and they will offer up the opportunity to another soul. Perhaps this new soul has no direct connection to the parents, but who might wish to be born into that set of circumstances in order to utilize the experience. Not every child born has a karmic connection to the parents, although many do."

"It is so complex," I said, marveling at the ever-expanding set of possibilities that accompanied the seemingly basic act of childbirth. "What if a soul wants to be born to someone but the woman or man is having difficulty creating the conception?"

"Remember, Joshua, that there are no coincidences, there are no accidents; there is a lesson or a benefit in everything. If there is no baby to be born, it is for a reason. Even something that you would call a one-night stand that results in a pregnancy is not an accidental baby. Whether it is for the child's purpose or because of the requirement of one or both of the parents, there is a reason and a purpose to it.

"Once a soul has been identified as a potential match, the incarnating soul will spend time visiting, if you will, with the others who are associated with the coming event in order to gauge whether this is the set of conditions they desire. The soul may not fully engage with the physical body of the baby until the actual birth is imminent. This may be a few days, weeks, months, or even a few minutes until the actual birth.

"In terms of you and Julia, through your recent series of interactions, you have both indicated that you wish to be together to continue to explore the love you have known. If you do choose to be with Julia is this next lifetime, you do need to carefully consider the fact that you will not be together as lovers; in this instance, you will be together as mother and child."

CHAPTER THIRTY-FOUR

From my vantage point in the upper corner of the room, I watched as she awoke and looked around the darkened room. I had learned that I had acquired the ability to read her from an emotional perspective as well as a physical one, and while I could not read her thoughts, I could understand the basic substance of what she was feeling.

There had been a marked increase in the number of interactions between Julia and I since my recent discussion with Sophia. I was quite intrigued by the intensity of this most recent dream interaction that we had both just taken part in. It was not surprising that the dream had caused Julia to suddenly sit up in bed, fully awake.

During this period of time, I did not continually inhabit the body of the developing child. I knew, of course, that it would be necessary to complete the full commitment. Sophia had already advised me that immediately following the birth, my birth, that I would still be aware of Sophia's presence as my spirit guide, but that this awareness would progressively fade as the newborn became more and more immersed in the slower vibration of the earth plane. As was often the case, she told me, that by the age of three or four years my conscious memory of Sophia as my spirit guide, and my memory of the time between lives, would become quite obscured. The clarity of that insight would be lost to the clamor of the physical reality surrounding and distracting me.

From my comfortable little nook, I watched as Julia adjusted the pillows behind her back and head. There was a rustling beside her as the father of this child, this new man in Julia's life, turned from his side and then settled on his back. Being connected to Julia as I was, I could sense when her emotions changed. I could feel her slipping toward a melancholy mood as she looked at the sleeping figure beside her, and then she stared off into the dark of the room.

She did not know I was with her in the room; I would not be visible to her, that much I knew. From what Sophia had shared with me, at best Julia might wonder why I was so ever-present in her thoughts, why she would be thinking so intently of her lover who had died a few years before. As I focused on her energy, I could tell that she was still feeling a sense of loss as it related to her time with me. This was despite the new man in her life and the approaching birth of her second child. I was aware from our many interactions, and that she still strongly carried her love for me. I also understood that Joshua Davidson was now only a memory for her, and that indeed my memories of Julia would also fade from my conscious awareness as I prepared for this new lifetime.

Julia sighed, and her hands stroked the risen flesh beneath her nightgown. As her hands rubbed her belly, the body of the baby moved in response to her rhythmic caress. I could not feel the physical touch of her hands, but I could easily feel the increased glow of love around me. Watching as she continued to massage the tiny body within hers, it felt odd to know that I was a part of that body and yet, for now at least, still quite apart from it.

"Will she know me?" I sent the thought out to Sophia; I could feel her presence nearby. "And, I wonder, if I will know her?"

"Yes, you will know each other," the response came back. "But not by name, not as you know each other now."

"Why is that? Why does it have to be that way?" I asked.

"There are reasons, Joshua, many reasons, not the least of which is the rigid manifestation that is present in the reality of physical time. On the earth plane, time still needs to move in one direction. You can know certain elements, you will be drawn to particular situations, experiences, and people, based on your inner awareness, but in most cases the specifics of those lifetimes will not be available to you.

"To know the personality of someone that you are familiar with is not so important, to bond with the energy of that person, that is what is important. In this new lifetime you will be born as a female child to Julia, that is the role you will assume in her life. That is all you need to focus on."

"I understand," I said. "When will the birth occur?"

"Soon," Sophia said. "Though you generally don't feel the need for sleep as a way of renewing your energy, you will find yourself entering into longer periods of meditation as the time of birth approaches; this is how you will embrace the final bonding process. At some point before the physical birth, your soul will fully engage with the body of the child and your mind will be the mind of the child. You will retain the core elements of your being, all of your past life experiences will be connected to this new life.

"For every entity that reincarnates to the earth plane, there is a method in place to protect the physical mind. This involves wrapping what you could call a veil of forgetfulness around yourself to separate your higher self from the physical reality around you. The purpose, as we have discussed, is simply to protect you from the rush of knowledge that would overwhelm your consciousness before you are properly able to accommodate it.

"The lessons and knowledge you have acquired will remain part of the fabric of your soul, this will help shape the personality that you will express outwardly to others.

"Always remember the laws of truth and love, Joshua; let these be your guiding light. The choices you make in this life will be yours and yours alone to make, and if you are true to yourself, you will always find yourself on the right path for you, the one that leads to your oneness. The spirit of the universe resides within you, you are the universe, the universe is you."

At last, as Sophia had intimated, the time arrived, and I felt myself beginning to drift into the slow peaceful spiral toward a deep meditation. A mist rose up around me and I floated toward it, entering deeper and deeper into it until it obscured my vision. It was like being in a plane and flying through a cloud.

After a while the vapor cleared and there I was, stretched out on my back, floating once again, comfortably ensconced in a warm body of water. I was staring up into the night sky filled with pure white stars. The points of light beckoned to me and I felt myself expanding to join with them. As I mingled with the points of light, I felt their energy flow into my body and I let their vitality nourish me.

I was aware of the stars and planets all around me, and that their position, relative to me, was of importance. They formed some sort of blueprint that I felt was, I don't know how to put this, so I will say that I felt like some sort of program was being downloaded into me as you would do with a computer. It was like my operating system was somehow charted to these points of light and energy. I felt comfortable surrendering to this feeling and, as I did, I felt the energy move deeper into my mind and body until it began to dissolve the atoms and molecules that held my shape together. I felt myself begin to tingle and vibrate at an extremely fast rate and then it began to slow until I was aware of a soft pulse of light that appeared in an elliptical pattern that hung in the dark sky, fully calling on my attention.

Soon the pattern became more circular in shape and then it compressed into a small glowing ball that beamed with an intense luminescence. I felt the light enter me, it was now emanating from the center of my being, shining outward as I was being pulled deeper and deeper into it, drawn toward its nucleus. As I reached the heart of it, I surrendered to it fully, and I was overcome by a brilliant radiance that consumed me.

"Go ahead, little one."

It was Sophia's voice that I heard. I could not see her, but the softness of the vibration in her voice was soothing.

"All is well. I'm right here beside you, all is well."

I was floating in a sea of warm water. I knew this sensation and I was reassured by the familiarity as the water lifted and rocked me in the gentle swells of its motion. I drifted peacefully in this way for quite some time. And then, I felt a surge within the water. It was slight at first, but then it increased in strength until I felt I was moving in a current that had begun to pull me along its course.

Suddenly I was plunged into a coldness that shocked me. My body tingled as cold air rushed over my exposed skin and I began to tremble. The water that had been such a comfort was now choking off my breath as I tried to pull air into my lungs. At last I was able to swallow a gulp of air; as it entered my throat, it was harsh and dry. I heard the encouraging words of Sophia's voice telling me to open my eyes, and as I did, I felt a sharp pain as the strong light burned into my eyes and I quickly closed them.

I was shaken and tossed about, not feeling that I had any control over the situation until, at last, the activity ceased. Something nudged at my face and I instinctively opened my mouth and was rewarded with a sweet and warm taste that I eagerly swallowed and demanded more of as it soothed the singed channel of my throat. The more I drew on the source, the more comfort it brought to me.

Hesitantly I opened my eyes again, this time the light did not hurt as much, the air was not as cruel. I opened my eyes wide and gazed up into the face that looked back at me.

"This is the person I have been telling you about," Sophia's voice said softly. "She will take care of you now, little one. You are now her little girl, and our time is done, for now. You know her, and she knows you, very well. You are safe, so be happy and be well. Remember to always listen to the voice inside of you that speaks from the place of love."

As Sophia's voice faded away, the soft warm light that radiated from the eyes that were looking back at me so intently brought me a renewed sense of comfort.

I felt at one with my universe. I felt at peace.

ABOUT THE AUTHOR

Paul Fisher is a former radio announcer, media executive, and now author. Recently retired from the radio industry, Paul enjoyed a long and successful career working with several major Canadian media companies including Rogers Media, CHUM Radio, and Bell Media.

When Paul was twenty, his father died at the young age of 47. Paul was with his father during the last few days of his father's life, and in fact was with him in the Intensive Care Unit as his father's heart failed on several occasions resulting in a series of near-death experiences. His father, upon resuscitation from these events, told Paul that there was a world that existed beyond this life, and did his best to describe the feelings and philosophies that he had been exposed to during his brief sojourns into the "other side".

Currently living near Toronto Canada, Paul enjoys listening to jazz music as well as writing. Entertaining with friends, family, and other interesting guests at dinner parties and gatherings, are a regular feature at the Fisher household.

If you liked this book, you might also like:

Dancing with Angels in Heaven
by Garnet Schulhauser
A Very Special Friend
by Dolores Cannon
Where the Weeds Grow
by Curt Melliger
The Anne Dialogues
By Guy Needler
Judy's Story
L.R. Sumpter
Time: The Second Secret
Kathryn Andries
Croton
Artur Tadevosyan

For more information about any of the above titles, soon to be released titles,
or other items in our catalog, write, phone or visit our website:
Ozark Mountain Publishing, LLC
PO Box 754, Huntsville, AR 72740
479-738-2348
www.ozarkmt.com

Other Books by Ozark Mountain Publishing, Inc.

Dolores Cannon
A Soul Remembers Hiroshima
Between Death and Life
Conversations with Nostradamus,
   Volume I, II, III
The Convoluted Universe -Book One,
   Two, Three, Four, Five
The Custodians
Five Lives Remembered
Jesus and the Essenes
Keepers of the Garden
Legacy from the Stars
The Legend of Starcrash
The Search for Hidden Sacred
   Knowledge
They Walked with Jesus
The Three Waves of Volunteers and
   the New Earth
A Very Special Friend
Horns of the Goddess
Aron Abrahamsen
Holiday in Heaven
James Ream Adams
Little Steps
Justine Alessi & M. E. McMillan
Rebirth of the Oracle
Kathryn Andries
Time: The Second Secret
Cat Baldwin
Divine Gifts of Healing
The Forgiveness Workshop
Penny Barron
The Oracle of UR
P.E. Berg & Amanda Hemmingsen
The Birthmark Scar
Dan Bird
Finding Your Way in the Spiritual Age
Waking Up in the Spiritual Age
Julia Cannon
Soul Speak – The Language of Your
   Body
Ronald Chapman
Seeing True
Jack Churchward
Lifting the Veil on the Lost

Continent of Mu
The Stone Tablets of Mu
Patrick De Haan
The Alien Handbook
Paulinne Delcour-Min
Spiritual Gold
Holly Ice
Divine Fire
Joanne DiMaggio
Edgar Cayce and the Unfulfilled
   Destiny of Thomas Jefferson
   Reborn
Anthony DeNino
The Power of Giving and Gratitude
Paul Fisher
Like A River To The Sea
Carolyn Greer Daly
Opening to Fullness of Spirit
Anita Holmes
Twidders
Aaron Hoopes
Reconnecting to the Earth
Patricia Irvine
In Light and In Shade
Kevin Killen
Ghosts and Me
Susan Urbanek Linville
Blessing from Agnes
Donna Lynn
From Fear to Love
Curt Melliger
Heaven Here on Earth
Where the Weeds Grow
Henry Michaelson
And Jesus Said – A Conversation
Andy Myers
Not Your Average Angel Book
Holly Nadler
The Hobo Diaries
Guy Needler
Avoiding Karma
Beyond the Source – Book 1, Book 2
The History of God
The Origin Speaks

For more information about any of the above titles, soon to be released titles,
or other items in our catalog, write, phone or visit our website:
PO Box 754, Huntsville, AR 72740|479-738-2348/800-935-0045|www.ozarkmt.com

Other Books by Ozark Mountain Publishing, Inc.

The Anne Dialogues
The Curators
Psycho Spiritual Healing
James Nussbaumer
And Then I Knew My Abundance
The Master of Everything
Mastering   Your   Own   Spiritual
    Freedom
Living Your Dram, Not Someone Else's
Each of You
Sherry O'Brian
Peaks and Valley's
Gabrielle Orr
Akashic Records: One True Love
Let Miracles Happen
Nikki Pattillo
Children of the Stars
A Golden Compass
Victoria Pendragon
Sleep Magic
The Sleeping Phoenix
Being In A Body
Alexander Quinn
Starseeds What's It All About
Charmian Redwood
A New Earth Rising
Coming Home to Lemuria
Richard Rowe
Imagining the Unimaginable
Exploring the Divine Library
Garnet Schulhauser
Dancing on a Stamp
Dancing Forever with Spirit
Dance of Heavenly Bliss
Dance of Eternal Rapture
Dancing with Angels in Heaven
Manuella Stoerzer
Headless Chicken
Annie Stillwater Gray
Education of a Guardian Angel
The Dawn Book
Work of a Guardian Angel

Joys of a Guardian Angel
Blair Styra
Don't Change the Channel
Who Catharted
Natalie Sudman
Application of Impossible Things
L.R. Sumpter
Judy's Story
The Old is New
We Are the Creators
Artur Tradevosyan
Croton
Croton II
Jim Thomas
Tales from the Trance
Jolene and Jason Tierney
A Quest of Transcendence
Paul Travers
Dancing with the Mountains
Nicholas Vesey
Living the Life-Force
Dennis Wheatley/ Maria Wheatley
The Essential Dowsing Guide
Maria Wheatley
Druidic Soul Star Astrology
Sherry Wilde
The Forgotten Promise
Lyn Willmott
A Small Book of Comfort
Beyond all Boundaries Book 1
Beyond all Boundaries Book 2
Beyond all Boundaries Book 3
Stuart Wilson & Joanna Prentis
Atlantis and the New Consciousness
Beyond Limitations
The Essenes -Children of the Light
The Magdalene Version
Power of the Magdalene
Sally Wolf
Life of a Military Psychologist

For more information about any of the above titles, soon to be released titles,
or other items in our catalog, write, phone or visit our website:
PO Box 754, Huntsville, AR 72740|479-738-2348/800-935-0045|www.ozarkmt.com